EMERGE

Hosting Gods

Book One

Lena Mae Hill

DEDICATION

For the muse

ACKNOWLEDGMENTS

Making a book takes a village. Writing it is only one small part. A huge thanks to all the people who helped Emerge... well...emerge. My son, who went without my attention for a month while I drafted and several more while I wrestled it into shape. My talented, encouraging editor Rebecca Jaycox who made me believe this book didn't have to sit on my hard drive gathering dust forever (and who patiently began to break me of my comma addiction). My cover artist, Elena Dudina, whose three pieces of art captured Bifrost perfectly. My typographer, Angela Fristoe. My beta readers, Kate Marin-Andrew, Tina Merritt, and Kim Owens for helping me catch last minute errors and smooth rough edges.

Thanks, y'all! I couldn't have done it without you!

CHAPTER ONE

Gwen

I blinked into the harsh sunlight that streamed through the door to our storage locker as it rattled upward on its rolling track.

"It's time," Mom said, her hair disheveled and an all-too-familiar frenzied look in her eyes. "Let's get out of here. Now!" Rushing in, she began scooping up our meager possessions, grabbing toothbrushes and dirty laundry, throwing items at random into a banana box.

"What about your job?" I asked, already knowing the answer. On autopilot, I stood from the bed and began to roll up the foam mattress with the sheets still on it.

"They've found us," she said, ignoring my question. She ran out to toss the box in the trunk of our latest car, a brown boxy thing she'd bought a month ago, when we'd landed in St. Louis. The continual, annoying ding alerting us that the keys were in the ignition answered all the questions I really needed to know. We were getting the hell out—and fast.

"Who found us this time?" I asked, carrying the mattress out.

"I saw a raven," she said, grabbing up an armload of folded clothes, dumping them into the backseat. They cascaded across the stained upholstery, unfolding themselves like fans as they went. At least she'd taken the time to gather our things this time. Sometimes, she dragged me out of sleep in the middle of the night and we ran, taking nothing but our latest car.

She jumped in the driver's seat and slammed her door as I closed the trunk, having thrown in the last random pieces of our lives. I hurried to the front door, my heart in my throat. Every time it happened, terror gripped me, as if her crazy were somehow contagious. As if I were afraid that one of these days, she'd be in such a hurry that she wouldn't wait for me.

The car lurched forward before I'd had a chance to buckle my seatbelt. I grabbed the dash as we bore down on the exit to the storage facility. The numbered doors ticked past like a counter, counting down to the moment when one of her episodes didn't end.

Talking kept her from sinking into the scary, semi-catatonic state she did sometimes when she saw things, so I tried again.

"Where are we going?" I asked, rifling through the stack of maps in the glove box.

"Just let me drive," Mom said. "Look for ravens."

I gave up on conversation for the moment, telling myself she'd calm down when we were out of town, away from the demons that had caught up with her yet again. Sometimes they were literal demons that only she could see, but sometimes they were giants or trolls or even dragons. Only she could see those, too. I worried more about the things I could see, like policemen, freezing temperatures, and people knocking on the car windows when we were sleeping in it. But most of all, I worried about us.

"Raven," my mother screamed. I jolted upright, grabbing for the wheel. A truck on oversized tires loomed in front of us, and I swallowed a scream, yanking us back into our lane.

"Mom, calm down," I said firmly. "Do you want to pull over so I can drive?"

Renewing her grip on the wheel, she took a couple deep breaths. "No, we can't risk it. You don't have your license. If we got pulled over…"

"You don't have a license, either," I pointed out.

"I'll be fine," she said, shooting me a forced smile. "Just let me get us out of here and away from that giant."

"Ah," I said, nodding. "So it was a giant this

time. What kind?" If I played along, she'd calm down faster, and I wouldn't worry for our lives quite so much.

"Frost," she muttered, her eyes darting around as she pulled to a stop at a red light. Her fingers drummed frantically on the steering wheel as she waited for the light to change.

Come on, come on, I urged the light, my hands curling into fists. The longer we sat there, the more agitated she'd get.

"Better than a fire giant, right?" I offered as the light turned green.

She stomped on the gas, and the car hesitated, then charged forward into the intersection. Mom didn't answer, so I began the tedious process of yanking my seatbelt out of the door, one halting inch at a time. The cars she could get with her limited cash were usually not in great shape, so I was lucky to have a seatbelt at all, even if it took five minutes to pull it out.

Once my seatbelt was on, I leafed through the pile of maps until I found the Missouri map. Flipping it over to the oversized city map of St. Louis on the back, I looked for a street sign outside the car, then found it on the legend, then placed my finger on it on the map. My heartbeat had already begun to slow, and as I directed Mom towards I-70, a sense of purpose descended over me.

Get us out of St. Louis, and we'll be okay again.

Maps were predictable. They didn't make

sudden changes. Sure, sometimes they led us into construction or to a closed road. But unlike us, the symbols and place names on maps remained in the exact same place for a whole year, until the next year's map appeared in the rest stops and visitor centers across the country.

"There," I said, nearly choking with relief as the overpass came into view, looming above the red-and-blue, shield-shaped signs with interstate numbers. It didn't really matter which way we went, which highway we took. The center of the country was safe that way—you could run in any direction, disappear into another town or city, and you'd still be in mid-America.

Mom swung the car onto the on-ramp, and I started to breathe normal at last. We'd made it. We were okay. As okay as we ever got, anyway.

For now.

CHAPTER TWO

Gwen

Two days later, I sat in shocked silence, trying to absorb my mother's latest announcement. By now I thought there was nothing she could say that would surprise me. Turned out, I was wrong.

"Gwen…?" Mom prompted.

I had to say something. She was waiting for my reaction. If I looked at her now, though, I might laugh, or cry, or scream. After a minute, I pried my lips open. I tried to keep my voice neutral, so it didn't break as I forced out the word. "You met a guy?"

Mom nodded, a tight smile on her lips. Before I could ask, she answered one of the million questions I had. "On the internet."

"But…how?" I asked, letting the incredulousness out. I stared across the picnic table, wondering if this was her total break from reality.

My mother did a lot of crazy things, but she

did not use the internet if she could help it. That's how the government spied on people. And she definitely didn't talk to men in chat rooms.

There were a lot of other things my mother didn't do, but I loved her fiercely. She may have had trouble holding a conversation without lapsing into ramblings about the end of the world, but she was my mom. She had literally pulled me from a burning building once.

"When we went to the library in St. Louis, they let me sign in as a guest, so I got online," she said. "Don't worry. I didn't give any personal information or sign in with any identifying details. He wants us to move in with him. He's giving us a home, Gwen." She put a hand over mine, smiling wanly at me.

"Who is this guy?" I asked, narrowing my eyes. "Exactly what kind of site did you meet him on?"

"A site for people who have been…left behind," she said, avoiding my eyes.

Since my mother wasn't religious, I knew she didn't mean it in the sense that the *Left Behind* books did. Which could only mean one thing.

I twisted a strand of my long blonde hair around my finger. "By Dad?"

"By love," Mom said, a faraway look in her eyes.

I knew my mother loved me, but I didn't think I'd ever heard her use that word before. I'd never really thought about being lonely because I always had her. And I'd never considered that she might be lonely, either. Now I studied her, wondering if I'd done something wrong. If suddenly, I was no longer enough.

Nothing had changed that I could put a finger on, which meant this creep had somehow gotten to her. My mother didn't trust the chick behind the counter at McDonald's, but somehow this guy had convinced her over an anonymous chat that we should go to his house...and stay? What the hell had he said to gain her trust that fast? There was exactly one person in the entire world my mother trusted. Me.

Not that my mother didn't have qualities that would make her a wonderful companion—she could be kind and brave and funny—but trusting? Never. I didn't want to be rude, but what kind of man would want a woman who had been voluntarily homeless for over a decade? Whose only permanent addresses had been storage lockers because the metal would block the giants from tracking us?

Now she wanted to move in with some random guy?

I gripped the edge of the table so I wouldn't pass out. My head was spinning, my stomach churning. This was wrong, all wrong. "Did he blackmail you?" I blurted.

"No, of course not," she said. "This is a good thing, Gwen."

"But…you don't even know him."

"That's true," she said slowly. "We'll get to know him when we get there."

"Where?"

"He lives in Massachusetts," she said, slipping a scrap of paper across the table with an address scribbled in pencil. "I wrote it down."

"And that's all you have? An address?" I tried to keep my voice level so I wouldn't freak her out. I didn't want to feed her paranoia, but this was batshit crazy. She couldn't just drive across the country to meet some internet weirdo. Blood rushed in my ears as I tried to figure out what to do. I had no one to call. No family but Mom. No relatives, no friends. All I had was her. She'd always told me we didn't need anyone else, that we couldn't trust anyone else.

And now that I needed help with her, I had no one to run to. That was the thing. We didn't run towards things. We ran away.

Mom and I sometimes talked, when she had good days. But I'd never questioned her method. Over the years, I'd gotten used to the way she was. For a long time, I hadn't realized it wasn't normal to be woken in the middle of the night, hurried into a car I'd never seen before, and driven to another state. That was just how we lived. And even now that I knew it wasn't normal for other people, it didn't bother me that much. It was normal for us.

Meeting random men on the internet? Not normal.

Driving across the country to meet some guy instead of running away from imaginary monsters? Not normal.

I couldn't tear my eyes from the gum wrapper blowing across the patchy, brown grass of the rest stop in Akron, Ohio, where we'd spent the night. That gum wrapper was *us*. Always moving, blowing from one place to the next. We might get caught up in one town or another for a few months, but only until we saved enough money to move on. Then we'd blow away again.

Back in the car, I closed my eyes and prayed that she'd snap out of this. That I'd fall asleep and wake up to find her being her usual self instead of a stranger who met guys online. I wished I had a real phone like pretty much everyone else on the planet so that I could Google this guy. My mother couldn't tell me a single meaningful thing about him. She didn't even know what he did for a living.

By midway through Pennsylvania, I'd worked myself into a panic. I couldn't sit still in my seat, shifting around every few minutes to try to get comfortable. This turned out to be impossible, since the discomfort was in my insides, churning like a stomach flu that cramped my guts and nauseated me. What if he was going to lure us in and murder us? Chances were, he didn't even live in a house. He was going to want to ride around with us in the car. And since we basically lived in a bubble, no one would miss us. If the TV shows I'd seen in laundromats were to be believed, that's how serial killers operated.

"Mom," I said at last, when I thought I'd explode from holding it together. "Can we talk about this?"

"About what, honey?" she asked, as if she didn't know.

"About moving in with a stranger. What if he's dangerous?"

"Giants are dangerous," she said. "I don't think he's a giant."

"How do you know?" I blurted, then immediately cursed myself. I didn't want to freak her out. I just wanted her to snap out of her weirdness for a minute, stop acting so un-momlike.

"I saw him," she said.

I grabbed the door handle, my head spinning. "What? When?"

"In here," she said, tapping her temple. "I knew he would find us the same way I know the ravens are reporting back what they see. I didn't know when, but now it's happened."

"If you told him you saw some guy in your visions, and he said he's that guy, he's lying," I said through clenched teeth.

"I know I haven't given you the best in life," she said. "Always on the road, always running. It's time to slow down. I want you to be happy. And maybe I can be happy, too."

Hands shaking, I covered my mouth, forcing the words to stay inside me. How could I deny her that? How could I argue with something that would make her happy?

Needing a distraction, I picked up one of the paperback novels on the floor at my feet. The pages were yellowed at the edges, the cover creased and worn. On the front stood a tall man, his long hair flowing in the wind, his shirt open at the neck to reveal bulging, tan pectorals. A woman was draped over his arm in a swoon, her enormous bosoms bursting from the top of a red satin dress and her blond hair hanging to the ground behind her. In the background, a crimson sunset shone over a prairie. Big, jagged letters spelled out the title, *Her Savage Passion*.

I opened the book, folded my knees against the door, and started reading. We'd picked up a whole box of similar titles at a garage sale for one dollar, paid in cash. This was my social education, since school was out of the question. This was where I learned about flirting, sex, and dating; about the Scottish Highlands, the Old West, and England's Regency era. I'd read my way through hundreds of classics, sci-fi tales, and tearjerkers, too. But today, I needed a happy distraction.

Somewhere in New York, I fell asleep. I woke up when Mom cheered. Unfolding my legs from where I'd curled them in the front seat, I stretched and looked around. It was morning. We'd driven all night.

"Where are we?" I asked, kicking some

paperbacks under the seat and reaching for a gallon jug of water at my feet. We were getting low. We'd have to fill up at a rest stop soon.

And then Mom's declaration the day before came crashing back. It seemed like a dream now. I'd been so worried about the guy, but in the stark light of morning, I found something new to worry about. Mom.

She'd never done anything like this, but there was no denying that she could sometimes go off the deep end. Once, she'd made us hitchhike into the Ozark Mountains and live in a cave for a month. She kept telling me we were fine, even when we saw crazy things in the woods. But one day she saw a wolf and a raven together at the same time, and she freaked out so bad I thought she'd never recover. Still, she'd never actually hallucinated before. Unless the imaginary villains we were always running from counted.

Did that count?

She'd been manufacturing dangers all my life, hadn't she? Satellites, government agents, giants, monsters, and God himself were out to get us. But not this rando. He was A-okay.

Maybe there was no man at all. I glanced over at Mom, dread building in my stomach. How would she handle it when she showed up, and there was no such address? How would I handle her?

CHAPTER THREE

Gwen

Turned out, Massachusetts was a long-ass state. But by afternoon, we'd made it across Boston, past a lot of towns with tribal names, and were crossing a large bridge. I rolled down the window using the old-fashioned window crank and took in a breath of salt air. I could smell the ocean.

I allowed myself one selfish minute of enjoyment before rolling up the window and checking on Mom. She didn't like the ocean. When you were at the beach, your back might as well be up against a wall. Nowhere to run. Mom liked places where you could escape in all four directions.

"Mom?" I asked, looking at the scrap of paper with the address. "Did you miss a turn?"

"No, I don't think so," she said, pushing an old atlas into my lap. "Check for me, will you? I know it's not as current as our folded maps, but we don't have one for Massachusetts. Look for a town called Wellfleet. It's about halfway down the Cape."

"Is this some kind of joke?" I asked. I may not have gotten a proper education, but I was probably the country's number one expert on United States geography. I knew that Cape Cod was bordered by water on not one, but three, sides. We didn't have a Massachusetts map because Mom didn't like this state even three hours inland, and she'd sure as hell never crossed a bridge onto a peninsula before.

"No joke, Gwen," Mom said. She shot me a weak smile and gripped the wheel with both hands.

I watched her for the next sixty seconds. I knew all her tells. She licked her lips three times and adjusted her grip on the steering wheel twice.

Shit.

"Mom?" I placed a gentle hand on her arm. "Are you sure about this? I mean, maybe there's somewhere we could go to get help."

"No hospitals," she said sharply.

"What about some other place," I said. "Maybe they can help us."

We'd stayed at homeless shelters before. Maybe they could have someone come there to check on Mom. She hated hospitals, so she'd never consent to that. I'd been to a hospital exactly once in my life—the time I'd been burned in the fire that took Dad's life. She'd barely let the hospital treat my burns before checking me out and taking off. Since then, she'd never been the same, but she'd taken care of me

15

the best she could. And I took care of her. For ten years, we'd had to keep moving so we'd be harder to track. That's what she always said. And now this.

"Neil will take care of us," she said, gripping the wheel. "He promised."

"Will you please stop being weird and tell me what's really going on?"

"I know you love the beach," she offered, shooting me another nervous smile. "I'm sorry we haven't spent much time there. Better late than never, right?"

"Still being weird, Mom."

"I'm just a little nervous," she admitted, darting glances at me as we passed one exit after another. "I've never met this guy, either. All I know is that he's got kids your age."

"Kids?" I asked, swallowing my own nerves. I'd been so busy thinking about Mom that I'd almost forgotten the guy. He had a family. Kids. *Teenagers.* Why couldn't they be under five years old, so they wouldn't notice that we were complete freaks?

Now Mom had gotten me nervous, too. I barely paid attention to the changing scenery as we got farther onto the Cape and regular houses gave way to empty tourist shops and summer cottages, now boarded up for winter. We stopped for a more detailed map of the Cape, and the salt smell almost knocked me flat. Cold wind whistled across the empty streets and blew sand across the parking lot, plastering my hair against my mouth like a gag.

I found myself unconsciously scanning for ravens, almost praying for one. Maybe Mom would take it as a sign to leave the Cape, like she took it as a sign to run from everywhere else.

A lone seagull swooped by against the white sky overhead. No ravens.

A chill ran up my spine, though, the kind that's supposed to mean someone is walking on your grave. "This place gives me the creeps," I told Mom as we climbed back into our car.

She checked the mirrors, and I caught her shivering once, too. But after a single car passed us on the road, she pulled back out, and we headed towards our final destination.

***

"Just a little farther," I said, craning my neck to read the mailboxes. The car crept along a road that was a mixture of chunky grey gravel and sand. To our right, a flimsy wooden fence held back a tangle of rosehip bushes. To our left, there were more rosehips, then a stretch of sea grass, and then a beach.

The Cape hooked around, with the Atlantic Ocean off to the east. We'd seen it coming in. Now we were on the inside of the hook, seeing the calmer waters of the bay on the Cape's western shore.

We weren't exactly enjoying the scenery, though. Mom had licked her lips raw. My cuticles were bleeding. What the hell were we doing? It was obvious we didn't belong here. It was obvious that no one at all was here. We were driving into an abandoned tourist trap that was ready to snap shut on us. The serial killer theory that had seemed so far-fetched now made my stomach curdle. This place was a ghost town. The guy could murder us and stow our bodies in a cottage, and they wouldn't be found until next summer.

I'd crumpled the scrap of paper with the address into a ball in my fist. I smoothed it over my thigh with shaking fingers, though I'd already memorized it.

"It looks like the road ends here," Mom said, pulling the car to a stop and leaning forward. "But I guess the driveway continues on from here."

"Can we go back now?" I asked. I didn't know what we'd go back to. Nothing, nowhere. Our nomadic life.

Better than a psycho killing us and tossing our bodies in the ocean for the fish to devour.

"It must be this one," Mom said, turning up a driveway that was even narrower than the road we'd driven in on. This one sloped gently uphill. The wind gusted, rocking the car and pelting it with sand. At the top of the drive, the road flattened out, and we pulled to a stop in front of...something. I didn't want to call it a mansion, but it sure as hell wasn't a regular house or a little cottage like the cute ones we'd passed on the way in.

It had the same grey shingle and white trim as the other houses, but it looked like a Cape Cod style house had taken steroids and grown six times as big as it should be. Its entire front side was glass, which gave the impression that it was watching over the ocean below.

"Mom, I told you—" I started, then broke off. I hadn't told her. I'd let her drive all night and all day to get us here, to some house she must have seen online. Or hell, maybe she'd just seen it in a magazine somewhere. I'd tried to talk her out of it, but like usual, she couldn't be swayed once she got something into her head. And now here we were, at a mansion overlooking the ocean, in the middle of October, when not even the rental company would be around. And I was going to have to convince her that there was no one here.

"Mom?" I said carefully, waiting for her to start screaming when she realized we were on a tiny strip of land with ocean on three sides. Thank god I knew how to drive, even if I didn't have a license.

"Well, I guess this is it," Mom said, shutting off the engine and turning to me. She wasn't screaming, but I could see the panic welling in her eyes.

"Okay, we saw it," I said. "We can go now."

She stroked my hair back with cold fingers. "You're growing into such a beautiful young woman," she said, her voice quavering. "I hope I didn't screw up too badly."

I had to try twice to swallow as bile rose in my throat. I clutched her fingers, holding onto the only thing I knew to be real, because this couldn't be.

"Why are you talking like that? Are you leaving me here?"

"Of course not," she said. "It's just that I've been selfish, keeping you to myself all these years. It hasn't been too bad, though, has it? Just us, on the run, like Thelma and Louise."

"Thelma and Louise died, Mom."

She sighed. "Let's just go in and meet them."

I closed my eyes and called on the heroine of my favorite book. Scarlet O'Hara would never run away before knowing what she was up against. I took a deep breath and looked Mom square in the eyes. "Okay, let's do it."

At this point, the best I could do was to let my mother see for herself. When she got something in her head, no amount of arguing could get it out. Though I had no desire to meet anyone who lived in that house, real or imagined, I'd lost the battle. Resigned, I followed her to the house. It didn't look like anyone was home, but maybe the car was in the monstrous garage to the right.

We climbed the wooden steps to the house, and Mom knocked while I stood awkwardly, half hoping we'd find it empty and half scared for the same reason. If no one lived there, maybe we could break in and squat there until spring. We'd done plenty of squatting before, a month here or there.

After the second knock, even Mom started to look uncertain. But I knew not to pressure her. She had to work this out herself. While she did that, I turned to the view. It was gorgeous, even on a cloudy day. The water was choppy and grey under the low clouds, and the salt in the air was not just a scent but a palpable texture.

Suddenly, the door swung open. My heart knocked around in my chest as I turned towards the door. A tall, devastatingly gorgeous guy was standing there wearing nothing but a pair of grey sweatpants. He held a bowl in one hand and a spoon in the hand that was wrapped around the doorknob. For a second, no one spoke. He took us in, and we took him in.

He looked a few years older than me, with unkempt black hair and piercing blue eyes that seemed to see into my very soul. His strong jaw was shadowed on one side by a nasty bruise, but it didn't detract from his good looks. His bare shoulders were broad, his skin sun-kissed tan, and just being within arm's reach of him, I could feel an inferno of animal heat coming off him in waves that nearly knocked me flat.

When my gaze traveled back to his face, I was jolted back to reality. The reality that I'd been rather obviously admiring the view. My face warmed as our eyes met, but his face remained hard and angry.

Apparently, he did not appreciate my admiration.

His eyes held mine, and I caught a defiant edge to the tilt of his chin. Something inside me tightened, coiling in on itself like a snake drawing back to strike. Heat crackled up my arms like static electricity, making the hair on the back of my neck stand up.

His nostrils flared. "Who the hell are you?" he said, his words sharp as razor blades.

"Leaving," I blurted. "We're…just leaving."

He stared at me like I was short a few brain cells.

"You must be one of Neil's," Mom said. "Is it Ezekiel?"

"No," the guy said, pulling his eyes from mine. Something weird had passed between us. I felt almost dizzy. My heart was throbbing hard in my chest, but I was glad he'd broken the connection. I wasn't sure I'd liked the feeling.

"I'm Olivia," Mom said, holding out her hand.

He stared at her hand like it was toxic. Then he took a bite of cereal and stood there in the doorway, just chewing and looking at us like he was deciding whether to shoot us or welcome us in.

I bit at a hangnail.

"Is Neil around?" Mom asked.

"No."

"Oh, right," Mom said with a nervous laugh. She licked her lips and looked to me, as if I had answers. When I didn't, she licked her lips again. "I forgot he'd be at work. Of course. I hadn't thought of that. What time did he say he'd be home?"

The guy shrugged his broad shoulders, and I

watched in fascination as the muscles in his ripped shoulders and taut arms glided under his skin with the movement. He had a black tattoo on his shoulder, but I couldn't make out what it was. His chiseled abs and lean torso drew my eyes again, despite his hostile attitude. He looked so much more real than the airbrushed covers of the romance novels I read. I'd rarely seen a shirtless male before since Mom didn't like the beach and where else was I going to see shirtless men? I was disconcerted by my urge to touch him.

"Xander, get out of the way, you oaf," interrupted a voice. A short, Hispanic woman with salt-and-pepper hair emerged from another room, pushed past the guy, and ushered us inside. Without sparing us a backwards glance, Xander turned and stalked off.

When he did, I caught the full shape of the tattoo on his shoulder. My heart skipped a beat, and I grabbed my mother's arm again. "He has a raven tattoo," I whispered.

She looked as anxious as I felt.

Xander had crossed the spacious foyer and entered a sitting room, where he flopped onto a brown leather sofa and resumed eating his cereal in front of the TV. "Would you mind taking them up to one of the guest rooms?" he called. "I'm awfully busy."

"You must be Mr. Keen's new daughter," the woman said to me, smiling warmly. "Which makes you Olivia, yes? I'm Rosa."

My mother nodded, looking relieved, though I was reeling with confusion. Mr. Keen's new daughter? What the hell did that mean? After Mom's weirdness in the car, I couldn't help but panic. Was she getting rid of me? I'd been scared she'd leave me in one of her freak-outs, not in a premeditated move. My fingers closed around her arm, anchoring myself. I wouldn't let her go even if she tried.

Every instinct in my body told me to turn and run. All my alarm bells were ringing at once, and red flags were popping up like fleas appearing from the carpet in a cheap hotel. Mom didn't seem to notice. She'd started across the foyer with Rosa, dragging me along. I couldn't leave her there alone. I'd have to wait it out, the way I did her weird fugue states and her manic flight-mode fits.

As we climbed the circular staircase after Rosa, I tried not to gape at everything, but it was impossible not to. The entire front of the house was glass, so as we climbed the stairs, we could see more and more of the ocean. I took back my assessment that this wasn't a mansion—it totally was. The foyer was so big it could have fit a few storage lockers *and* a car. Vertigo gripped me, and I grabbed at the railing, my head spinning.

I barely knew the names for the things around me—vaulted ceiling, exposed beams, hardwood floors—and I'd never seen them in real life. Yanking my hand back from the railing, I pulled my sleeve down over my hand and rubbed at the place I'd touched before continuing up. With every step, I was keenly aware of my scuffed, second-hand Converse. I was probably leaving dust on the immaculate steps. That, or some kind of used-shoe residue visible only to those who would stick up their noses at a pair of shoes that might contain traces of someone else's foot sweat.

When Rosa had left us in a bedroom that would have fit at least three of our five-by-ten storage units, I grabbed Mom's arm. "Why did that woman call me his daughter?" I hissed. "You said you weren't leaving me here."

Mom took my shoulders in both hands. "Gwen, I would never leave you. Never." She pulled me in and gave me a quick, fierce hug. We weren't huggers, so it meant a lot when we did. It sealed us together for a moment, like a promise.

"What is this place?" I whispered when she released me. "Who is this guy?"

"I don't know," Mom said, licking her lips rapidly. "I think he's rich."

"Mega rich," I said. "Did you know?"

She shook her head, her eyes wide as she took in the light, spacious room. It had hardwood floors with a dusky-blue area rug next to a huge canopy bed that must have been at least king sized. The walls were decorated with paintings of boats bobbing in the water, and I was pretty sure I recognized one of the cottages we'd passed in the background of one painting.

We even had our own bathroom, though I was a little afraid the bathtub might be used to harvest kidneys. What else could a rich guy want from a couple nutcases like us?

CHAPTER FOUR

Xander

I tried to get back to my busy day of playing video games, but my brain was short circuiting every two minutes. It was those crazy people upstairs. Finally, I got sick of restarting the level over and over, so I tossed down the controller and headed for the garage to fuck around with my bike.

I debated whether to jet and let Dad deal with this shit when he got home, but I wasn't sure what the crazies would do if I left them alone in my house. Probably burn it down. Not that a new start would be a bad thing. They'd get thrown in lockup, and we'd get the hell out of the state, go somewhere new, where no one knew us. But as tempting as the thought was, I couldn't just bail on my brothers and let them walk in on…whatever she was. Not without warning.

Dad had already blindsided us. He'd sprung

this on us all of a week before, telling us he met some lady in a grieving spouse support group. Wasn't that some shit. And now she'd shown up with no warning, and I'd had to deal with Dad's mistake on my own. Big surprise there. He'd conveniently failed to mention that she had a pretty blonde daughter who looked dangerously doe-eyed and ready for corrupting. Too damn innocent to be sleeping in an unlocked bedroom down the hall from the likes of the Keen brothers, that was for sure.

I grabbed a couple wrenches and started changing the oil on my bike. I wasn't sure what had gotten me so worked up. Everyone in Wellfleet knew that Xander Keen was unattainable—not that it stopped the girls from trying. I might fuck with them for kicks, but they could never fuck with me. I was an impenetrable fortress. But as soon as these wackos showed, everything inside me got all fucked up and crazy. My stomach, my head, my nerves, my adrenaline. And yeah, my dick.

On a scale of fugly to fuckable, Gwen did not register. Not because she wasn't hot—she was—but because I couldn't be thinking that shit about the daughter of Dad's girlfriend...or whatever the hell she was. Not that Dad was going to marry her. He hadn't spent his life building an empire from his dream with Mom, then fighting tooth and nail to keep it, only to throw it all away for two homeless nut-bags off the street.

They wouldn't be the first people who had

tried to discredit the men in this family and take us down with them. But no one had succeeded yet, and these psychos weren't going to be the first. It pissed me off that I'd even allowed them into the house. For all I knew, they were in there taking pictures of the shit they meant to steal when they pulled their con. It didn't help that the girl had been...whatever. It was more than how she looked. It was how she *felt*. Her presence had unsettled me, gotten me all turned around.

My wrench slipped, and my knuckle slammed against a bolt, the skin peeling back in a flap. Blood started dripping like gasoline onto the garage floor. I swore and wrapped it in a rag. I wanted to kick the shit out of something, but I wasn't about to kick my bike or anything that might hit it. And I wasn't stupid enough to kick the Bugatti.

Instead, I stalked out of the garage and glared up at the house. Rosa had taken them to a guest room on the third floor, but I couldn't see anything through the window. The curtains hung still, and they hadn't turned on the light inside. And yet I stood there, staring up for a good minute. I knew it was just the surprise, but it still sucked to feel like that girl had gotten me by the balls for even a second.

Disgusted, I turned away and circled the house to the car they'd driven up in. There was no way these crazies were going to take us down. No one fucked with the Keen family. Not at school, not anywhere else in life. I made damn sure of that, appointing myself guardian of our name at school, even if it got me suspended every now and then. Dad's lawyers took care of the rest of the world.

Where were they now, when he needed someone to knock some sense into him? It was one thing to have gold digging bitches trying to scheme their way into our lives and another thing entirely to invite them in.

I didn't care if they caught me going through their shitty little car, so I yanked open the door. The handle almost came off in my hand. I didn't give a fuck. I'd find some incriminating evidence and pass it on to Dad. If he wouldn't listen, which he probably wouldn't, I wasn't above going to his lawyers or even the board of his company. He wasn't going to ruin our lives because of some whack-job he found on the internet.

I rooted around in the glove box, but there wasn't much there. A pink slip, a manual, a receipt for an oil change. Hell, she didn't even have insurance cards. I slammed the box and searched under the seats, where I found a bunch of cheap paperback romances and dirty socks. By the time I'd finished with the car, my stomach was sour and hollow. It didn't seem right to call them homeless as an insult anymore. Not when I was pretty sure they actually were homeless.

I took out two battered duffle bags from the trunk and searched around the spare tire. I pulled up the mats in the front seat, and felt for lumps in the carpet in the back, where the mats were missing. Nothing too incriminating. They didn't seem to be carrying any evidence, but that didn't prove much. They could still be scammers. I knew one thing for sure. They were poor as fuck, and they were after our money and our family name. And I wasn't about to let them get it.

CHAPTER FIVE

Gwen

Mom had driven all night, and she passed out cold as soon as she lay down on the bed. I had to stay alert in case anyone came upstairs. The nervousness of a trespasser clung to me, and I felt guilty just for existing in this luxurious space where we clearly did not belong.

After a while, I began to relax despite myself. Mom would have a fit soon enough, and we'd run then. We hadn't even unloaded our bags, so the car was packed and ready. This was just a hiccup. When she snapped out of it, we'd laugh with disbelief that we'd gone into a mansion and taken a nap. I was just freaking out because she'd never had an episode quite like this before.

While I waited, I couldn't resist taking a peek at the small bookcase that was in the bedroom. It was mostly crime thrillers and courtroom dramas, but I took a stab at one, lying down gingerly on the soft, clean bed. My dirty hair would probably stain their high-dollar sheets, but I wasn't about to undress in this place. I didn't want to be caught in a vulnerable moment when someone came and told us to get the hell out of their palace.

I tried to read, but my eyes kept glazing over, and I had to start over at the top of the page again and again. But eventually, I must have dozed off. I woke to the faint sound of voices downstairs. I bolted upright, listening hard. Outside the window, the sky had grown a murky, gunmetal grey. I'd slept until evening, and my mother was nowhere to be found. Heart racing, I slipped off the bed and ran to the door. When I flung it open, I almost tripped over my duffle, which someone had carried up and set in the hallway outside. I hauled it through and left it in the middle of the bedroom floor. Then I slipped back out and tiptoed down the hall, quietly this time.

When I reached the second floor landing, I could hear my mother below, her voice low and serious. My legs turned to mush, and I had to steady myself against the wall. At least she hadn't ditched me. No matter how many times she promised, it was a constant fear. I had nothing without her.

A man's voice answered my mother's, but they were both too quiet for me to make out their words. Gripping the railing, I took a step down the stairs, then another, careful to keep my worn sneakers from slipping on the polished wood. I leaned forward, craning my neck and listening with everything I had.

"—been years—didn't think I'd ever—almost time—"

Mom was just talking about how long she'd been on her own with me. Suddenly, I felt guilty for spying. I should be happy for her and stop freaking out about being in a strange house with a dude I'd never met and his incredibly rude son. Mom would never lead me into danger, and she'd promised never to leave. Despite my irrational fears, I knew that deep into my bones, as surely as I knew I'd never leave her. She'd spent her whole life keeping me from anything even remotely, hypothetically dangerous. Whatever was going on, there wasn't anything sinister about it.

I had to trust her. If I didn't, I'd go completely mad. She was the only person in the entire world who knew me, the only person I knew. She anchored me. Without her, I'd fly right off the spinning world and into outer space, where her mind resided half the time.

Hating myself for doubting her, I stepped up a step, creeping backwards until I reached the top floor. When I took the final step, a chill exploded along my arms and up my back. I froze as a soft, warm breath stirred the fine hairs on the back of my neck.

"Hey there," said a low, masculine voice behind me.

After nearly jumping out of my skin, I turned

slowly, trying to come up with an excuse for when Xander raked me over the coals for eavesdropping. But the guy standing behind me wasn't Xander.

A stranger towered over me, so close we were practically hugging. Instead of stepping back, he stared down at me from behind his round spectacles. I stared back in an exaggerated way, hoping he'd notice how rude it was, but apparently his father hadn't taught him any more manners than he'd taught his other son.

After a second my resentment melted, and I found myself studying him as closely as he was studying me. There was something about him…had we met? Or was it just a slight resemblance to the brother I'd already met? This guy had a sculpted, handsome face with well-defined cheekbones, chin, and nose. His black hair was cut just long enough on top to hold a curl. Behind his glasses, his eyes were an intense, warm brown, which kept his sharp, angular features from looking severe. He stood with a slight slouch to his shoulders, as if he weren't quite comfortable being six feet tall.

For reasons I didn't completely understand, I wanted to pull him closer, to put my arms around him and comfort him. I tugged my sleeves over my hands and balled them into fists. What was wrong with me? Aside from my mother, I never touched people—and I was used to that. Why did I suddenly have the urge to start petting everyone?

A voice called up the stairs that dinner was

ready, and we both jerked back, startled. How long had we been standing there, silently drinking each other in? I suddenly felt not just awkward but disconnected somehow, as if I'd zoned out on an especially vivid daydream. The guy standing over me looked just as bewildered as I felt.

"So…uh, dinner's ready," he said, gesturing for me to go at the same moment I gestured for him. After another awkward pause, I turned and escaped down the stairs.

Rosa, the woman who had greeted us so warmly, ushered us into a dining room with a long table topped with a white linen tablecloth. Above it hung a crystal chandelier that probably cost more than Mom had made in her entire life. She, Xander, and Neil were already there, scooting in at the table when we walked in. Neil immediately jumped up and strode down the length of the table to greet me with a firm handshake. One look at him, and I knew where the good looks of the two sons came from.

He was tall like them, with a modest tan and black hair shot through with strands of silver. He wore tailored pinstripe pants and a lavender dress shirt with the sleeves rolled up to his elbows, showing off muscular forearms and an expensive watch.

Every inch of him stank of money.

I was suddenly aware that I literally stank of something much less pleasant than money. The vague scent of dirty hair that I usually didn't notice was amplified by my nearness to this suave, clean-shaven man with his faint traces of cologne and expensive taste. I swear, I could smell it on him.

"You must be Gwen," he said, holding onto my hand. "I'm Neil."

"I know."

He kept holding onto my hand, studying me, until I pulled away. What was with all these weirdos and their staring? Why had my mother brought me into a house full of people who did the one thing I hated more than anything—paid attention to me. We spent our lives trying not to draw attention. The only exception was when Mom had an episode and stopped caring. But when my eyes moved to her, she licked her lips and smiled. No screaming, no dragging me out to the car or even muttering about ravens.

"I see you've met Eliot," he said. "And I trust Xander greeted you warmly when you arrived."

I glanced over at Xander and I caught something in his eye. Maybe a challenge? "We couldn't have asked for a more hospitable welcome," I said, turning back to Neil.

"Glad to hear it," he said. "I'm sorry my daughter isn't here to join us for dinner. Peyton's about your age, your mother tells me. She's at cheer practice, but she should be home in time for dessert. You'll like her."

"If she's anything like your sons, how could I not?" I asked. "Your family is so friendly and normal."

Mom shot me a startled look. Ah. So she

hadn't told him everything. Maybe he thought *we* were friendly and normal.

"I'm afraid Gwen hasn't had a chance to make many friends," Mom said, shooting Neil an anxious smile. "With how often we moved."

"Well, she'll have lots of friends here," Neil said cheerfully, taking his seat again.

"Sorry about your wife," I blurted.

Everyone in the room stared at me. My toes curled inside my shoes.

"Smooth," Xander muttered with a smirk.

I swallowed hard. "You know, because she died."

"No need to apologize," Neil said, but I noticed he'd gone a little stiff. He turned to Eliot. "Where's Finn?"

Eliot shrugged and pulled a phone from his pocket and started texting.

"Sometimes, I think they really are telepathic, the way they're connected," Neil said, busying himself with shaking out his cloth napkin and laying it across his lap. "They say that about twins."

"Wow," I said, scooting in next to Mom. "Big family."

"Let's eat," Neil said, clapping his hands together. As if on cue, Rosa came in carrying a huge serving pan. My stomach growled loudly, but I put down my fork when I saw that no one else had started eating.

"Lobster with truffle butter," Rosa whispered,

sliding a piece of white meat with pink skin onto my plate. I gave her a grateful smile, relieved to have an ally here even as the surreal moment made my head swim. Two days ago I would have been ecstatic if my mother had gotten a job like Rosa's. Now, I was being served herbed fingerling potatoes by an actual maid.

To my surprise, after serving us, Rosa sat down with the rest of the family.

When everyone started eating, I picked up my fork and went right for the lobster. Of course I'd never had lobster before, but I'd read about it in lots of books. Guys were always feeding it to their dates when they wanted to impress them with their money. The thought gave me pause, and I looked up to see if Neil was checking my mother's reaction, ready to boast about the dinner he'd served us. But Mom was engrossed in the food, and Neil wasn't paying her much attention. In fact, he was looking at me.

I quickly pushed the bite of lobster into my mouth. It was sweet and tender and buttery, and my stomach begged for more. Before I could take another bite, though, something zinged up my back like a needle of electricity. My fork slipped from my fingers and clattered to the table. The hair stood up all along my arms, almost crackling with stiffness.

Xander muttered something, and he and Eliot exchanged a look. Neil's eyes followed our every move like a hawk's. He wasn't just watching me. He was watching his kids, too. When his eyes moved to the door, I turned to see another guy shuffling in.

Finn, I supposed.

For a second, he looked just like...I couldn't think of the person he looked like, but he felt so familiar, as if I'd seen him before. I wracked my brain, trying to remember if we'd ever been here when I was younger, before Dad died. Or if I'd met him somewhere else. But I'd been so many places and seen so many faces, it was impossible to know where I'd run across him before. I was sure I had, though. The sense of familiarity was undeniable and unsettling.

"Sorry," he said, his eyes circling the table and landing on me. Like his brothers, he was cute, but he lacked the tall, dark, and handsome thing. He was average height, with light brown hair falling in loose waves around his shoulder. His handsome face was highlighted by dark, voluptuous lips that made me immediately wonder what they'd feel like.

What the hell, Gwen? He's cute, big deal. Get a grip and stop perving.

His jade green eyes caught mine, and electricity zipped up my arms and through my entire body, as if it sensed that he was somehow different than the many cute strangers I'd admired in passing. As if this time, there was more to my random attraction.

I felt my face warm, and I tore my eyes from his, more ruffled by the open longing I saw on his face than my own unexpected desire. Not that a guy had never given me an appreciative glance before. I got the odd smile or once-over as often as the next girl in the diners where my mom worked, but not when I had bedhead and was wearing the same rumpled clothes I'd slept in…twice.

A rush of shame washed over me. He was probably wondering why there were dirty strangers at his table, not admiring me.

"Your lobster's getting cold," Rosa said, gesturing with her fork towards Finn's plate.

"Right," he said, shuffling forwards and taking his seat. He swung around, sliding his paint-splattered jeans under the table. Tiny droplets of black ink spotted one tan forearm, and a drop had landed on his left cheekbone.

"Gwen, your mother tells me you're an avid reader," Neil said after a minute of awkward silence.

I looked up, startled, and cast my mom a worried look. She didn't like anyone to know anything about us, not even the smallest detail. What else had she told him?

"She reads at least a book a day," Mom said with an encouraging smile.

"Out of necessity," I muttered. I knew she wanted me to make conversation with her new guy, but it was just too bizarre.

Mom smiled apologetically and took a bite of lobster. The moment washed over me in all its ridiculousness. We were eating lobster in a freaking mansion. A giggle threatened to bubble up inside me. Struggling to keep it inside, I pinched my lips together.

"I like reading," Eliot said quietly, pushing his glasses up on his nose. He was slouching at the table the same way he did when he stood—with his shoulders folded in, as if he were trying to be smaller, to disappear. I knew that position well from times when my mother had drawn public attention, and a protective longing unfurled inside me again.

"Cool," I said, offering him a small smile. "We'll have to compare reading lists after dinner."

Eliot looked surprised, which endeared me to him even more.

Xander snorted. "That sounds *fascinating.*"

What was his problem? Was he the reason Eliot was so shy? I could see it now, the cocky older brother with his dangerous scowl overshadowing the geeky, quiet brother. All the girls in romance novels fell for guys like Xander. The hot, mean ones. But I thought they were jerks.

"What else do you like to do?" Eliot asked, watching me intently.

I looked to my mother for help, and she smiled and nodded for me to answer. I wiped my hands on the linen napkin beside my plate. "I like...maps."

I cringed even before Xander scoffed, right on cue, with exactly the curl in his upper lip I expected. Not that I cared what he thought. But...well, maybe I did. It was hard not to feel self-conscious around a guy who looked like he did—and who clearly knew it.

"Maps?" Finn asked, his head cocked to one side.

It had just popped into my head when I tried to think of what I spent most of my time doing. Now, they were all staring at me again.

I squirmed in my chair, concentrating very hard on taking a bite of lobster. I knew basically nothing about boys, or human beings in general. Sometimes, I could forget that, but now was not one of those times.

Just then, a thump sounded in the front room and footsteps approached. Peyton. If Xander was the asshole, I knew the girl would be even worse. Cheerleaders were always bitches in the books I read, and I knew girls could devastate each other in ways guys couldn't even comprehend.

"Something smells delish," said a perky voice. A petite girl skipped into the room, her glossy, baby-pink high ponytail swinging. Well, she wasn't blonde as I'd expected, but everything else fit my image of a cheerleader—the hairstyle, the pretty face, the tiny, perfectly proportioned body that probably didn't have a single burn scar on it.

She was followed by a guy wearing athletic shorts and a T-shirt despite the wintery chill outside. He had a sports duffle over one muscular shoulder, so I assumed he must be her football player boyfriend. Cheerleaders always had those.

His Wellfleet Oysters T-shirt was molded to

his sculpted body, which looked like it was made of pure muscle. His ripped shoulders and washboard abs strained against the fabric, as if they longed to be seen in all their glory, without the impediment of clothing. The thought made my face warm as my eyes traveled upwards. I couldn't help but feel a twinge of regret that he was already taken. With his chiseled jawline and blonde, military-cut hair, he looked like a movie star from a small-town football romance.

His eyes met mine, and that crazy sense of familiarity washed over me again, this time so strong I had to grasp the edge of the table. I felt myself sway as if I might topple over. *Déjà vous* swept through the room like a gust of wind. I'd been here before. I had met these people before. I didn't remember, and yet, I *knew* in that strange way that I only knew a few things in life.

I may not know where I'd get my next meal, how we'd pay for gas, or when we'd pack up and take off again. I may not know a single real-life person besides my mother. But I knew that no matter where we went, the earth was below and the sky above, the sun rose in the east and set in the west, my mother loved me, and that whether a day was the best or worst one ever, it would end as time marched on. And I knew these people.

It was impossible, but somehow, I did.

"Oh my God, look at us. We could be real sisters," Peyton said, drawing my gaze from her boyfriend as she skipped over to stand beside me so everyone could compare us.

Her hand landed on my shoulder as our eyes met, and something sizzled through the room. It wasn't just inside me this time. I felt rather than heard a crack somewhere far below us, as if a fissure had broken in the earth's crust. The house tremored. Little sparks fizzled across the tablecloth, the way sparks of static electricity hop along a sweater you peel off in the dark. Rosa jerked back, knocking over her glass of wine. Peyton grabbed onto my chair, her mouth frozen in a little O shape. Static shocks crackled along my legs.

And then it was over. My mother's fork, which had been poised halfway to her mouth, sank back to her plate. Neil's shoulders relaxed as he righted the glass and threw a napkin over the spilled wine. Rosa started putting lobster on the two empty plates.

"Um, hello, what just happened?" Peyton shrieked.

Well, at least I wasn't crazy. The adults were acting so normal I'd almost thought I'd hallucinated the whole thing.

"The heater kicked on down in the basement, that's all," Neil said with a tight smile.

"Dude, did you see those sparks?" the football player asked. "That was wicked!"

"Maybe I should check the fuses," Eliot said, pushing back from the table.

"It's fine," Neil said. "It's happened before.

It's no big deal."

No big deal? I felt like I'd been halfway electrocuted, and they were acting like nothing had happened.

But it had. I stared at Neil, who gave me a quick smile before pouring himself some wine. Eliot said he was going to check the breaker box, just in case, and loped out of the room. Peyton sat down, chattering on about how crazy that was, and then moving on to how sorry she was that she hadn't been here when we arrived. Only Xander was openly glaring at me, muttering curses under his breath. I anchored my eyes to him, relieved that someone else was acknowledging what had happened, and it wasn't so easily brushed off.

A spot of wine soaked up through the napkin Neil had thrown over it like blood leaking through a bandage. Physical proof. Did they really believe that was just the heater? What was wrong with these people?

Suddenly, I couldn't take it anymore. All the changes and the weirdness overwhelmed me, and I thought I'd be sick. I jumped up from the table. My chair crashed to the floor behind me. Though I usually avoided drawing attention, I didn't care right then. I had to get out of there.

This is how Mom must feel when she completely loses her shit.

"I—I'm going to go lie down," I said, staggering backwards.

"But I just got here," Peyton said, jumping up and grabbing both my hands in hers.

Dizziness washed over me, and I stumbled, my knees giving way. The football player rushed forward and caught me. "Whoa there," he said in a deep, amused voice.

A bolt of electricity shot through me when he touched me, and I almost cried out. Was this how my mother felt all the time? Was I losing my mind like her? Is this how it happened, a psychic break with reality, everything distorted like a funhouse mirror so you couldn't tell what was real and what was part of the crazy?

"I must be allergic to lobster," I mumbled.

"But you haven't even had dessert," Xander said, laughter edging his voice. His taunting tone made my suspicions from the day before rise to the surface. Had they drugged me?

"I was going to show you the library," Eliot added. I hadn't even seen him return. Had I blacked out for a second?

I did really want to see the library, if that's what it was. But for all I knew, that was code for "torture chamber."

"Let her get some rest," Mom said, holding up a hand to stop the protests. "This is a lot to take in."

"She's right," Neil said. "We've all been a family for a long time. This is her first night here."

I wondered distantly what that meant, but my

brain was jumping all over the place and I couldn't focus. I didn't know about the fuses downstairs, but my brain was definitely shorting out.

As the football player scooped me up in a threshold carry, my head swam. What was happening? Had my mother betrayed me, sold me off to a bunch of psychos for the only thing they could offer that she'd want—secrecy?

"Mom?" I called, struggling to get free of the strong arm circling my waist.

"Go lay down," Mom said. "It's all right, Gwen. We're safe here. Just get some sleep."

Unlike Peyton's two tall brothers, this guy was thickly muscled, his chest and shoulders hard as I pressed my palms against them, trying to push myself away.

"Chill, I'm just going to help you to your room," he said. He smiled, his face a mix of boyish charm and Hollywood good looks. Momentarily dazed, I gave in as he strode out of the kitchen and up the stairs. There was no way I could fight my way out of his muscled embrace, anyway.

As he climbed the stairs, I let myself be Scarlet O'Hara for a minute, being whisked off by Rhett Butler. But my mind quickly raced ahead to the next scene in that book, and awkwardness replaced any romance in the moment.

"Sorry I wasn't here earlier," the guy said. "Me and Peyton almost always have practice at the same time, so we just ride together."

"You live here, too?" I blurted out. "How many of you are there?"

He laughed and pushed open the bedroom door where I'd slept earlier. "Just the four of us and Peyton," he said, letting me down at last. "And she's basically one of the guys. So five of us."

I wiped my hands on my jeans, then let them hang limp, not sure what to do with them. Now that I was standing here with just him, I felt silly for making a fuss in the dining room. The dizziness had passed, leaving only a faint urgency buzzing in my blood, as if I had drank a lot of coffee because I needed to be somewhere, but then I forgot where I was supposed to be.

"I'm Ezekiel," he said. "But my friends all call me Zeke." He thrust out a hand in an oddly formal gesture, considering we'd just had our bodies pressed together.

"Hi, Ezekiel," I said, feeling shy as I placed my hand in his. A wave of vertigo rolled over me, but it quickly passed, thanks to his steadying grip on my hand.

The corner of his mouth quirked up, and he lifted his eyebrows. "Don't you want to be friends?" His tone was teasing, but in a nice way, not like Xander's.

I felt my face warm, and I pulled my hand from his. "Sure."

"Sure…?" he asked, still raising his eyebrows expectantly.

"Sure, Zeke," I said, testing it out like it was a word in a foreign language. I may not have had a single social skill, but I'd never thought I was particularly shy, either. But this was a whole new ballgame. I was standing in front of a guy who looked like he could be on a show on the *CW*, considering his height combined with the muscular build, blonde hair, and easy, infectious smile.

"Cool, Gwen," he said, the corner of his mouth quirking up again. His blue eyes sparkled with humor as he said my name. And though I'd never thought much about my name one way or another, it sounded fun and carefree on his lips. When he said my name, I didn't picture boring old me, reading paperbacks in the car while Mom did odd jobs in another nameless town. I pictured a girl with her blonde hair in the kind of ponytail Peyton wore, a girl who drove a red convertible with her name on the custom license plate, and deserved a guy like him.

"I guess I'll let you get some rest," Zeke said. "Unless you wanted me to stay? If you don't feel good, I could just hang out for a minute, in case you need anything."

"Thanks," I said, sitting on the edge of the bed. "I don't know what happened down there. Sorry." My face warmed thinking of the spectacle I'd made. In Zeke's presence, I'd forgotten the sparks and the mini-earthquake. Thinking about it now, it didn't seem like a big deal. I knew it was weird, but my body was relaxed, like I had nothing to worry about.

Definitely drugged.

I couldn't summon the anxiety that thought should have caused.

"Tell you what," Zeke said. "I'm going to hit the shower since I probably stink. You can use the ensuite bathroom in here if you want to clean up."

An inferno of shame washed over me, immobilizing my tongue in my mouth. I nodded mutely, staring at my shoes. I could feel the grime between my toes.

Zeke didn't seem to notice my discomfort, or he was too polite to comment. He went on like everything was cool. "I'll meet you on the deck in like thirty." He smiled and held up both hands, palms out. "If you want. No pressure."

Without waiting for an answer, he stepped out and closed my door. I fell back on the pillows, grabbing one and hugging it to my chest, biting back a smile.

Though all Neil's kids were attractive, there was something about Zeke that made my heart melt. I was pretty sure I was having my first crush.

CHAPTER SIX

Gwen

The door had barely closed behind Zeke when Mom stepped into the room. The high of being with Zeke began to fade as soon as she walked in dragging reality with her like a ball and chain. Before I could think, a flicker of resentment darted to life inside me. For once in my life, I wanted a moment to feel normal. A moment where I wasn't the daughter of the crazy lady, where I was just a girl reveling in the rush of new feelings overtaking her.

Guilt quickly replaced my resentment, and I remembered everything that Zeke had made me forget for a moment. "Mom," I said, sitting up and replacing the pillow I'd been holding. "What happened?"

"I don't know," she said, sinking to the edge of the bed. "But I'm going to find out. We're going to figure it out together, okay? Just like we always do."

"We're leaving?" I asked, a knot of conflicting feelings tangling inside me. An hour ago, I'd been waiting for this. Now I wasn't sure. I wanted a few more minutes of normalcy before I went back on the road for another ten years. That glimpse was not enough.

"We don't have to run," Mom said. "Not now. Maybe not again for...forever."

I blinked at her stupidly, trying to imagine what we'd do with ourselves if we stayed in one place. If we had a real home, a place to accumulate things, to get comfortable.

It was dangerous to think that way, though. We'd never stay. That was as delusional as thinking there were giants after us.

"I talked to Neil a little," Mom said. "He says this kind of thing sometimes happens. Maybe not as...spectacular as what happened tonight. But odd things."

"And that makes you feel safe?"

Mom shook her head. "I don't know what to feel right now," she said. "I'm being careful, though. And you should, too."

"What does that mean?" I asked, my fingers worrying at a tear in my jeans.

"It means there are things besides giants that can hurt you," she said, her voice low. "People can hurt you, too, Gwen."

"I know," I said, examining the thread I'd pulled loose.

"Good," she said. "I didn't realize…well. When Neil said he had kids, I guess I didn't fully realize what that meant until I saw them. If anything happens that makes you uncomfortable, you can come to me. You know that, right?"

"Mom," I said, my face warming. "I'm fine."

"It's just that you've never dealt with the problems most teenagers face. Peer pressure and hormones and…"

"God, Mom," I said, standing and pacing the room. "This is so not necessary. I read a lot of romance novels. I know how things work."

Now Mom looked uncomfortable. "I know you do," she said. "I brought you into this house, though, so I want you to know that I'm on your side. These are teenage boys who have lived a different life than you. If one of them did anything…"

"Thanks," I said. "I think I'm going to take a shower. Will you stay in here?"

She gave me a wary look, then nodded. "Of course."

I grabbed a few clean clothes from my duffle, then stopped in the bathroom doorway, a new thought forming. "Are you going to sleep in Neil's room?" I asked.

It was silly and immature to need her to sleep with me, but I'd never slept in a room without my mother. Not really. Sometimes I slept in the car, or a storage locker, or even a break room at whatever job she got. But that didn't really count. She was working during those times. When she slept, I always slept next to her.

"I can sleep in here with you as long as you need me to," she said with a reassuring smile. "I'm not going anywhere, Gwen. I told you that. I'll be right here when you get out of the shower and right here all night."

"Oh," I said, glancing into the bathroom. "I might...well, I might go out and talk to the others for a while.

"I might stay up and talk to Neil a while, too," she said. After a moment's pause, she smiled. "It's strange having other people to talk to besides you."

"It is," I agreed, a smile forming on my lips. "I think I like it."

"Me, too."

In the bathroom, I undressed on the plush carpet beside the tub. My grubby toes sank into the soft, thick threads. The room was big, with a full clawfoot tub surrounded by a circular rod. The curtain hanging around the tub was a dusty blue linen with tiny sailboats printed on it. Muted blue, green, grey, and tan tiles across the floor brought back the memory of the beach that afternoon. Not so much as a speck of dirt or a random hair was visible anywhere. It was so clean that I winced as I stepped onto the tiles and into the tub.

I quickly turned on the water, scrubbing away the dirt on my feet with almond-scented soap. Instead of using an entire mini bottle of hotel shampoo, I only had to use a little of theirs to get mounds of soft foam in my hair. Heavenly, scented steam filled the bathroom in clouds, and the hot water didn't run out after five minutes like it did at the laundromats or rest areas where we usually paid to shower. I indulged my greed, washing my entire body with the fine soaps and even conditioning my impossibly long hair.

When at last I felt clean and fresh enough to step out of the tub, guilt replaced the greed. I'd used up tons of hot water, and taken advantage of their generosity. But then, I figured they could afford the soap, so I tried to quell the feeling of being an intruder. They had invited us. We hadn't broken in.

I pulled up short when the full-length mirror reflected my image back to me, as if reminding me that I could never belong in this perfect house. With my clothes on, I could pass for normal until someone talked to me. Without them...

Drawing a slow breath, I ran my fingers over the mottled red scar tissue that covered my body from the bottom of my right breast to my left hipbone in a swath that barely missed my belly button. My skin was puckered and shiny, almost reptilian. Though I saw the scars every time I undressed, they were just a part of my body. Seeing them in a mirror was like seeing them from an outsider's perspective. What would this beautiful family think if they saw how ugly I was under my clothes?

I barely remembered the fire that had taken

Dad's life and half of Mom's sanity. The pain and trauma of my wounds had made the memories of that night and a few months after into vague and shadowy nightmares. But my body didn't forget so easily. I'd been marked by that fire as surely as Mom had, just in different ways. Neither of us belonged in this house with its perfect people and fancy food.

Turning away from the mirror, I quickly wrapped myself in a luxurious, fluffy white towel that must have been half an inch thick. I'd had the same towel for a year, and it had been secondhand when I'd gotten it. How ridiculously rich did a person have to be to afford towels that cost more than my entire wardrobe? The extravagance both awed and horrified me. How many rooms in this house stood empty while people like my mother and me slept in cars—or much worse?

As I wound my hair up and prepared to leave the bathroom, my mind returned to something my mother sometimes said. We were the lucky ones. We weren't completely homeless—we had our car, and she always managed to get jobs that paid cash. It was true.

At those jobs, she made friends, however briefly. She told me stories about them, about her kindly coworkers and cranky managers, quirky customers and clients. I never talked to anyone. And yet, I hadn't been lonely. The thought that she needed more should have made me sad, but instead, that little flame of resentment flickered again. Why did she have to need other people? I didn't need anyone else.

Then I remembered Peyton skipping over to stand beside me and saying we could be sisters. And the way I felt when Zeke turned that dazzling movie star smile on me. Mom had always told me we didn't need anyone else. But if she could change her mind, then maybe it was okay for me to start needing other people in my life, too.

CHAPTER SEVEN

Zeke

I stood in the shower scrubbing my nasty feet, thinking about what had just happened. I didn't know what it was about this girl, but I wanted to know more. Something weird was going on, and she was the key. I'd felt it when I walked into the dining room at dinner, and I knew she'd felt it, too. Whatever was going on, I was going to find out.

I'd wanted to hang out in her room a while, but I was getting the vibe that she needed space. Girls didn't regularly give me that vibe. They were usually the ones hanging on like left tackles while I tried to shake them loose.

Still, when I got done lathering up, I decided I'd stop by and remind her of the invitation to hang. The others must have been dying to get to know her, too, and they'd all gotten a shot first. Ever since Dad had announced that he'd invited a mysterious lady and her daughter to come stay with us, I'd been going nuts with curiosity. Dad didn't do stuff like that. Since Mom died, he'd had his hands full with the five of us. Having five teenagers in the house couldn't have been easy for anyone, even if one of them hadn't been Xander.

Now the lady had arrived, and though she was a little strange, I was way more interested in the mysterious daughter. I didn't want to waste my shot at getting to know her by hanging out in the shower too long, but I also didn't want to gross her out with my stinky pits.

When I was scrubbed clean as a newborn baby, I shut off the water and stepped out of the shower. The bathroom was so full of steam I could barely see the full length mirror that stood next to the sink. I stepped up to it and wiped a spot clean, leaning in to check for budding zits. My skin was clear, though—that junk Peyton had given me must have worked. Not that I'd ever let on that I used girl's skin cream.

I flexed my arms in front of the mirror, checking out my muscles. Then I gave my bicep a little kiss for getting me so far on the football field, not to mention with the ladies.

"Wake up."

My head jerked up, and I squinted to see through the steam. Who the hell had come in the bathroom while I was showering? It couldn't have been Gwen, could it? That wasn't her voice. Or was it? I couldn't even say for sure what the voice had sounded like or which direction :t had come from, though I'd heard the words clearly.

"Who said that?" I asked, swiping at the steam around me. It billowed and swirled, but I couldn't make out a shape. I karate chopped the steam, searching for someone—was it her mom? I'd barely gotten a glimpse of her before I carried her daughter off. Maybe she was pissed about it.

Sometimes I remembered weird shit that hadn't really happened, like I was sure I remembered walking around some pond in Boston, feeding ducks with Mom when I was little. But that couldn't have happened because Mom hated birds and said the smell of them made her sick. But hallucinating something in the present was more real than hallucinating a memory, and a lot freakier.

The weirdest part was, I couldn't find anyone in all that steam and fog. After I'd freaked myself out, I threw on a towel and got out of there with a quickness. Not that I was afraid of steam monsters or anything, but I was sure I'd heard a voice. I'd never had a hallucination before, not even the time that asshole Joaquin had given me a brownie at a party and then laughed at me because I didn't know "special" meant "drugged."

Besides, wasn't a hallucination when you *saw* trippy shit that wasn't there? I didn't know if you could hallucinate a sound. Maybe that was called something different, like a hearlucination.

I hurried down the hall, threw on a T-shirt and some sweats, and rubbed the towel over my hair one more time. In my mirror, I looked totally normal, and no creepy fog monster lurked behind me. Tossing my towel on the end of my bed, I headed for Gwen's room. After all the excitement downstairs, I expected someone to have come up to check on her, but I couldn't hear a peep behind her door.

A funny thing happened in my gut before I tapped on the door, but I figured it was just because I'd skipped dinner. When I pushed open the door, Gwen was lying on the bed, propped up on pillows, with a book open across her knees. Her wet hair was twisted up into a giant knot thing on top of her head, and she was wearing different clothes. She looked up and offered me a shy smile.

"Hey," I said. "You ready to go sit on the deck?"

"It's kinda cold," Gwen said in a small voice, hugging herself and rubbing her arms to warm up.

"I'll grab you a jacket," I said. Then I fixed her with my best puppy-dog eyes. "Come on. Please?"

Another smile tugged at the corner of her lips. "Maybe for a minute," she said, swinging her legs off the bed.

"Really?" I asked, surprised for some reason. But I didn't want to look too eager, so I tried to hide it by shrugging and saying, "Cool."

She stuffed her feet into a pair of ratty Converse sneaks and shuffled over to me, not seeming to notice that she'd turned the smooth operator Zeke into a total dork. I was just glad I'd gotten to her before my brothers told her too many of my less stellar moments. Xander was especially fond of doing that around girls.

"How big is this place?" Gwen asked as we stepped into my bedroom. "Do you each have your own room?"

"The twins used to share," I said. "But that was by choice." I snagged a Wellfleet Oysters hoodie from the back of a chair and handed it to her, covertly kicking a pair of boxers under my bed while she was distracted. I didn't want her thinking I was a total slob. The girl was fine, but unlike the girls who usually caught my eye, she wasn't all dolled up. Not that I didn't dig the natural look, too, but it was cool to know a girl had put in some effort for me, especially if I'd gotten myself all spiffed out for her.

Gwen pulled on my hoodie, reaching up to dig her topknot out of the neck of the shirt before pulling her head through. She looked even better in my sweatshirt. With a jolt, I caught myself checking out her Levi-clad legs. I had to remember she was there because our dad was interested in her mom, not because she was keen on the Keen. For a minute, I'd totally forgotten. But hey, it wasn't my fault Dad had the hots for her mom.

"Let's hit the deck," I said, shrugging off the weird pull she had on me. I wanted to get out of my room before she noticed the seashell nightlight plugged into an outlet in the corner. Obviously, I hid that shit away in the bottom of my closet when I invited girls over.

As we headed downstairs, I gave myself a pep talk. It was only natural for me to check out a fine female, especially a new girl in town. Wellfleet wasn't exactly a happening place in the off-season. Summer was when the beach babes showed up—high school girls with their parents, nannies watching the kids of vacationing doctors, Ivy League college girls bonding with their parents on their time off school. This time of year, I was deep into a dry spell, since I'd already dated all the girls at school I was interested in.

Gwen shoved her hands into the pocket of my hoodie as I led her out onto the back deck. We could hear the little waves in the bay slapping the shore below. Gwen huddled deeper into my hoodie, which swallowed her up in the cutest way. I brushed off the urge to put my arm around her. After throwing some logs into the outdoor fireplace, I crouched and lit it, calming myself with the familiar task.

When the fire was lit, smoke started churning out in my face, and I jumped back, halfway expecting a weird smoke monster to speak to me. Before that could happen, I opened up the flue so the smoke would go up the chimney. I stood back and smiled at my handiwork.

"Pull up a deck chair," I said. "I'll go grab some snacks."

I ducked inside and headed straight for the dining room, where Rosa was cleaning up. "Save me any lobster?" I asked, grabbing a handful of glasses and following her to the kitchen.

"For you? No way," she said. "You'll wolf it down in two bites without enjoying it. There's a microwave dinner in the freezer for you."

"Aww, you're killing me," I said, giving her my puppy dog eyes as I opened the freezer.

"I'm kidding, you lug head," she said, pulling a foil-wrapped plate from the fridge. With a grin, I tossed the frozen dinner back, ruffled her hair, and grabbed the plate. I was famished.

"How is she?" Rosa asked, giving me a guarded look.

"I don't know yet," I said, peeling the foil off my plate. "Dad tasked me with making her feel at home, so I'm going to try."

"She's not too upset about what happened at dinner?"

"No idea," I said. "How come you're not asking if I'm upset?"

"You're fine," Rosa said, rolling her eyes.

"Why wouldn't I be?" I slid the plate in the microwave and turned it on before reassuring myself. "Dad said it was just the heater, so it was just the heater."

"Exactly," Rosa said, turning away.

While my food heated, I saw a shadow slip down the stairs and towards the deck. Damn. I'd missed my chance to have Gwen to myself.

Oh, well. I didn't mind sharing, as long as it was with one of my brothers.

CHAPTER EIGHT

Gwen

When the French door slid open, I gave a guilty start, though I hadn't been doing anything but arranging two chairs close to the fire like Zeke had asked me to. It would take me a while not to feel like an imposter in these lavish surroundings.

When I looked up, it wasn't Zeke coming out, though.

"What's up?" Peyton asked, bouncing across the deck, her ponytail swinging.

I shrugged, studying the floor. I hated this feeling, the one I'd been worried about when I heard Neil had a family. They were all typical teenagers, and I...well, I wasn't. The minute I opened my mouth, they'd all know what a weird, awkward, socially inept person I was.

"I figured we could hang out," Peyton said. "We can get in the hot tub if you want."

"No," I said quickly, imagining their horror if they saw my childhood scars.

"Okay, then," Peyton said. "What do you want to do?"

"Stop feeling like I'm squatting here illegally and you're going to kick us out of your mansion at any minute?"

Peyton stared at me. I swallowed and turned away, cursing myself for voicing my thoughts. There were a couple ways I could have answered her question, but apparently, the honest answer wasn't the right one. Asking if she was a cheerleader bitch like the ones in all the books I read probably wouldn't have gotten us off on the right foot, either.

I was avoiding the question of why meeting her had caused a minor earthquake. That would lead to questions about my sanity, which might lead to questions about Mom's sanity, and we tried not to raise those questions with outsiders. Outsiders being anyone besides me and Mom.

How was I supposed to know what to say to a bubblegum-haired cheerleader?

"Soooo, anyway," Peyton said after a long, awkward pause. She had a slight Boston accent like her brothers.

"Yeah," I said. "So anyway."

She gave me another odd look. "Our dad told us you were coming, like, a week ago," she said. "Kind of a shock. How long have you known?"

I felt like I'd been slapped. Mom had known

for that long?

"Uh…a day?"

"Oh, wow," she said, her eyes widening. "That's nuts."

"No, it's not."

"Um…okay," she said. "But your mom just told you that you were moving halfway across the country to meet some guy she met online. Yesterday. How crazy is that?"

"She's not crazy," I said quickly, pulling my hands into the sleeves of Zeke's hoodie. "We're not nuts. We're totally normal."

Peyton laughed and pulled over a piece of deck furniture that looked like a couch but was made of some kind of twisted wooden sticks, topped with sand-colored cushions with little blue seahorses on them. "Normal is boring," she said. "And I can already tell you're not boring."

"Sure I am," I said. "Move along, folks. Nothing to see here."

Peyton laughed again and plopped down on the couch thing. Even the way she sat down was cute and bouncy. "How do you like the place?" she asked, gesturing around.

"It's…amazing," I said, then winced at the bald awe in my voice. I should have played it cool, acted unimpressed.

"It's nice of your mom to give up your house and just move all the way out here," she said. "I can't imagine doing that. I'd be so mad if Dad had wanted to move to St. Louis. No offense, I'm sure it's cool, but all my friends are here, you know?"

"Totally," I said, though of course I didn't know anything about friends or missing people. When I thought about Mom leaving me, I thought I'd die. So maybe missing people was like that.

"What about you?" Peyton asked. "Are you going to miss your friends a lot?"

I thought about telling her my best friend was Buffy the Vampire Slayer from the show I'd watched in its entirety at a library in Little Rock while my mom went to work every day. Or maybe I should pick Scarlet O'Hara from *Gone With the Wind*, because I could talk to her anywhere. That kinda interfered with the whole sanity thing, though, and I'd already gotten enough funny looks tonight, so I just nodded.

"Tell me about your best friend," Peyton said, leaning back and watching me expectantly. Apparently this was some kind of game.

"I…didn't really have a lot of friends," I admitted.

Just then, Zeke stepped onto the deck with a plate in one hand and a soda in the other. He took a seat on the far end of the couch from Peyton and started eating.

"Don't worry. You'll have tons of friends here," Peyton said. "We'll make sure of it, won't we, Zeke? And we're going to be best friends. We'll be like sisters."

"You're not like a sister to me," Zeke said,

giving me a smile that made me feel like we had our own little secret.

"Don't be mean," Peyton said, swiping his soda.

"I'm not being mean," Zeke said. "I already have one pain-in-the-ass sister. I don't need two."

Peyton just laughed.

I watched her take a drink, envying the easy way they had with each other. I didn't even have that kind of relationship with my own mother. During her good times, we were close, but there was always that barrier between us, that thing we didn't talk about. I knew the good times wouldn't last, that we'd be back on the run again too soon. Before now, I'd never fully realized what I was missing.

Sitting on the deck, watching Peyton try to steal a bite from Zeke's plate as he held it away, both of them laughing and taunting each other, I couldn't help but ache. A knot formed in my throat as I thought of the words she'd dropped so casually.

We'll be like sisters.

I'd never thought about having a sister. I'd never known it was an option. Suddenly, my entire life felt narrower than a one-lane bridge. I'd been to so many places, but I'd never done the simplest things. If we stayed with the Keens, a whole life would be open in front of us instead of just a road. I would interact with other humans instead of just reading about them in books and watching them on TV. Any one of those people, those interactions, could change the course of my life.

Gripping the seat beneath me, I tried to steady myself. It was all too much, the endless possibilities racing by. And though these kids were both kind of what I'd expected—she was perky and petite, he was hot and confident—it wasn't as clear cut as I'd imagined. She wasn't a bitchy mean girl, and I hadn't figured him out within minutes of knowing him.

Turned out, my books hadn't taught me everything. These people were real and unpredictable. I couldn't memorize my lines and know what they'd say next. And there were three more of them in the house, probably not doing what I pictured—painting, doing homework at a computer, and lounging around in a leather jacket, respectively.

If I went to school, it would be full of people who didn't say the lines I gave them in my head, who didn't react the way I predicted when I saw them and matched their type to the characters in the paperbacks under the seat of Mom's car.

Suddenly, my social isolation seemed like a bigger deal than it ever had before. I had no idea how to relate to normal people. If Mom really wanted to stay here and didn't whisk us away in the morning, if we moved in with these strangers, I might as well be visiting another planet. I knew as much about aliens from reading as I did about teenagers.

CHAPTER NINE

Gwen

When I went up to bed later, I was tired but strangely elated, as if I were floating on a cloud. I was still scared shitless, don't get me wrong. Figuring out real people was a whole lot more complicated than figuring out whodunit in a murder mystery. But I thought I was really going to like my new pseudo-family.

If it happens, I warned myself.

After a few hours with Peyton and Zeke, I was no longer anxious to jump back in the car. Now, I dreaded the moment when Mom's illness reared its ugly head and scared them off. It was one thing to have strangers witness me chasing her down the street while she shrieked about unleashing the hounds of hell. It was another thing to have people I actually knew witness it.

Not that I really knew these people yet. But I

wanted to. I was a dry sponge soaking up information about how real people my age lived, what they did, how they talked. I was fascinated. Captivated. I wanted to know more, to be part of what they had. Maybe in some way, Mom had sensed how much more humiliating it would be to have friends witness her episodes, and she'd sheltered me from it by making sure I never got close to other people.

It wasn't fair, but Mom had never let me believe in the myth of fairness. I didn't expect life to be fair, and I didn't expect some rich guy Mom had met online to want us around after he experienced one of her episodes in person. I doubted she'd even told him about it, and seeing it was in a whole other realm. My scars could be hidden forever, but hers always surfaced eventually.

To my relief, Mom was snoring quietly in the room they'd given us, just like she'd promised. I kicked off my shoes, peeled off my garage sale jeans, and realized I was still wearing Zeke's hoodie. I didn't want to take it off. He'd made me feel comfortable here, like I belonged. For a few hours, sitting on the deck with him and Peyton, I'd forgotten about Mom, and running, and the constant feeling of waiting for something to catch up to us. I'd felt like I was living someone else's life—a normal life.

Shame washed over me when I caught sight of Mom's face, her lips parted, small wrinkles lining her skin. It wasn't her fault.

Without allowing myself to indulge in any

more sentimental feelings, I peeled off the hoodie and tossed it on a chair in the corner, my T-shirt still inside it. I'd bring it back tomorrow.

As I reached for my duffle to find my pajamas, the door swung open. Instinctively, I dropped to the floor in a crouch, wrapping my arms around my knees as Eliot stepped in. He froze, too. The longest three seconds in history ticked by before I lifted one of my arms to block his view of my boobs straining against my dingy second-hand bra. "Did you see anything?" I blurted, praying I'd covered my scars in time.

Eliot covered his glasses with one hand, but I could see a grin fighting to break loose on his smooth lips. "I saw you come up like two minutes ago," he whispered. "I thought you'd still be up."

"I am up," I whispered back.

"I didn't realize your mom was in here. You can have your own room. We have plenty."

"We're fine."

"Right," Eliot said. "Cool."

"Want to let me get dressed?" I hissed, glancing at my mom as she stirred.

"Not really," Eliot said. "But I will. Goodnight, Gwen."

With that, he stepped back out of the room, his hand still covering his eyes, and pulled the door closed.

The awkwardness had nearly choked off all my oxygen, leaving me lightheaded. I slid onto the bed, checking that Mom was still sleeping, and tried to catch my breath. In the books I read, guys like Eliot were always the nerdy virgin type. I'd been wrong about the others, so maybe I was wrong about him, too. But I didn't think so. If he'd never seen a girl in her underwear before, that explained why he didn't want to leave. But still. He'd been awfully unruffled by my appearance. He hadn't even blushed.

To be fair, I hadn't either, but it was probably just out of shock. If I'd thought about it, I would have. I was just glad he hadn't seen the ugly burn scars. I squeezed my eyes shut, but instead of being humiliated, I found myself smiling. Giddiness rose inside me, and I couldn't help smiling the whole time I got ready for bed and fell asleep.

I woke in the night to the all-too-familiar sound of my mother having a nightmare. She spoke in tongues, yelling garbled sounds that weren't even words.

"Mom," I cried, grabbing her and shaking her shoulders, fear thundering in my chest. "Wake up. It's just a dream."

Selfishly, I had hoped we'd get to stay in this luxury resort for a couple more days. Try a few new foods, sleep in a bed that seemed to hug my skinny body, talk to other people my age who didn't look at me like I was a pariah with unwashed hair and unfashionable clothes.

But it was over now. I could hear footsteps running our way.

Instinctively, I huddled over my mother's body, blocking her from the inevitable scrutiny of whoever was approaching.

"Fenrir is coming," Mom howled.

"It's not Fenrir, Mom. It's probably Neil," I said. If that wasn't an innocuous name, I didn't know what was. It seemed to calm Mom, who opened her eyes and looked at me blearily. Behind me, the door opened. I positioned my body to block her from view, though I knew I couldn't avoid the questions.

At first there would be concern and curiosity, but it would be quickly replaced by pity, then distrust, and awkward self-consciousness as the people made quick excuses to get away. This wasn't their problem, and they didn't want to get involved.

"Is she okay?"

Not random people, but Neil. A man whose house he had opened to us for reasons I still didn't understand. Until I did, I wasn't going to reveal my mother's condition any more than I had to.

"She's fine," I said. "She has nightmares, that's all. She's okay now that she's awake."

I tensed as he entered the room instead of going back to bed as I'd hoped. Circling the bottom of the huge bed, he studied my mother. When he'd reached the far side, he sat down on the edge of the bed. He was wearing a pair of flannel pajamas, but even they looked chic instead of frumpy on him. He ran a hand through his salt and pepper hair and sighed.

"How long has she been like this?" he asked, looking down at her glazed, confused expression.

I'd woken up with stark clarity, but she looked like she had no idea where she was.

"It's just a nightmare," I said. "She'll come out of it in a minute. Sometimes they linger, that's all."

We don't need your help, I screamed at him silently. I wanted to shove him off the bed, to claw his eyes out so he'd stop looking at us like that. I took a breath to calm my nerves. He was already at the pity phase. I prayed for a quick transition to the escape phase.

"I'm sorry," Neil said, looking straight at me.

Go away, go away, go away...

"I didn't know she was like this," he went on. "I don't know how much she told you, but I've been looking for you for years."

My heart bucked in my chest, and I had to swallow sour bile in my throat to keep from choking. "What?" I whispered.

That sense of familiarity that had raced over my skin like goose bumps when we met... Did he know us?

Memories were strange things. They didn't work like photographs. They weren't visual. I remembered the feel of my dad's presence, for instance. I remembered riding on his shoulders, and that he was tall. Sometimes, I'd pass the greeter at Wal-Mart or the guy standing in line at a gas station bathroom, and Dad would flash through my mind. But I didn't actually remember what he looked like. I didn't know what prompted those flashes of memory—the way someone stood, his cologne, a physical feature, or something else entirely.

And I didn't know how I knew the Keens, but I was sure that I did.

"Who are you?" I asked, my voice like an accusation as I pulled my mother's head into my lap, away from him.

"I'm someone who knows you've been taking care of your mother for a few years if not longer," he said. "You don't have to do that anymore. I'm here to help you both in whatever way you'll allow. A child shouldn't have to take care of her parent, Gwen. Let me take that burden off your shoulders. We have plenty. You don't have to live that way."

"We're fine," I said through clenched teeth. "How many times do I have to tell you? It was just a nightmare."

He gave me a pitying look that said he knew I was full of shit. I didn't know who he was or what Mom had told him, but he knew more about us than I wanted him to know.

"You said you were looking for us. Are you a friend of my dad's?" I asked, cradling my mother in my arms.

"The chain can't hold Fenrir forever," Mom said dreamily. "The giants will come, and the gods will die."

"Do you know who Fenrir is?" Neil asked, his eyes following my every move.

"Of course I know who he is," I snapped. "That's what gives her nightmares. It's a wolf in a myth. It's not real."

But to her, it was real. She never told me about her nightmares, but she often woke up screaming about Fenrir and the giants. So I'd looked him up once when we were at a library. It hadn't clarified much, but at least I knew it was a Norse myth and not someone from her past trying to hunt us down.

"Why don't you get some sleep?" Neil suggested. "There's another guest room at the end of the hall. I can take it from here."

"I'd rather stay with her," I said, holding her head to my chest. "We'll be fine, really. We'll leave in the morning."

"You don't have to do that," he said, standing. "I'll leave you two alone. But I meant what I said, Gwen. This shouldn't be your responsibility."

"Well, it is," I said, watching warily as he walked to the door.

"It doesn't have to be," he said again. "We'll talk in the morning."

I waited for him to close the door behind him before I slid down in the bed beside my mother. My heart hammered. What if he called someone, a mental institution or child protective services? I didn't think he'd call the cops—they'd believe me when I said it was just a nightmare. But what if they tried to take her away? Or me? I couldn't let that happen. I wasn't abused or neglected. I was loved fiercely. And my mother may not have given me a conventional upbringing, but she didn't belong in a nut house.

Once when I was a kid, I asked my mother if we were homeless. "Right now, we don't have a home," she'd said. "But that's by choice. We don't know what it's really like to be homeless. We're just traveling."

But as the years went by and we never had a home, I wondered. Mom tried to make it seem like a fun adventure, our gypsy lifestyle. Sometimes, it was like that. Just me and my mom, laughing as we crested a hill and saw the Hollywood sign across the valley or the ocean sparkling in the distance. It was fun crossing off every state on the map as we traveled through. It was fun flying over the Golden Gate Bridge or the Mississippi River in our rattle-trap car, or cruising the Vegas strip and gazing out across the Grand Canyon.

But it wasn't fun to wake up with flea bites all over because the latest car was infested with them. It wasn't fun running out of gas and having to walk miles on an icy road to the nearest gas station or risk being picked up by cops or creeps. It wasn't fun not being able to stay at hotels like other travelers because we didn't have a credit card, or driving all night because we couldn't find a place to pull over behind some bushes to sleep. It wasn't fun having our car found and being chased off someone's property.

As I held my mother and waited for morning, I knew I wouldn't be able to sleep again that night. My heartbeat had returned to normal, but every little sound made it race again. I was sure they were coming for us—not monsters but people. If Mom was in any condition to drive, I'd insist we leave before I had to face that humiliation. She was always kind of dazed and unresponsive after a vision or nightmare.

All I could do was lie there and wait, my stomach churning with nerves, my limbs heavy with dread. My brain refused to stop cycling through the last day, every event and conversation, every incredible and terrible feeling. I thought again of what Neil had said. My heart throbbed with adrenaline, and I clung tighter to my mother, praying she'd snap out of it soon.

Maybe she wasn't as crazy as she seemed, because now I was the one who wanted to get the hell out of there, despite the comfort and apparent hospitality around me. I shivered under the warmth of the blankets, glancing at the window. It stared back like a black, sightless eye. Outside, the wind whistled through the marsh grasses, and in the distance, the waves lapped the shore. The hour before dawn was always the darkest, and tonight, it was the longest.

All those years, Mom had known someone was watching us, chasing us. Now, it seemed she'd led us straight to him. But why?

CHAPTER TEN

Gwen

As Mom began to stir, I slipped from the bed and ducked into the bathroom. When I came out, she was standing in front of the dresser, braiding her hair.

"Mom, we need to get out of here," I said, shoving yesterday's clothes into my duffel. I yanked my t-shirt from inside Zeke's hoodie, barely registering his garment as I tossed it onto the bed. Hanging out with him on the deck the night before had been a sweet dream. This was reality.

"What are you talking about?" Mom asked. "We just got here. Calm down, Gwen."

"Don't you remember last night? Neil came in when you had a nightmare. He's not going to want us around, and if he does, it's with questionable motives."

She smiled sadly at me in the mirror. "I'm sorry I didn't bring you here sooner," she said. "If I'd known about him, I probably would have. But it's okay now."

I narrowed my eyes at her. "What does that mean?"

"I told you, it's safe here," she said.

"What makes you think that?" I asked. "What if we move in and Neil refuses to let us leave when it's time to go?"

I couldn't ask the question I really needed her to answer. What would happen if she was trapped, unable to run when her demons caught up to her?

"There's power here," she said, locking eyes with her reflection. A strange edge entered her voice, the one she got when she'd told fortunes for people in New Orleans or Conway or Vegas. But it turned out that people only wanted to hear the good stuff. Fortune telling wasn't a very lucrative business when half the time you were told that you would toil in frustration all your life and never get ahead, or die of a heart attack before making amends with your father.

"Mom, seriously. We need to leave before the others wake up."

"It's too late," she said to the mirror, her eyes boring into their reflection. "The pieces are already falling into place."

I threw my hands up in frustration. This was the reason I never tried to persuade her to stay somewhere when she wanted to run. All I got back was nonsense when I tried to talk sense. I wanted to grab her and shake her, tell her this was our lives she was messing with.

Before I could argue further, there was a tap on the door.

Well, the knock eliminated at least two people in the family.

I opened the door to find Finn standing there, looking a bit lost. A flicker of confusion crossed his face, as if he didn't know who I was or why I was in the room he'd just stopped at.

He flashed a quick smile. "Hi."

"Hi."

Maybe it was the fact that I'd never been around guys my age before, but I couldn't seem to get enough of them. Every time I saw one of them, I wanted to drink him in with my eyes. Today, Finn's long hair was pulled up into a topknot that probably would have looked ridiculous on most guys. Somehow, he pulled it off, maybe because it looked like an afterthought rather than someone trying too hard. With his hair pulled back, his angular features stood out, highlighting his good looks and those gorgeous, dark lips.

"Have you been down to the beach?" he asked.

I shook my head.

He shifted nervously and stuck his hands in his jacket pockets. "Uh...want to?"

I hesitated, glancing back at my mom. I did want to. I wanted to a lot. Mom had let me go to the beach lots of times—for about five minutes. Just long enough to dip my toes in the water, or, if she was feeling generous, a quick swim. Then it was back on the road, heading inland.

For once, she wasn't telling me to pack up, to get in the car, that we had to go. I opened my mouth to turn him down, but then I closed it. This was my chance to do the things I'd never done, things I wanted to do so badly it ached inside me. I'd missed so much of life while I sat in the car.

"You should go," Mom said, as if sensing my indecision.

I kept glancing at her as I pulled on my jacket, waiting for her to do what she always did after a nightmare. When I had my jacket snapped—the zipper didn't work—I turned to her. "Are you sure? You'll be here when I get back?"

"Of course," she said, looking hurt.

"Right. Sorry, Mom." I crossed the room and bent to quickly kiss the top of her head. "Come get me if you need anything. I won't go far."

Outside, Finn led me down a set of winding steps with a handrail all the way down to the sand. The wood looked new, still tan instead of weatherworn grey like the shingles on the houses. The stairs led through rosehip bushes, their red fruits bright against the grey stems, other bushes, and tufts of beach grass. As we descended the steep staircase, I ran my hand along the railing, afraid I'd lose my footing and pitch headfirst down the stairs.

Finn trotted down the steps ahead of me, his

stride as easy and comfortable as an athlete. His shoulders were broad and square under his jacket, and a few wisps of hair had escaped his topknot and curled against his skin. I had the weirdest urge to reach out and touch them, to see if they were as soft as they looked, or to nuzzle my nose into the little nook at the back of his neck.

When he reached the bottom of the steps, he stood back and watched me descend the last few.

"Those are steep," I said, relieved when my feet were on the flat sand. Stairs were not a popular activity with Mom. Like beaches, high buildings did not offer ready escape routes.

"You'll get used to them," Finn said with a small smile.

I searched around for something to say as we turned right and began to walk. Finally I settled on something I'd read in a few books. "Come here often?"

As soon as the words were out, I cringed at my stupidity.

Crap. That's a pickup line guys use in bars!

Finn either didn't notice or was too polite to mention it. "Every day. I like to walk while I think. It makes the ideas flow."

"For painting?" I guessed, remembering the colors splattered on his jeans the night before.

"Stories," he said, turning right and beginning to walk.

"You write?"

"Comics," he said. "A little writing, a lot of inking."

"I noticed your fingers last night."

Does that make me sound like a pervert?

"My fingers?" He pulled his hand from his pocket and studied his nails, as if just noticing his fingertips were stained black. "Huh. I'm sure that's attractive," he said, stuffing his hands back into his pockets.

"I wouldn't worry," I said. "You can tell girls you enjoy long walks on the beach."

He shot me a strange look, and I bit my tongue. Did he think I was flirting?

Was I?

I wasn't sure that I actually knew how to flirt. I'd definitely never had the opportunity, and I didn't know if it was something that came naturally or had to be taught. I couldn't deny that he was attractive, with those jade-green eyes and that moody artist thing going on. I, on the other hand, was wearing a jacket with someone else's name written on the inside. I had no business flirting with this rich boy.

"I don't really talk to girls," he said, turning to approach the water's edge.

I almost laughed at that, but Finn's face was serious as he contemplated the horizon to the west. The sky was a pale pink that reflected the sunrise to the east, and for a minute neither of us spoke. The waves in the bay were tiny, rolling up on the beach rather than crashing. The rushing sound of the water on the sand filled the silence between us. But I couldn't hold back my burning questions. The more I talked to real people, the less I understood about them.

"Why don't you talk to girls?" I asked at last.

"I leave that to my brothers," he said.

"You're talking to me."

"You're...different, I guess."

"Different from what?" I asked, tugging my sleeves over my hands. I didn't want to be different. I was trying so hard to act normal, so they wouldn't see what a weirdo I was.

Finn laughed quietly, pushing his hands deeper into his jacket pockets and glancing sideways at me. "That sounded like a line, didn't it?"

"We just met," I pointed out. "How do you know I'm different?"

"It wasn't a line."

"Okay." I studied him from the corner of my eye, standing there at the edge of the water, with the morning sunlight glimmering on his tan skin. He looked so beautiful it made my insides ache. I wondered if anyone would ever look at me that way. If only my hair wasn't so freaking long, I could let it blow across my face and look all sexy like the girls in movies, and maybe he would. Instead, I had the world's biggest granny bun and the inability to sound like a normal human being.

"I actually want to talk to you," Finn said after a silence. "That's how I know you're different."

I tried to laugh. "I don't think Eliot would find that reasoning sufficient."

"Now who's assuming she knows us so well?" he said. "What happened to *we just met*?"

"You're telling me Eliot's not the smart, literal, logical type?"

Finn paused, watching me with a slight smile and his eyes all squinted half shut. "No, he is," he said slowly.

Relief swelled inside me. I had gotten it right for once. Maybe I'd survive this after all.

"Want to walk?" he asked.

"Yes. I've only been to the beach a few times."

We started off down the tideline, where a ridge of seaweed tangled with clumps of seafoam with a brown skin on top. Now that the sky was lightening, I could see that the water wasn't crystal blue, either, but kind of murky.

"It's clear on the ocean side," Finn said, as if reading my mind. "Over here, on the bay side of the Cape, the water is a lot warmer. But not many people swim here because of the color of the water."

"I don't blame them," I said.

"It won't hurt you, though," Finn said. "You can surf on the ocean side with a wetsuit and a lot of courage, but no one swims in the winter up here. You'd die of hypothermia."

"No kidding." Wind swept along the beach, right through a thin spot in my jacket.

"You said you'd been to the beach before?" Finn asked. "Which ones?"

"A few," I admitted. "But we never stay long."

"How come?" he asked, looking genuinely curious.

I bit my lip, trying to come up with a good reason. But when I opened my mouth, something completely unexpected came out. The truth.

"We didn't really come from St. Louis," I said. "I mean, we did. It was the last place we lived. But before that…"

"What?" Finn asked, his brow creasing with concern.

"We were on the move a lot," I said. "I've been all over the country. Mom doesn't like to stay in one place for too long. That's why we could pick up and move so suddenly when she met your dad online. Why I've never really had friends, and I have zero idea what to say to you or any other normal person, and you probably think I'm a total freak right now."

"You're doing fine," Finn said, his hand resting gently on my arm. "After the life you've lived, no one expects you to be perfect."

"Thank you," I whispered. I took a breath before going on. I found myself spilling the story to him, if only the abbreviated version. I didn't tell him all the gruesome details that would send him running to call social services or make him think we were pathetic losers. But I outlined a few of Mom's beach-related quirks and other eccentricities. When I finished, there was a moment of awkward silence.

"I'm so sorry, Gwen," Finn said at last.

Hearing him say my name brought a strange comfort, a sense of safety and stability, as if he'd anchored me in this world, made me real, when he'd uttered my name aloud. I was unbelievably grateful for his simple statement and the simple way he said my name, as if it was an undisputable truth.

I shoved my hands deeper into the pockets of my lumpy jacket. Some of the stuffing had migrated when I used it as a pillow, so it was fat in some places and empty in others. "I've probably been to all the famous beaches in the continental U.S.," I told Finn. "Even if I only saw them out a car window, not everyone can say that."

"I guess if it was fun for you…" he said, looking doubtful.

"It wasn't," I admitted with a sigh. "It isn't."

"Well, it's over now," he said, his hand slipping down my arm and tugging mine from my pocket. When he linked our fingers and squeezed, a swell of emotion made my eyes blur over with tears.

"I don't know," I said, not sure why I was telling him all this. "I keep waiting for her to tell us it's time to go. Honestly, that's how I've spent the last ten years. Waiting to go, waiting for her to get worse, waiting for something to happen."

"Now it has," he said. "We found you. You're with us. The wait is over."

It was irrational, but I believed him. I didn't know how to explain it, even to myself. Just that his words sounded so logical. It was time to live. I could finally stop holding my breath.

But then what? What if I made friends with these people, and then Mom ripped us away again, like she'd ripped me away from every other place in my life. I'd never even had a friend. Now I had a chance to make five friends in the same house, but what then? If I let myself get attached to these people, to these comforts, I'd be worse off than when I started. Now I knew what I'd been missing all my life.

But I wasn't going to let that fear scare me away. I wasn't going to run like Mom. I was going to embrace every chance, to wallow in every opportunity. I was going to hold Finn's hand, and laugh with Peyton and Zeke, and pretend, even if only for a week, that I was normal. Every moment was precious, and I would relish every single one. I offered Finn a shy smile, and my heart throbbed inside my chest when he offered me an equally shy smile in return.

CHAPTER ELEVEN

Finn

I knew I should drop Gwen's hand. Though I'd only taken it to reassure her, she held onto me like I was a lifeline thrown out to a drowning girl. I couldn't bear to pull away, to make her think I didn't want to touch her or be near her. She was such a strange mixture of trusting and suspicious, of blind innocence and defensiveness.

She reminded me of an abandoned seagull chick Eliot and I had found down in the dunes when we were kids. It had been so shy, and yet, so trusting once we had it in our hands. We'd taken it home and kept it alive in a box until it was old enough to go off on its own, thanks to Eliot's endless research on how to raise it and reintroduce it into the wild.

Now, I had this other kind of baby bird in my hand. I couldn't help but think of how she'd reacted when I'd said she was different. Any other girl would have thought it was a line. From any other guy, it probably would've been. It was an easy line because it was true. Other girls knew this stuff. She'd be in trouble when she started school, if she didn't know better than to trust any guy who said she was different.

We made our way past one of the stone piers jutting out into the water. The tide was sinking, and little rivulets of water wavered across the wet sand. From the corner of my eye, I watched Gwen breathing in the sea air, strands of her blonde hair ribboning out in the wind.

I was glad she'd trusted me with her truth. I had a feeling she didn't share that story with just anyone. But then, what did I know? I'd never even held a girl's hand before. Holding her hand implied some kind of ownership, and I didn't own Gwen. She didn't own me. In the classes I'd taken at church, they'd told us not to do things like this.

But maybe it was okay if she was like a little sister to me.

I knew I was making excuses even as I made them. She wasn't like a sister to me. Even if Dad married Olivia—and he wouldn't do that—that would make what I was doing worse, not better. And Dad had just met her mom. In the two years since Mom died, he hadn't gone on a single date, despite the locals and tourists lining up for a chance. No matter how long he knew a woman, he'd never replace Mom. They'd been high school sweethearts who had never dated anyone else. Their whole lives had been about loving each other.

Their love had taught me what love was. Growing up, I'd watched them, knowing that one day, I'd have that kind of love. Since then, I'd been saving my love for someone I could share that kind of bond with.

As we approached the stairs, I watched Gwen from the corner of my eye. Her lips drew my attention. Even without makeup, they were red and full. She had no idea how beautiful she was, but it was more than that. She was magnetic. I was drawn to her with a constant, unrelenting pull. Was she the girl I'd been waiting for? Was the attraction some kind of divine sign? I definitely wasn't holding her hand in the way I'd hold hands with a sister. I knew it, and yet I was too weak to stop.

Her fingers were soft and cold inside my hand, as fragile as that baby bird we'd rescued. It was my job to protect her, just like we'd protected it. A primal instinct had risen inside me, telling me to take care of her. I would treasure her trust and guard her secrets because I knew they were sacred. There were guys at school who would be all too eager to take advantage of her trust and innocence. I may not have been one of them, but I knew exactly what those guys were like, because my brothers were the worst of them all.

CHAPTER TWELVE

Gwen

Even though I knew I should let go of Finn's hand, I didn't want to. It was warm, for one thing, but that definitely wasn't all. Touching him was nothing like touching my mother. Every nerve ending in my hand had come painfully alive. My entire body was gone, leaving nothing but my palm, my fingers, my skin pressed to his. I was a shadow following behind my one living, radiant limb. When he squeezed my hand, his fingers pressing between mine, I forgot how to breathe.

I'd read plenty of books where people did this casually. But it wasn't casual. It was electrifying, almost unbearable. Since it was my first time holding hands, I tried not to beat myself up about the fact that holding hands with him felt so good I wanted to close my eyes and swoon into his arms. But in my jeans and stuffing-challenged jacket, I didn't think I could pull that off quite like Scarlet O'Hara in her big dresses.

I contented myself with imagining it instead, with wringing every sensation I could from the moment. We walked along the beach in silence, listening to the water lapping at the shore as the tiny waves receded, leaving behind a strip of wet sand. Hermit crabs scuttled along the beach, disappearing into holes when we came close to stepping on them.

I didn't dare squeeze Finn's hand, lest he notice we were still linked and pull away. I prayed he wouldn't see that I could barely put one foot in front of the other. Though I tried not to overthink it, it was hard not to. I was walking on a beach at sunrise holding hands with a boy. The spaces between my knuckles cradled his fingers, our hands fitting together like they had been sculpted for this exact moment, this exact purpose.

"This is going to sound like another line," Finn said when we'd reached the wooden steps leading up to the house. "But...I feel like we've met before."

I swallowed hard and managed a nod. "I feel it, too."

"Really?" He glanced at me, surprise creasing his brow.

"Yeah," I admitted. "I feel like I've always known you. All of you, actually. That's weird, right?"

"Definitely weird," he agreed, fingers still entwined with mine as we climbed the steps together.

They were just wide enough to allow us to walk up side by side. With his hand in mine, climbing up didn't scare me.

"Do you think…maybe you'd show me some of your comics sometime?" I asked.

"Oh," he said, glancing at me sideways. "Yeah, maybe."

He sounded like it was the last thing in the world he wanted to do.

"I'm sure they're amazing," I said. "And I love reading everything. Even comics. I promise I won't judge."

Finn shrugged, looking uncomfortable as he dropped my hand at last. A wave of loneliness washed over me when his hand left mine. He slid open the glass door for me, and I stepped inside, tugging my hands inside my sleeves to have something to hold onto. Inside, we were greeted by the smell of frying bacon. Low voices murmured in the kitchen.

"Oh, good, you're back," Mom said as I followed Finn into the kitchen. Mom was seated at the table, along with Peyton and Zeke.

"Would you go grab your brothers?" Neil said, sliding a spatula full of sizzling bacon onto a plate.

Finn ducked upstairs, and a few minutes later, he reappeared with Eliot on his heels.

"Hello, lovely," Eliot said, flashing me a grin.

My face warmed as I remembered the last time he'd seen me, wearing considerably less clothing.

I cast a guilty glance at Finn. Despite the intimacy of our walk on the beach, he didn't seem bothered by his brother paying attention to me. In fact, he didn't even seem to notice.

Had I imagined the whole thing—the connection, the moments that had passed between us? Confused and a little stung, I slid in at the table without looking at either of the twins again.

"Where's Xander?" Neil asked, scooping steaming heaps of scrambled eggs onto the plates already set at the table.

"He's coming," Finn said, sliding into a chair.

Eliot grabbed a pitcher of orange juice from the fridge and began pouring some into each glass like we were guests at a fancy resort.

"Where's Rosa?" I asked to distract myself. I was determined to make it through the entire meal, though I'd begun to feel overwhelmed again.

"She's getting the venue ready," Neil said just as Xander shuffled in and plopped down in the chair next to mine.

"What venue?" he asked just as I opened my mouth to ask the same thing.

"Olivia and I talked it over, and we don't see a reason to wait," Neil said. "It will be a small, simple affair, but we've decided to get married."

"Are you fucking kidding?" Xander asked, jumping up from the table. His chair scraped against the floor, and orange juice sloshed in the glasses.

The world tilted dangerously under me, and I

grabbed the edge of the table. My throat was so tight that my voice came out as barely more than a whisper. "What?"

"Just a little wedding," Mom said, giving me a tight smile.

"Mom, you can't," I blurted out.

"Oh my god, Dad, I'm so happy for you," Peyton said, clapping her palms together in a quick little burst of applause before leaping into her father's arms. "I was about to set up a dating profile for you online. I can't believe you're doing this. It's so overdue."

I swallowed back a painful lump in my throat. This wasn't supposed to happen. I knew I shouldn't have left her and gone to the beach. What had Neil done to her? This wasn't how our lives worked. It was me and Mom. Mom and me. Thelma and Louise. Not Thelma and Louise and an entire family of weird rich people.

"Be happy for me," Mom said, cutting her eyes at Peyton, who was babbling on about how her dad needed to get out more, and she'd been worried about him, and he obviously needed to start dating again, although she hadn't expected him to get married quite so fast...

"That is fast," Zeke agreed, looking confused. "They just got here. You're already getting married? You don't even know each other."

"You didn't waste any time, that's for sure," Xander said, glowering at Neil.

"It's been two years," Peyton said, glaring at him. "Don't you want Dad to be happy?"

"What's the rush?" I asked Mom, not quite able to swallow this new development. It was one thing to go stay with people and get off the road for a few days. It was another thing entirely to learn that she was making something permanent. She'd have to sign documents, create a paper trail. I knew something had to be wrong, but I didn't know how to get her out of it. She was the adult. How could I rescue her if she refused to let me?

She twisted her fingers around her napkin. "No rush. We just thought it would be easier to get it out of the way. You'll be starting school on Monday, and this way you'll have at least an address to give them."

"Monday?" I asked, panic rising in my throat. But along with the sheer terror, a thrill of hope went through me. If this was real, I'd be going to school with the rest of the group sitting around the table. I could make friends, maybe have a boyfriend. I couldn't even begin to imagine what it would be like. I'd always wanted to go to school, to live like the girls in the books I read. But until now, I'd never believed it was possible.

"I'll call up first thing Monday morning," Neil said. "They'll probably want to give you a few placement tests to get you in the right classes, but they'll let you start right away."

"This calls for a shopping trip," Peyton said.

"We can go to Boston today and get our bridesmaid's dresses."

I stared at her like she'd just sprouted tentacles. How could she be so blindly accepting, without a single qualm about this madness?

"I hope you aren't expecting me to wear a tux to this charade," Xander said, ripping a strip of bacon in half with his teeth. He chewed and glowered at his father, breathing hard like he was about to explode.

"A nice shirt will be fine," Neil said.

I'd been starving, but my stomach was so knotted with nerves I could barely eat. I managed to swallow enough to satisfy my rumbling stomach, but when Mom rose from the table, I abandoned my plate and raced up the stairs after her.

"Mom?" I said, stepping into our bedroom behind her.

"Mmm," she answered, crossing the room to stand at the window.

"Can we talk?" I asked, my voice tentative. I didn't like to argue with my mom. Pushing her buttons could result in more ugly scenes. I went along, knowing we were doing what she needed to do. In some way, I'd understood her madness. Maybe that made me crazy, too.

I didn't understand this.

Mom raised her eyes to mine. They were placid, not straining like a caged animal, not darting around. That freaked me out more. Even when we stopped for a few months in one town or another, when she settled down for a bit, she never looked peaceful. Wary, expectant, determined…not calm. Never that.

"What's going on?" I asked.

"I just came up here to think," she said. "This house is so busy."

She turned as if to go, but I held out a hand to stop her. "No, Mom. Wait. I need to ask you why you're doing this. This isn't like you." I dropped my voice to a whisper. "Is Neil threatening you somehow? I noticed neither of you mentioned love when you talked about getting married."

"Gwen, sweetheart," she said, looking almost pained with affection as she reached out and brushed my cheek with her fingers. "I hope one day you'll marry for love. I married your father for that. But there are other things in this world, things bigger than love. There are things in other worlds, straining to break free, and we must do our duty to keep them from being unleashed into this world."

I closed my eyes, calling on my patience. I wished I could understand her when she went off on her rambling tangents, but they never made sense to me.

"So we're staying here forever?" I asked. "No more running?"

"There's no reason to run," she said. "He found us, didn't he? And if marrying Neil forms the closest bond I can form to help our world, I'm happy to do it."

"Wait," I said, my heart stammering in my chest. "What do you mean? All those years of running...you were running from Neil? And now you're marrying him, just like that?"

"I don't know if you've noticed, but Neil has a lot of money."

"Why does that matter? If he's dangerous, we have to get away."

"He's not dangerous. But if he can find us on an anonymous login at the St. Louis library, he can find us anywhere. And so can the giants."

My heart was racing so hard I had to sit down on the edge of the bed, afraid I'd pass out. "So he is threatening you."

"I knew this day would come," she said with a sigh, sinking down beside me. "I was ready to stop running. I'm so tired, Gwen."

"That doesn't mean you have to marry the Fenrir, or one of the giants you're always talking about. Is that what Neil is? I mean, he's obviously not a giant, but is he a monster?"

She shook her head. "Neil's just a man, honey. A very determined one, maybe, but just a man. And giants aren't twenty feet tall, like in fairytales. They can be any size, even as small as you." She smiled a little, as if this was all slightly amusing.

"But Mom," I said. "Why was he looking for you? Why does he want to marry you?" Maybe that sounded mean, but I was done playing nice. I wanted a family, and I wanted to be normal, but none of this felt right. When I was with them, it felt perfect, but when they weren't there to reassure me, I couldn't seem to shed the defenses I'd been building for the past ten years. We didn't let in outsiders. They weren't safe. Mom had taught me that. She couldn't just say it was all okay now and think it would all be erased.

"Neil knows the dangers of this world, too," she said. "If marrying him brings us closer, makes us all a family, and that will save this world from the giants, don't you want to do it?"

I wanted to scream and shake her until she really heard how crazy she sounded. For some reason, Neil had her convinced that he saw the same things she did. I didn't know why he was playing along with her hallucinations to gain her trust, but I wasn't falling for it. He had the money, the house, the name. We had nothing. It didn't make sense. Mom's nonsense reasoning was as sound as anything I could come up with.

I had nothing to lose. This was real, and it was really happening. So I voiced the one concern that I hadn't spoken aloud yet. It took all the courage I had to spit the words out, and even then, I only managed a whisper. "What if he marries you and then has you committed?"

She turned and took my face between her hands. "Gwen, stop worrying. Please."

I snorted, halfway between a sob and a laugh. "Seriously, Mom?"

"You know how hard I've tried to protect

you. That's my job. All your life, we've run from danger. I would never lead you right into it. Can you just try to relax and trust me a little tiny bit?"

"Okay," I said, nodding. My throat was tight, but I couldn't argue with that. She had always been there for me. She had never led me into danger. Maybe for once I could relax and have the life I should have had all along.

"Promise you're with me?" she said. "I need you on my side. We're still a team of two, like we've always been. Don't make me do this alone."

"I won't," I said, leaning in to hug her. "I promise."

"Good," she said, pulling away. "Because if you make me go shopping alone with Peyton, I might explode with good cheer."

I laughed and shook my head. "She's so bubbly I think she's half human, half soap."

"It really can't be healthy," Mom agreed.

An hour later, Peyton and I climbed into Mom's old beat-up car and headed towards Boston. Peyton chattered away about the boutiques she liked in Boston, Walden Pond, and Harvard Square. I suddenly felt guilty for saying she was too much. She was exactly the distraction I needed from worrying about Mom. I'd never been in a car with a friend, but for a moment, I felt like a normal teenager going shopping with her friend.

Still, I kept glancing at Mom, wondering what was going on in that head of hers. I could only hope she wouldn't get cold feet and decide not to go back, kidnapping Peyton in the process. In a way, it was a relief to stare out the window at the road rushing by beneath the wheels, to be moving again. It was all I'd ever known. There had been days when I was so sick of driving I literally puked, and I'd never have imagined I could miss it. But today, the familiarity comforted me.

When we got to Boston, Peyton gave Mom directions, looking at her phone the whole time. At last we parked, put some coins in the meter, and headed down the sidewalk. It was Saturday afternoon, and people were out shopping, but it didn't feel busy. We were in a nice part of town with shops under every awning. I'd been to tons of cities, and each one had its own personality. Boston was no different.

"I love Boston," Peyton sang, spinning around with her arms out. "Don't you love it, Gwen?"

My name coming from her lips sounded different than I'd ever heard it before, like someone who was loved and trusted by default. It was the name of a best friend who had shared secrets since childhood, painted her toenails while confessing her first crush, and giggled in the dark at a slumber party. I wanted to be that person so much my chest nearly turned inside out.

In reality, I would never be that person. I wasn't a kid anymore. I'd never have a best friend who had been there my whole life, unless Mom counted. And she'd certainly never done any best friend things with me. The closest she'd come to trying new hairstyles was when she had me braid sections of my hair as she combed lice out of it after buying used pillows at a garage sale.

A dried leaf skittered along the sidewalk, and I stomped my ratty Converse on it, crushing it like a bug. Undeterred, it tumbled away when I lifted my foot. It reminded me of the gum wrapper tumbling across the rest stop the day my mother had told me she'd met Neil online.

Only three days ago. It seemed like an eternity.

"But first, Starbucks," Peyton said, linking her arm through mine like she didn't care that I didn't know how to be her best friend.

"But first?" I asked.

"Yeah, you know," she said. "Like, *but first, coffee?*"

"I don't get it."

She laughed and bumped our shoulders together as we walked down the sidewalk ahead of Mom. "You'll learn. My girlfriend says I'm the most basic white girl ever."

"You seem pretty interesting to me." I glanced back at Mom, making sure she was okay by herself.

"I love pumpkin spice everything, fall is my favorite season, and Uggs are my spirit animal," Peyton said, pulling her arm from mine to count off on her fingers.

"Okay…"

"Oh, and I totally rock sweaters with scarves and yoga pants."

I surveyed her outfit. She'd described exactly what she was wearing. I was a little less fancy in my standard jeans and hoodie.

"And you're a cheerleader," I offered.

She gave me a funny look. "That's not basic white girl."

"I guess I don't know what that is," I mumbled.

"Don't you ever get on the internet?"

"I have before," I said, not wanting to explain the situation with the internet, and how we couldn't reveal our identities. Sometimes, libraries would let us use their computers under a guest login, but usually they wanted us to have a card first. Logging on with a card left a digital footprint, and those were trackable, according to Mom. Besides, in order to get a card, we had to have an address.

"Where's your phone?" Peyton asked. "I'll show you the memes."

"The what?" Mom asked.

"I don't have a phone," I said to the sidewalk.

"What? How do you live without a phone? Oh my god, I would die. Seriously, Olivia. You should get her a phone. It's practically neglect not to."

"It's not neglect. I don't want one," I said quickly, my heart speeding at the words I'd dreaded hearing for years. The words that could take me away from Mom. I pulled my sleeves over my hands and tried not to squirm at Peyton's attention as we stepped into the coffee shop.

"We'll get you a phone," Mom said, sounding perfectly normal for once, like there was a logical reason she'd never gotten me a phone.

"What do you want?" Peyton asked. "My treat. Well, Dad's treat, actually. He sent the credit card for today's shopping festivities. And that starts with fuel."

"I don't know," I said. "I've never had Starbucks."

Instead of laughing at me, Peyton looked up at the menu. "Normally, I'd say we should start you out with a safe choice, like a latte, but since you can only get pumpkin spice in the fall, we'll start you off at the pinnacle of coffee drinks."

Her confidence made me feel a little better. A few minutes later, the three of us left Starbucks, armed with sweet coffee drinks. The awkwardness quickly faded as Peyton looked on her phone for dress shops. Soon, we were trying on everything we could find that didn't require alterations, and I forgot about being out of place.

Peyton wanted to come in the dressing room with me, but I quickly shut down that idea. I wasn't about to have her gawking or asking questions. Not when she had the absolute perfect body. She looked a little insulted when I told her I wanted to change alone, but by the time I came out to model the dress, she seemed to have forgotten any hard feelings.

I'd never shopped at a new clothing store in my life, and to my surprise, I got almost as into it as Peyton. Really, we were just there to be accessories to Mom. I'd never seen Mom in a dress before. It completely transformed her, and tears sprang to my eyes when she came out of the dressing room wearing the first one. After that, the afternoon passed in a blur of dresses and shoes, hair and nail salons, more dress shops, and finally, a makeup store. I didn't even know such a thing existed—a store just for makeup.

It was evening by the time we piled into Mom's old car, the trunk stuffed with bags and boxes, shoes, dresses, sashes, and even a tiara.

Peyton exclaimed over our collection of CDs, which she called "so retro," not knowing that we didn't listen to the radio because the antennae could be used to track us. I didn't share that detail with her.

"Listen, I know it probably seems like I'm crazy for wanting a sister so bad, but it's not just that," she said ejecting a Lana Del Rey CD. "Dad would never admit it, but I know he's been lonely since Mom died. I honestly didn't think he'd ever meet someone. I mean, my girlfriend's mom got divorced, and she got married like three months later. And Dad hasn't even looked for a date—in two years. I was afraid he'd gotten all complacent and set in his ways and he'd never put any effort into meeting someone new. So I'm just happy for him."

"That's nice of you," Mom said.

"Not really," Peyton said. "I mean, not that I have anything against you. You both seem cool. It's just that mostly I think it would be a tragedy for my dad not to be happy again. He went through so much when Mom was sick. He needs someone to take care of him for a change. And he's a catch, so you're getting a good deal. It would be a tragedy for him to end up old and alone in that big house. We're all graduating in the next few years, so I was getting really worried about him. And then you came along."

She beamed, and I tried not to feel guilty about the fact that Mom had already told me this wasn't a marriage for love. But whatever Neil's intentions, I could tell Peyton wanted only the best for him. Unlike the cheerleaders I'd read about, she wasn't fake or mean at all. She obviously worshipped her dad and wanted him to be happy. If only I could so blindly go along with Mom's decisions, trusting that they were for the best.

Soon, we were crossing the Sagamore Bridge again, the one between the mainland and the Cape. I realized when we hit the Cape side that I'd been on edge the whole day, nervously awaiting the moment when Mom would declare that we weren't going back. A silent sigh spread over my entire body, from my toes to the crown of my head. Mom was right. It was time to relax. We weren't going to run. We were going home.

CHAPTER THIRTEEN

Gwen

That night we unpacked the car, sneaking the boxes in with lots of giggling from Peyton, who was determined that the guys didn't see any of our stuff. I thought it was just the groom who wasn't supposed to see the bride, but what did I know about real weddings? Plus, it was fun dashing up and down the stairs with my sister-to-be. Being around Peyton infected me with a strange high, and I couldn't help but join in her scheme.

When we'd finished unpacking and eating dinner, Mom said she was going to turn in early, so she'd be rested for the big day. The idea of a wedding still felt strange to me, but I tried to adopt Peyton's attitude. I read for a bit, then wandered out of our room. The house was dark—I must have read longer than I'd meant to—and quiet except for the sound of the wind moaning through the pines outside. The eerie sound put me on edge, and I crept along the hallway, feeling as if I were being watched.

Light was coming from under one of the doors, but the others were dark. I knew which room was Peyton's, since we'd put the dresses in there, and I'd seen Zeke's room the other day. I debated knocking on the door with the light under it. Maybe it was Finn, up late drawing. But maybe it was Xander, up late devising evil plans to be more evil. So I passed the door without knocking.

Tiptoeing down the stairs, I froze on the second floor landing. Like the last time, I felt a breath on the back of my neck. Goosebumps exploded up my spine, and a shiver of dread settled in my belly. Summoning my inner Buffy, I turned slowly.

No one was there.

My first instinct was to bolt headlong down the stairs. But I took a few deep breaths instead. I wasn't going to wake Mom in the night, or Neil, whose room was downstairs, just because a breeze had tickled my neck. It was probably just the heater kicking on, blowing warm air out all of the vents. Besides, I knew way too much about running from imaginary demons to think it actually worked.

Clutching the railing just in case a mischievous ghost was around, I made my way down. When I reached the bottom of the stairs, I breathed a sigh of relief. That's when I realized I had no idea what I was doing there. I couldn't remember why I'd wanted to come downstairs at all.

Not wanting to immediately turn around and go back upstairs, I headed to the kitchen, made myself a cup of tea, and grabbed a blanket from the couch. I was about to sit down when I hesitated. Something inside me urged me to go outside. For a second, I resisted. Was this how Mom felt? Following hunches, jumping at every current in the air, afraid of shadows? Maybe whatever had happened to her happened to all the women in our family when they reached a certain age. It might start slow like this, so people just thought we were quirky.

But I could tell this wasn't all of it. That's what scared me the most. Some gut feeling told me this was just the beginning. Suddenly, I was stepping through the glass door onto the deck, though I didn't remember making the decision to go out. Eerie shivers gripped me, climbing my vertebrae like the rungs of a ladder.

I stepped closer to the outdoor fireplace, where a heap of coals glowed. I'd never actually seen a real-life fireplace before. The fact that it was outdoors, and didn't even warm the house, both fascinated and impressed me. I'd spent so much time worrying about staying warm and not being wasteful that I couldn't help but gape in awe at the extravagance. I'd tried to hide it when I was out here with Zeke and Peyton, but now I let myself marvel.

"Do you always sneak around in the dark?" a voice asked from the shadows behind me.

I spun around, holding back a cry of surprise.

My heart hammered in my chest, and adrenaline burned through my limbs, making me shake all over. A little bit of it was fear, too. I hadn't been alone with Xander before, and I had no desire to start now. Something about him terrified me, even as a part of me was inexplicably drawn to him.

"Do you always sneak up on people in the dark?" I asked after a few seconds too long. My throat was tight, and I wanted to edge towards the door, but I stayed where I was. If we were going to be part of the same family, part of the same household, we'd have to learn to live with each other. If I let him push me around now, it would never end.

"What are you doing here?" he asked, suddenly stalking forward out of the darkness. The firelight played off the lines of his gorgeous face, and a dangerous thrill ran through my body at the sight of those delectable lips, now twisted into a cruel sneer. It was all I could do not to reach out and run my thumb across his full lower lip, feel its softness for myself.

I wrestled to get my thoughts under control. I did not need to be thinking about his lips. I didn't even know why my mind had gone there. He obviously hated me, and I should feel the same about him.

"I just came out to get some air," I said, tightening my hands into fists to keep them from shaking. "I didn't know you were here."

"That's not what I meant," he growled, stalking closer to me, until I could feel the fiery heat of him crackling up my arms.

"Your guess is as good as mine." I refused to step back, though my heart was rattling around in the cage of my ribs like a trapped bird. I would not let him see how much his nearness affected me. I'd dealt with scary men before. He was no different.

"You shouldn't be here," he said.

I tried not to let his harsh words cut through me, but they did. I'd gotten dirty looks all my life, but it had never felt personal before.

"Then I'll just be going," I said, scooting around him. The heat of his body climbed mine as he leaned in just as I passed.

A chuckle followed me as I scurried for the door. "Run away, little mouse," he said, his voice an alluring purr. "This house is full of tomcats."

Upstairs, I lay in bed shaking. I didn't think he'd come in and snatch me from the bed while my mother slept, and yet dread pinned me to the mattress. Something wasn't right here, no matter how right it felt at times. There was something dangerous here, some kind of trap. And we'd walked right into it.

I rolled over, staring at the window. I knew how to drive. I could take the keys and run, just keep driving until I hit the west coast, then turn around, pick a different highway, and drive until it ran out. It was easy to get lost and stay that way. We'd been doing it all my life.

Mom's deep breathing told me she still slept.

She didn't want to go, and I couldn't just leave her. Not after all she'd done for me. She'd told me that everything she did was to protect me. Though her rambling never made sense, that much was consistent. So why had she brought us here? How did this fit into her madness? There must be a piece to the puzzle that I was missing.

I had to find it before something happened. Though we'd stopped running, I was still waiting. For the first time in my life, Mom was the one content to stay, and I could feel the urgency pressing down on me, as if something ominous approached, just out of range of my senses. The premonition gripped me, the sense of dread. I'd always thought it was fear of having to run again or mom leaving me. But maybe it was more than that. Maybe I shared her madness.

She'd found peace here, but I hadn't. I had to get back on the same page so I could understand what was happening to us. If I stopped resisting, opened myself to the possibilities and looked at this situation in a different light, from different angles, I might find the answers. I might make sense of how these people fit into our lives.

CHAPTER FOURTEEN

Gwen

The next morning caterers and florists invaded the house, and I spent most of the day worrying that the noise and people would upset Mom. Even the Keens got overwhelming—every time I turned around, one of the guys was there. Finally, I had to go up to our room to be alone for a minute. I found Mom in our bedroom, staring out the window. I could see in her unfocused eyes that she wasn't peering down towards the beach, enjoying the sunshine reflecting off the water.

This was my last chance to be alone with her before she signed documents, made it permanent. Our last chance to go back to our old life.

I approached her with caution. I never knew when her blank stare meant she'd just zoned out like a normal person, or if she was hallucinating. This was not the time for her vague, cryptic statements, though. We needed sharp minds, snap decisions. It was now or never.

I opened my mouth to speak, but then I stopped. If it was never, if we stayed, I'd have a family. I'd belong. I could have a normal life with everything that entailed, just like Peyton and the guys did. A life I'd spent the last ten years dreaming of, when I was brave enough to let myself dream.

Instead of bringing peace, the thought fanned that ember of resentment inside me, and a flame of rage flickered to life. If something connected our nomadic lifestyle of waiting and wanting to the wasteful luxury of this house, why hadn't we come sooner? If Mom knew they'd find us eventually, she could have contacted them.

Instead, she'd kept me on the road, barely surviving through harsh winters, close encounters with scary, armed homeless guys and even scarier, more heavily armed cops. I'd endured crazy flights of terror, nights of hunger when she hadn't found a job that would pay cash under the table, and weeks without bathing. And all that time, these people had been looking for us. We could have lived in splendor all along.

"I just came to say best freaking wishes, Mom. Marry Neil and live crazily ever after."

I spun on my heel and walked away. Just as I reached the door, a knock sounded. I flung it open, ready to snap at whoever was unfortunate enough to be on the other side. But I stopped short when I saw

Rosa.

"It's time, Ms. Olivia," she said.

Mom joined us and took my hand, holding it in a firm grip, as if she were afraid I'd run away without her. She smiled at me despite my glare. "Soon, you will understand," she said. "Today, accept your new family. This is where you belong. Where you always belonged. Now, you are one of them."

My stomach knotted as we descended the stairs. Neil had gone ahead with the boys, and the house was quiet. That was, until Peyton came galloping down the stairs. "Don't start without me," she cried. "Oh, this is going to be so much fun. Just us girls, getting ready for a wedding. No big deal, am I right?"

We helped Mom into her dress, an elaborately beaded, champagne-colored, A-line gown with long sleeves. I couldn't help but soften towards her. She needed me, and I was being selfish. I wanted to apologize, but I didn't want to admit what a bitch I'd been in front of Peyton, the most accepting, cheerful teenager in existence.

Mom looked so out of place in the dress I almost had to laugh. Peyton did Mom's hair while I applied minimal makeup. She looked little enough like herself as it was. I stood back from her, my throat constricting. Maybe she did look like herself. I was beginning to think I didn't know my mother as well as I'd thought. I'd always considered equals, teammates. Now, she shared secrets with someone else, making me feel like the child in our relationship. In a few short days, Neil had filled places in her heart I didn't even know were empty. She had joined a second team—the adults.

"Time for us to get dressed," Peyton said, taking my arm. A buzz went through me, but I barely noticed. I was getting used to the strange electrical charge these people had.

In the first-floor bathroom, I stood in front of the full-length mirror. I'd never been in a bathroom like this, but it explained the term *restroom*. The room was as big as the biggest storage locker we'd stayed in, about ten by twenty feet. In one end, there was the usual—a toilet, an inset tub and shower. The double marble sinks had a stretch of gleaming marble between them, on which fancy soaps shaped like bird nests with eggs in them looked so real I was afraid to actually use them and mess them up. The other end of the bathroom featured a soft rug on the floor and full-length mirrors on all three walls. Two plush chairs and a small table sat under soft, flattering lighting set recessed into the ceiling.

I didn't understand it. Who would want to sit in a bathroom and chat with a friend? The whole thing just reminded me all over again that I didn't understand this world, and therefore, didn't belong. A week ago I would have thought about trying to escape out a window, but now...I was ready for this, whatever it was. So I pulled on my sheath dress with the wrap skirt, trying to keep my eyes away from the whorls of scarred skin on my stomach.

When I emerged from the bathroom, Peyton covered her mouth with both hands and squealed. Mom looked a little misty-eyed as she smiled at me.

"Who knew that was under all those generic jeans and hoodies?" Peyton said, bouncing over to me. "Now, let's do your hair and makeup. Wait until my brothers see you. They won't know what hit 'em."

She caught my mom's startled expression and quickly added, "I mean, I'm sure you want to impress us, since we're about to become family and everything."

Peyton went to get her makeup, appearing a minute later with what appeared to be a small suitcase. She held it up and grinned, then skipped down to the bathroom. Inside, she opened her makeup case on the small table between the chairs. "Sit," she said. "I can't wait to put makeup on you. It'll be like when I first got makeup. Mom took me to Boston and I got everything you can imagine, and then she let me practice on her." She abruptly stopped speaking and began digging through the makeup, concentrating on lining up an assortment of items on the edge of the table.

After a long, awkward silence, I realized that maybe I should say something. That maybe she was expecting something from me. But what could I say to that? Anything I could say would sound pathetic.

Still, I knew she would have tried for me. What would she say if I told her about my dad?

"What was she like?" I asked at last. The moment I said it, I winced, remembering Xander sneering at me when I told Neil I was sorry about his wife.

Peyton shrugged, never looking up from the tubes and tubs and pallets as she spoke. "I know what I'm supposed to say. Peppy Peyton will say her mom was great, and tell some funny story. That's what everyone expects me to say."

"You've met my mother," I said, gripping the arms of the chair. "There's not much that can surprise me when it comes to moms."

I kept my voice light, but for some reason, I wanted to get up and flee the bathroom. I hadn't asked about their mother because it seemed insensitive, like I was comparing her to Mom. But maybe I didn't really want to know, either. Their lives were so perfect. Maybe I didn't want to hear about one more thing they'd had growing up that I hadn't.

Or maybe I didn't want to hear otherwise. There was something both appealing and sickening about their wealth and beauty, their perfection. Part of me didn't want to see below the flawless surface reflection.

Peyton took a deep, shaky breath. "No, you're right," she said with a small laugh. "What am I complaining about? Mom really was great. It's just the last few years, when she was sick, it was pretty hard. But at least I had her through the hard part, puberty and makeup and all that."

I didn't know what to say to that, but Peyton came around the table and sat down on the edge, her knees on either side of mine. The folds of our dresses fell together so I couldn't tell which was hers and which was mine. My heartbeat ratcheted up a notch, and I swallowed nervously, surveying the pile of products she'd selected.

"Don't worry," she said. "I picked good colors for you."

That wasn't what made me nervous, but I didn't correct her. I'd never been alone with her. Suddenly, I was nervous.

"It's brave of you to be so welcoming to my mom," I said. "I don't think all your brothers agree."

"I want Dad to be happy." She took my chin in her hand and raised my face towards hers. I dropped my gaze, aware of how intimately close we now were. "I'm going to dust some powder on first," she murmured. "Close your eyes."

Swallowing hard, I obeyed as her big soft brush began caressing my face. After dusting on powder, she dabbed blush on my cheeks and sat back. "Now I'm going to do your lips," she said.

Her fingers gently lifted my chin again. My senses all increased, taking in the pressure of her knees around mine, the whisper of her breath as she leaned close, the faint scent of freesia around her. As the pencil touched my lips, so many nerve endings started firing that I could hardly breathe. A trembling moment passed before the pencil began to move slowly across my skin. Her warm fingers curled against my jawline, steadying themselves as the tip of the pencil traced my lips.

A flood of sensation filled me, starting at the sharp tip of the pencil, moving to the softness of her fingers on my chin, the brush of her skin against my throat at she moved her arm. It swept down my body, making goosebumps rise on my flesh and a warmth spread through my belly. As she swept creamy lipstick across my lips, I fought to keep myself from leaning into her touch, begging for more. My whole body was alive, tingling, *wanting*.

"Open your eyes," Peyton murmured, her fingertips lingering on my skin.

My eyes snapped open as I remembered where I was. I was alone in a bathroom with Peyton, and my hormones must be going nuts, because all of a sudden, I had a random urge to lean forward and press my newly painted lips to hers. I shook my head, my heart racing. What the hell? Was this what happened when you grew up in isolation, only able to touch your mother? I was so desperate for human touch that now I was lusting after another girl.

"I'm just going to do a little bit of eyeshadow and a coat of mascara," she whispered. "You're so pretty you don't need more."

My face warmed as our eyes caught. Her gaze lingered on mine then slipped to my lips.

I swallowed hard.

Peyton sat back and turned to pick up the

makeup, fumbling the eyeshadow in the process. The pallet clattered to the floor. I may not be able to read people, but I was sure she was feeling what I was. It wasn't possible that I could feel so much without it spreading across the air between us and invading her body like a virus.

"Damn," Peyton muttered, leaning down to snatch up the makeup. "Okay, close your eyes and stop messing with me." She laughed nervously, then quickly swept a soft brush across my eyelids. Again, the sensation of her fingers on my face, touching the sensitive skin of my eyelids, sent tension coiling through my body.

When I opened my eyes this time, I tried to look anywhere but at her as she coated my lashes with mascara. My mind was whirling, my body buzzing. I was so confused I wanted to jump up and bolt from the bathroom. It was one thing to like being with her, to find her enthusiasm contagious, and another thing to feel like I was melting when she touched me. I'd almost accepted it with the guys. Anyone who'd never been around guys would go into overdrive when under the same roof as so many gorgeous ones at once. It was only natural to want them all. But I'd never wanted a girl before.

As soon as she finished, Peyton stood and held out a hand. "We should go."

"Right. Totally."

With a shy smile, she slipped her hand into mine and tugged me back towards the living room. A giddy laugh bubbled up inside me, sparkling like champagne. The comfort of her presence had melded with something else, something exciting and new. A secret. I'd never had a secret before.

I held onto her soft hand, never wanting to let go. The feeling coursing through me was too good. When Rosa told us a limo was waiting outside, I didn't hesitate to follow Peyton out and slide inside with Mom. Whatever this was, I wanted to be part of it.

The ride passed in a blur. Peyton chattered the whole way, checked her makeup in a little mirror she had in her purse and fussing with Mom's hair. In minutes, we were pulling into a large parking lot. Considering how cold it was, I was not surprised that there were only a handful of vehicles. When we stepped out, I heard the roar and crash of waves that was missing from the bay.

We helped Mom down a steep path to the beach, where a small group was gathered. They'd set up two speakers, and music began to play.

"Hot damn," Zeke said, and he gave a wolf whistle that made me smile despite the surreal nature of the moment.

Peyton grabbed my hand and gave me a huge grin, not seeming to notice the hum of energy that coursed through our connected hands. She looked absolutely stunning in her wrap dress, and I remembered her comment from the night we met, when she said we could be real sisters. We were almost the exact same size, but I had to envy the way the satin hugged her slightly curvier frame.

She started forward, and my legs began to move without instruction from my brain. The sand felt as if it were rolling under my feet like waves. A seagull swooped overhead, white against the charcoal grey sky. A buzzing filled my brain, and the rush and roar of the waves seemed to fade into the distance. An irresistible pull dragged me forward. Together, Peyton and I floated towards the guys while a photographer snapped pictures of us. I found my eyes moving across the men in the group ahead. My family.

Zeke was grinning like it was the happiest day of his life. Next to him, Xander stood motionless, his face so incredibly blank he could have been a marble statue. Beside him, Eliot was watching us with a closed-lip smile, a dimple sinking into his cheek. And then there was Finn, his eyes dreamy and unfocused as he watched our approach. Last, Neil waited for my mother, his eyes on us, his face a mix of emotions I couldn't read.

When we were a few yards away, Peyton dropped my hand and ran forward to throw her arms around him. "I'm so happy for us, Daddy," she said as he lifted her feet off the ground for a second.

He set her down, and she stepped to his other side, motioning for me to join her.

My mother's walk was quick and sure. Before I could quell the anxiety churning in my stomach, she was standing with Neil. A minister of some sort started talking.

This was it. She was really going through with it.

This was our last chance to run, to go back on the road. Our last moment to reclaim our old life, to dash up the dunes and back to the parking lot, hop into the car and burn rubber on our way out. Stop at the first house with a shady car in the yard with the words "for sale" scrawled across the windshield. Disappear into the anonymity of the road, of mid-America, and cash-for-hire jobs.

Two words broke through my thoughts.

"I do," Neil said.

"I do," Mom said.

A sucking sound drew our attention, and we turned to see a wall of water barreling down on us.

CHAPTER FIFTEEN

Peyton

I'd lived in Cape Cod all my life, and I'd seen some monster waves, but this was like a freaking tsunami.

"Get down," I yelled, grabbing Gwen.

I don't know why I yelled that. It was instinct. I know, I know, when there's a tsunami, you should probably get up, not down. But I didn't have much time to think about that as the monsterest wave of all time came rushing towards us.

The photographer, who was near the dune, took a picture of it and then turned tail and ran. I don't know what anyone else did, because just then the wave crashed over us. I lost my footing and was tumbled head over heels.

Icy salt water churned around us, rushing into my nose and mouth and ears. My dress tangled around my legs, and I couldn't tell which way was up or down. Instinct took over, and I paddled madly for a few seconds before I felt myself being pulled out with the water. Seconds later, my head surfaced. I looked around, bewildered, my brain registering the freezing water around me.

A regular-sized wave came barreling towards me. I ducked under and let it carry me towards shore. Staggering to my feet, I dragged myself from the water, my dress clinging to my legs. Around me, my brothers were stumbling out of the water, too. Eliot's glasses were gone, and he was coughing up water. Xander and Zeke were cursing up a storm. Along with the minister, Finn had been dumped farther up the beach towards the dunes instead of being dragged back by the wave. Only Rosa, who had been watching from the dune and was not part of the wedding party, had been spared.

Dad was looking around frantically. "Where's Gwen?" he asked.

Olivia, who was crumpled in a heap on the sand, suddenly shot up like she'd been electrocuted. Her bedraggled hair stuck to her face, her makeup streaked down her skin, and her beautiful dress was a ruined mess.

"Gwen," she shrieked, charging back into the water as fast as her waterlogged dress would allow.

I scanned the water, catching a glimpse of something bobbing out in the waves. "There," I yelled, pointing.

"She can't swim," Olivia screamed.

Xander and Zeke both dove back into the

frigid water, disappearing under an incoming wave.

Dad ran out and grabbed Olivia around the middle, lifting her up and turning back to the shore. "You'll drown yourself," he barked when she flailed and kicked to get to her daughter.

Tears stung my eyes and choked my throat, and I clung to Eliot, shaking uncontrollably. I tried to imagine how I'd feel if I had only one person in the world, and she was being sucked out to sea in hypothermic temperatures. I had all the love in the world compared to Olivia. Compared to Gwen. I had all these protective, loving brothers and an amazing Dad. They only had each other.

"Let's get up to the limo," Finn said. "We'll all die if we stay out here much longer."

As if confirming his fears, an icy blast of wind raked across my skin, and Eliot hugged me tighter. "He's right," he said, not moving towards the parking lot. "We can't do anything more than they can."

The thought of leaving them all out there and hoping for the best was unbearable. I knew Finn was right, but I couldn't tear my feet from the ground. Finn came to stand beside us, sheltering me from the wind with his body. We were all shaking so hard it felt like the earth was quaking under us.

Dad fell when a wave hit his back, but he staggered to his feet, dragging Olivia with him. Behind them, I saw three heads bobbing in a wave. It began to gather, cresting with all three of them on it. A second later it crashed with a deafening roar, and they disappeared under the water. When their heads came up, they were nearly on shore.

A sob of relief escaped my throat.

Xander stood, dragging Gwen's limp body in his arms. He charged up through the last of the water and laid her on the sand. One of the straps on her dress was broken, and her tiny boob was exposed. Somehow, it made her look more fragile and lost. Xander peeled back the wet hair matted to her face to find her mouth. Her lips were blue, her skin the white of a dead fish's belly. I squeezed my eyes closed, letting frantic, muddled prayers race through my head. Pleading she'd be okay, that she was alive, thanking the lord that my two oldest brothers had spent summers lifeguarding, and hoping it was enough.

Xander's hands crushed down on Gwen's skinny chest, then his mouth descended on hers. Again and again.

I heard a horrible choking sob coming from my throat, but I couldn't stop it. It couldn't be over just like that. It couldn't. I'd had a sister for exactly one second, and she was being ripped away. It wasn't fair.

"Let me take over," Zeke said, grabbing Xander's shoulder.

Xander shoved him back viciously, pumping Gwen's chest with renewed vigor.

"Dude, you're going to hurt her," Zeke said. "And you'll wear yourself out. Let me take a shift. Now."

His voice was commanding, and after a few seconds, Xander's shoulders slumped and he fell back in the sand, allowing Zeke to take his place.

Olivia screamed, fighting Dad, who was trying to reason with her, though she was obviously unreachable.

"Let's get the limo ready to take her to the hospital when she wakes up," Eliot said as Zeke continued working on Gwen. But as we all rushed up the slope, I couldn't help but think it had been too long. We could save ourselves, but we couldn't save Gwen.

CHAPTER SIXTEEN

Gwen

I didn't know where I was, if I was dead or alive. But my consciousness was there, and something was tugging at it. Calling it back. Telling me to come home.

"It's not time," a voice whispered into the nothingness I'd become. "Go back."

I didn't know who'd spoken. Someone trying to revive me or something inside me. As if watching from above, I could see a wet, bedraggled group huddling on the beach together. There was a body, her face obscured by someone trying to resuscitate her. Someone had been hurt or drowned in the wave. Anguish pierced me, a stark panic that it was my mother.

But no, the body on the beach had lilywhite skin and a crumpled dusty rose dress clinging to her in a sodden mess. Horror flooded through me.

Peyton.

As I searched the group to see if everyone else was safe, I saw her pink hair pressed against Finn's chest. Eliot huddled with them. Xander stood alone, watching Zeke bent over the body. Neil held Mom, whose beautiful wedding dress was ruined. And she was freaking out. I had to go back, to get her, to help her.

That's when I realized it was me down there on the beach. Zeke was trying to save me. I had to get back, but I didn't know how.

Help me.

I sent the plea out into the void, not expecting a response, but not knowing what else to do. Suddenly, a glowing light filled my vision, and I looked up from the beach below. Above, as blindingly bright as the sun, was a figure of some sort, as if the sun had morphed into a vaguely humanoid shape.

"You are bound together now, as one unit," a ghostly voice said. It was at once silent and deafening, overpowering and insubstantial. "When you become one, I become complete."

As the voice spoke into me, I thought I'd burst with the force of it. It was overpowering, a force as great as the sea.

"What are you?" I managed.

"You are a part of me now. The time is drawing near."

"I don't want to die," I screamed with every fiber of my soul, or whatever I was now. Panic like I'd never known gripped me, and I strained to find some way back to my life. If this thing was here to take me away, I wanted no part of it.

"You must go back now," the being said. "Put my pieces together, and I will speak to you again."

"I promise," I said with all the force I could manage.

"You must leave Midgard soon. You have a long journey ahead."

Before I could answer, a ton of ice thudded into me. Crushing pain shot through my limbs, and panic seared into my burning chest. I fought madly to get away, but my body only twitched, my eyelids fluttering open.

It was enough. Zeke rolled me over, and water poured from my mouth. Gurgling and gagging, I emptied my stomach and lungs.

Before I'd even finished, Zeke spoke. "I'm going to carry you up."

I didn't fight as he lifted me and tossed me over his shoulder, my head hanging down behind him. My body was simultaneously aching with cold and heat. My chest, lungs, throat, and stomach were on fire. Gasping for breath, I spit water and bile all the way up the dune.

When we reached the parking lot, Finn jumped out of the limo and opened the doors for us. Zeke slid in with me, and Peyton grabbed my coat out of the pile on the seat and wrapped it around me. Mom leapt onto to me, sobbing as she clutched me against her.

Violent shivers wracked my body, and I was only vaguely aware of everyone else's apparent nakedness under their jackets as they huddled together for warmth. The limo must have been warm, but I didn't feel it. I noticed Neil watching us intently, his brow furrowed with concern.

"Don't go to sleep," Eliot warned when I closed my eyes.

As the limo sped out of the parking lot, Peyton and Mom pulled off my dress, dropping it to the floor with a pile of wet clothes. I held the jacket tight around myself, determined not to let them see more than they already had. It could have been a lot worse than one boob.

My head was spinning, and I seemed to lose some time. The next thing I knew, we were pulling up to a clinic, and a couple nurses were covering us with blankets, lifting me into a wheelchair, and wheeling me inside.

For a while, I couldn't focus. Time seemed to stop and start. There wasn't a hospital in Wellfleet, just a clinic, but they treated the others for mild hypothermia. They'd gone up to the limo to take off their wet clothes before me and Zeke. We were held a couple hours longer, the clinic keeping us under warming blankets and asking us questions about what had happened and other random things that didn't make sense to me.

When I could finally answer all their

questions, and they were satisfied that we were out of danger, they let us go home. By then it was evening. When we got home, the house was oddly quiet, as if it were waiting.

There was no wedding reception, no party. Finn was at some kind of church function, and Xander had apparently taken his motorcycle and left without telling anyone. The rest of us ate clam chowder in a state of sober silence, each lost in our own thoughts. I kept picturing that angel thing I'd seen, turning over what she had said. Or he? I wasn't sure angels had a gender. I'd seen some crazy things in my life, but angels were not among them.

Had I been dead? Did the words mean anything?

"You looking forwards to your first day of school?" Neil asked, breaking the silence at last.

I nearly choked on a piece of potato. "Tomorrow?"

"They want you to get caught up as quickly as possible," Neil said.

"You've only missed the last ten or so grades," Peyton said.

"I can't believe you've never been to school," Zeke said. "It's awesome, Gwen. You're going to love it."

"I don't have a birth certificate," I blurted out. I didn't mention that Mom had burned that, along with all our other documents, in an elaborate ceremony in the desert when I was six.

"You don't need one to start," Neil said. "And we'll work on getting a copy from the state."

"The state?" I asked, my eyes darting between him and Mom. "They have a copy?"

"You can always request a copy," Neil said with a reassuring smile.

"From here?" I asked, turning to gape at Mom. "I was born *here*?"

"At Mass General, in Boston," Mom said.

I felt like I'd been blindsided. "Why didn't you tell me?"

"You never asked." She smiled and tried to pat my hand, but I drew away.

I ate the rest of my chowder in silence, not sure why I felt so betrayed. Mom was right. I could have asked her any time, and she would have told me. It wasn't like she'd lied. Yet the anger I'd felt earlier began to creep back. It was just that I'd always been so busy worrying about her, I'd never thought to ask the most basic things. Instead of being a normal kid who knew things like where I came from, I was her caretaker. She took care of me, too, but wasn't that her job? It wasn't a kid's job to make sure her mother didn't get arrested.

I should have been going to school and making friends so it didn't feel so strange when people were nice to me. Relating to guys so that I didn't go into this insane, gluttonous mode where I couldn't get enough of every single guy I came in contact with. Making casual contact with people so that I didn't feel like I was going to explode when someone touched me. I should have been learning how to relate to sane people, and how to be a sane person myself.

Instead, I knew how to read maps.

Of course I knew more than that. I knew my birthday, and if I asked about Dad, she did her best to satisfy my curiosity. When I was younger, we'd played a car game called "Did We Live Here?" Any time we entered a new state, I'd ask if we'd been there before. It was hard for me to remember places well. Everything blurred together, since we never stayed in any one place long enough for it to make an impact on our lives. Sure, certain places had more character than others—New Orleans, San Francisco, and yes, Boston. I just hadn't imagined that's where I came from. That I came from any one place and not just the broad stroke of the country's middle.

I lay in bed for a long time that night, trying to sleep. Nerves fluttered around my stomach. My first day of school was the next day, and I hadn't even prepared. I wasn't ready, but Neil said the sooner I got started, the sooner I'd catch up. After the day I'd had, Mom offered to let me stay home, but I was tired of hanging out with my mother. Not only was I getting more irritated with her the more we settled in, but I didn't want to watch everyone else go off to school while I sat at home. It would just highlight once again how different I was. I wanted to be like everyone else for once in my life.

No one at Wellfleet High would know me, so they wouldn't know that I wasn't a typical teenager like them. I'd read so many books about high school, seen it on TVs in laundromats and diners and break rooms. At last, I was going to walk the halls of a real school, just like every other fifteen-year-old in the country.

I was also going to be a hollow-eyed zombie if I didn't get at least a few hours of sleep. Try as I might, I couldn't shut off my mind, though. Finally, too frustrated to try any longer, I slipped from my bed and tiptoed down the hall, hoping I wouldn't have the bad luck to run into Xander again. He hadn't come home yet, so maybe he was staying the night with his girlfriend or in jail.

In the kitchen I made tea, but no sooner had I sat down, I heard footsteps on the stairs. A moment later, Eliot stepped into the kitchen. He was wearing what I called old-man pajamas, the kind with a button-up shirt and matching pants. His were light blue with thin vertical stripes of white and tan.

I was relieved it wasn't Xander, but I barely knew Eliot. In the few days I'd been there, he'd seen me in my underwear once, and my boob once, but otherwise, we'd barely interacted. He'd holed up in his room most of the time, appearing at family meals but otherwise remaining on the sidelines during all the activity. I'd been so busy that it had been easy to overlook him. I had a feeling he might get that a lot, especially with the brothers he had.

Making a mental note to give him more attention, I smiled over the rim of my mug at him.

He smiled back.

Crap. What now?

Say something...say something...

Eliot cleared his throat and shuffled his feet.

Okay, Gwen, now you've crossed over into creepy territory.

"Tea," I blurted.

Eliot blinked like an owl at me.

"Tea," I said again. "I'm, uh, drinking tea. Want some tea? I mean, it's your house, obviously you can get yourself tea. Or whatever you want. Do you even like tea?"

Okay, now I'd said the word *tea* so many times it had lost all meaning. Perhaps the silent staring was a good choice after all.

"Tea sounds great," Eliot asked, sauntering over to the counter. He had different glasses on—big black frames that slanted up at the corners. With his curls and dorky, open smile, he looked eerily like Buddy Holly.

"You couldn't sleep either?" I tried, wanting to make conversation but feeling ridiculous now that I'd been a complete idiot.

"Sure," he said, taking down a mug. "Or maybe I heard someone come down, and I was hoping it was you."

My face warmed, but I lowered it over my tea so he wouldn't notice. Despite his geeky exterior, he didn't seem to have any trouble talking to human beings. Maybe he recognized another socially inept soul. Or maybe he just wanted to make me feel better.

"Why would you hope that?" I mumbled as he poured hot water over a tea bag and sat down beside me.

"My brothers all had a chance to hang out with you," he said. "I hoped I'd get to know you a little before you started school. I'm sure you'll have more interest from guys than you can handle by the end of tomorrow."

I snorted, choking on my tea in the process. I was smooth like that.

Eliot patted my back until I'd recovered from choking. "It's a small school," he said. "A new girl is bound to draw attention. And you're not bad to look at, either."

My face grew even warmer, from both his words and his touch. I could feel my skin glowing with warmth where he'd touched the center of my back. I clenched my hands around my cup to keep them from doing something stupid. They were itching to touch him back, to see how it felt. But it would probably be weird to ask.

Hey, stepbro, mind if I touch you? Not in a weird way, but just to try it out. See, I've never really touched boys before, and I just wanted to see if you feel different from my mom. No? Okay, cool. No worries.

"How are you feeling?" Eliot asked.

It took me a second to come back from my

thoughts and realize he was talking about earlier in the day. "Good," I said.

A totally normal response. Score one, Gwen.

"That was pretty crazy, right?" His voice was casual, but his eyes were studying me as if watching for some kind of sign.

Instinctually, I found myself choosing my words with caution. I may have felt like I'd always known these people, but I didn't trust my own judgment of them. Sure, they felt kind and trustworthy, but what did I know about judging people?

"Was it?" I asked. "I'm not familiar with the wave patterns here."

Eliot laughed and stood, and I knew the test was over. I just didn't know if I'd passed or failed it. "How about that library visit I promised you?" he asked, holding out a hand.

"Now?"

"What better time?"

I hesitated, then slipped my fingers into his palm. Warmth spread up my arm as he pulled me to my feet, but I didn't want to let go. In fact, I wanted to tuck his hand against myself and roll up in him like a blanket cocoon. But that would definitely be weird. I was pretty sure, anyway.

He led me up the first flight of stairs along the second-story hallway, and I realized that with everything going on, I still hadn't seen most of the house. I knew the third floor pretty well because it was mostly bedrooms, but I hadn't explored the other floors.

"After you," Eliot said, twisting a knob and pushing open a door. I stepped into the darkness, the comforting smell of books greeting me. Eliot hit a switch, and soft, amber light filled the enormous room. An imposing wooden desk sat near two tall windows, but most of the furniture in the room was plush brown leather couches and chairs. Ottomans and a few other pieces were scattered about the cavernous room, and a thick, patterned rug covered most of the hardwood floor.

"Wow," I breathed, scanning the walls and walls of books. It was like something out of a fairytale, if fairytales were written for book nerds.

Eliot shot me a quick smile. "What do you like?" he asked, stepping inside and turning to face me. "Or would you like a tour of the whole library?"

"Yes, please," I said, forgetting all about my awkwardness. I couldn't hold back my smile. The place was too incredible.

Eliot cleared his throat and adopted a tour-guide voice, gesturing to the wall on our left. Shelves reached to the ceiling, each one lined with leather-bound tomes. I thought my eyes would orgasm from taking in such luxurious splendor.

"You really shouldn't have shown me this first," I said. "I may never leave."

Eliot laughed, his whole face lighting up. Maybe it was my imagination, but he seemed more alive in this room, as if a weight had been lifted when he stepped into its magic. "You and me both," he said. "I've spent so much time in here. I mean, this is basically the internet, before there was internet."

"I've lived my whole life without internet," I said. "But I couldn't live without books."

"And you shouldn't," Eliot said.

My statement wasn't strictly true. I could technically live without books, but I'd be a hell of a lot weirder. Books had been my friends and my teachers. Sure, real people were more complicated, and they didn't always say what they would've said if they existed in a fictional world. But without books, I wouldn't even know what they were supposed to say.

"Want me to show you the rest of the house?" Eliot asked. "I promise you can come back here at the end. And any other time you want."

I gazed longingly at all the shelves I hadn't even begun to examine, then turned away. "I guess it wouldn't hurt to learn my way around," I said. "This place has a lot to remember."

As we stepped out of the library, my palm itched almost uncontrollably to join with his again. My fingers twitched to reach out and touch him, to feel the broad planes of his back as he led me along the hallway. I curled my hands into fists and tucked them under my arms so I wouldn't accidentally reach out and stroke my stepbrother. That might be frowned upon by, you know, regular humans. I didn't know how girls who went to school dealt with this feeling all day long. How was I going to cope tomorrow, when I was around hundreds of guys?

Eliot showed me the other rooms one by one. First up was a small game room, which had two TVs, a wet bar, a pool table, foosball, and a couple other games. Then there was a "small" personal movie theater, where he said they showed movies once a week when they could get everyone together. There was a locked door, which Finn used for a studio when he worked on his art.

"You never have to leave the house," I said as we headed downstairs to the first floor. "You could just bring a girl here for a date and have a whole movie theater to yourself."

"It has come in handy," Eliot said.

"You've been on a date?"

Way to go, Gwen. That didn't sound incredulous at all.

"Well...yeah," Eliot said "Haven't you?"

"No."

I realized that no one in this family really knew what my life had been like. I'd told Finn, but he'd obviously kept it to himself. A swell of warmth rose in my chest. I'd known I could trust him. Now that we were family, I should probably tell the others, too, but I wanted them to see me as normal for as long as I could, even if it didn't last. I'd told Peyton we moved around a lot, but I hadn't told her why and how.

Without comment, Eliot showed me the

workout room. It had a barre and two walls made entirely of mirrors, since apparently Peyton had been into dance for a while. Half the floor was made of a tough rubber mat, the other half, hardwood. A bunch of weight machines, a treadmill, and some contraptions I couldn't even identify stood at one side of the room. The room after that was a soundproof music studio.

"Do people know about this?" I asked, gaping at the equipment.

"About what?" Eliot asked.

"About your house."

"It's not a secret," Eliot said. "Wellfleet is so small that all the locals know each other."

"You could totally impress the ladies with this," I said, backing out of the music studio. I wasn't great with electronics, having never gotten to use anything more than the car CD player and a few computers at public libraries. Everything here looked expensive and complicated.

"Are you saying you're impressed?" Eliot asked with a smile that was just a little smug.

"Uh, yeah," I said before I could think about playing it cool. How could one family have so much?

Eliot laughed and touched my elbow. "We're almost done."

Finally, he led me into a room at the end of the house that was almost entirely glass. Set into the floor was a long, clear blue pool, lit up from below. I could see our reflections in the glass windows all around the room. Even the ceiling was glass. I wanted to exclaim how insane this whole thing was again, but he didn't seem to notice. Of course he didn't—he lived here.

"And that door leads out to the deck," he said, pointing across the room. He circled around the pool and pushed the door open, and a blast of cold air made steam billow up from the pool. "There's a hot tub out here, if you didn't notice," he said. "And the fireplace, of course. If you wanted to get in...the hot tub, I mean, not the fireplace..."

I smiled, shaking my head. He'd already seen way too much of me—he didn't need to see my whole body. And suddenly, my exhaustion hit me all at once. I swayed on my feet, barely able to stand under the weight of it. "I think I'm finally tired," I said, stifling a yawn.

"Then my job here is done," he said. "Either that, or I've bored you to sleep."

"It's been a long day," I reminded him with an apologetic smile.

"You're telling me near-death experiences aren't the norm for you?" he asked, his eyes widening in mock surprise. "What kind of life have you been living?"

I laughed, but I wasn't about to actually answer that question.

Eliot strode back around the pool and smiled down at me. "I'll take a rain check on the hot tub," he said, his voice low and a bit husky.

Suddenly, it was hard to swallow, and I had to tear my gaze from his. "Okay," I whispered.

He chuckled and moved a half step closer, until we were almost in each other's arms. He smelled clean, like soap and freshly washed clothes. And for someone who didn't always make it to a laundromat until far past time, that was the smell of being okay again, getting off the road, having a few simple pleasures.

I closed my eyes and breathed it in, the safe smell of him, the reassurance of it. His fingertips grazed my elbow, and a sparkler ignited inside me, the sparks dancing across my skin. I sucked in a breath, ready to melt into his arms, to revel in his strength and comfort. Everything about him said that he was good and trustworthy. So much so that it scared me more than Xander, with his undue resentment.

I was used to people treating me like something pathetic and nasty, less than human. Xander's scorn, contempt, and loathing were familiar. True, when most people gave me that attitude, I didn't inexplicably find them mouthwateringly sexy, but still. I'd endured all that before. Xander might be dangerous, but he wasn't unexpected.

Eliot, however, terrified me. Not because of anything he did, or said, or even anything he was. I had a feeling he was just a nerd like me. But the fact that he could so easily and effortlessly melt my defenses, step through them as if they weren't even there…that's what scared me. My reaction to him scared me. I didn't care if he was my stepbrother. I knew better than to trust someone I'd just met.

And yet, I did trust him. More than that, I wanted to be near him. I wanted to get in the hot tub with him, wanted to sit so close our bodies pressed together under the water. I wanted to lean in and press my nose to the spot where his neck met his shoulder and inhale his scent, see if he smelled different up close. I wanted to move forward just another half-step, to close the distance between us and see if those sparks opened like sunbursts inside me.

My eyes opened, and I found myself gazing directly into his warm brown eyes. His eyes searched mine, then dropped to my lips. My heart lurched.

"I...I'd better get to bed," I said, stepping back and shaking my head to clear my strange thoughts. "Tomorrow's another big day."

"How about we skip the near-death experiences tomorrow?"

"I'll try," I said. "But from what I've heard about high school, I think it qualifies."

CHAPTER SEVENTEEN

Gwen

Monday dawned cold and damp, with clouds low in the sky. I stumbled out of my room to see Peyton dashing past me, a backpack slung over one shoulder, her pink hair bobbing in its high ponytail.

"We're late," she called down the stairs, skidding to a stop at the top. She turned back to me, her eyes wide. "You're just getting up?"

I squinted one eye open and mumbled, "Unghunga," which loosely translated to, "My body just woke up, but my brain hasn't caught up yet."

"It's your first day!" she squealed, looking way too excited for this ungodly hour. "I knocked on your door an hour ago. I thought you were getting ready."

"Mmnghhhk." I rubbed at my eye, my brain beginning to rouse. I'd finally fallen asleep around dawn, and I definitely wasn't ready to get up.

"Are you ready?" Zeke asked, stopping in my doorway, spinning a set of keys around one finger.

"We gotta go," Peyton said, dragging me back into my room. "Just throw on some clothes and let's go."

"I probably should shower," I managed.

Peyton looked me over, wrinkling her nose. "Yeah, you should. But hurry."

"What's going on?" Neil asked, stopping in the hall outside my room.

My head was starting to throb. Was it always so noisy here in the mornings? Mom wasn't really a morning person, and I must have inherited that trait. We liked our quiet mornings, with the wheels whirring by under us.

"New girl's not ready," Xander said, looking over his father's shoulder.

"You can take her," Neil said. "The rest of you, get going or you're going to be late."

"What? No," I said, my eyes flying to my nemesis. I was awake now.

Xander met my gaze with a cool smirk. He looked like he knew exactly how much he scared me.

Shit. I'd tried so hard to be tough with him.

"Gwen?" Mom mumbled from the bed behind me. "Gwen, where are you?"

I had a sudden urge to tell her to shut up, with some choice words sprinkled in there. Despite what I'd said to Eliot the night before, I was so excited to start school that I'd stayed up until it was nearly light out, replaying every TV show and movie about high school I'd ever seen. For the first time in my life, I was getting a chance to do something normal. And like usual, Mom was fucking it all up.

"Go ahead and get ready," Neil said to me. "You'll have a ride."

I shot a last fearful look at my new family, sure they'd leave me with Xander if I didn't stick around to fight it. But Mom was calling me again. My shoulders slumped, and I closed the door and hurried to the bed. It wasn't her fault that her mind didn't work right.

"What now?" I asked, crumpling to the bed with a sigh.

"I dreamed I got married," she said, her eyes faraway. "And a big wave almost killed you."

"Hate to break it to you, Mom, but it wasn't a dream."

"It's always a dream first," she mumbled. "Then comes reality."

"Well, this time reality came first," I said. "You're married." I held up her hand, showing her the fat diamond Neil had put on her finger right before the ocean decided to defy gravity.

Suddenly, her limp hand clenched around mine, yanking me towards her with inhuman strength. "The bridge is crumbling," she rasped. "You have to stop it."

My heart twisted in my chest, my blood turning to ice water. I'd known this was coming. And yet…for a few days, I'd let myself hope. I'd started to believe it could last, and I'd wanted it to.

But these words, delivered in the voice of a dying old man, were all too familiar. Next she'd start talking about Ragnarok, and Fenrir, and the end of the world. And the sick thing was, a part of me was relieved.

Yes, for a few days, I'd dreamed I could have a real family. A whole family. But my dream suddenly seemed as far from reality as hers—probably further. I smiled sadly down at my mother. Despite the pleasantness of this dream, in truth, I'd been waiting for this. I knew this. It was familiar and therefore predictable. As ironic as it was to find more comfort in moving every few days, or weeks, or months, than a huge house overlooking the ocean, with fancy food and plush beds, that was my reality.

"Gwen, you about ready?" Neil asked from outside the door. "It's okay if you're a little late. I'm sure the office has a helper to show you around."

I pulled open the door and tried to smile. "I'm not going."

"What do you mean?" A frown of concern creased Neil's brow.

"Mom's…I mean, I think she wants to leave."

"You just get ready for school," he said, stepping past me. "I'm working from home today, so

I'll be here with your mom. Don't worry about a thing."

Dear god, I wished it were that simple.

"Go," Neil said, a smile on his face but his voice firm and commanding.

I turned to the bed. Mom met my questioning look with a vacant smile. After a moment of indecision, I ducked into the bathroom to shower, vowing I'd stay if she was still talking nonsense when I came out. But when I emerged, the bedroom was empty. I dressed quickly, my heart pounding. I ran downstairs to the kitchen, where I found Mom eating an English muffin and drinking coffee with Rosa and Neil.

"Are you okay?" I asked, slipping in beside her.

"Of course," she said, like nothing had happened. "You just eat and get to school."

I should have been happy that she hadn't gone into an all-out fit this time. Instead, I wanted to shake the hell out of her. For the first time in my life, I had a chance to do something normal, with other kids my age. I'd been waiting my whole life for this, and she'd almost ruined it for five minutes of reassurance. Now, for her to act like it was no big deal…I wanted to scream.

When Neil yelled up the stairs for Xander, I spun around to face him, forgetting about Mom's questionable mental state.

"I can drive," I said quickly. "I'll just take Mom's car."

That way she couldn't leave me stranded if she did go into a full-on freak out, and I wouldn't have to ride with my evil stepbrother.

Neil shook his head. "You better wait until you have a license."

"Yeah," Xander said, gliding into the kitchen. "You wouldn't want to do anything *bad*. One arrest in this shithole town and you'll get lumped in with the likes of me."

I swallowed the bite of English muffin I'd been chewing, which had suddenly turned to stone in my mouth.

"Make sure Gwen gets to school and finds the office," Neil said to Xander. "They know she's coming. Get her settled in and help her find her first class, and she'll be fine from there."

He smiled at me, seemingly oblivious to Xander's scathing glare. "Don't worry, Daddy-O, I won't introduce her to my friends, if that's what you're worried about," Xander said. "I'm sure she'll get along better with the office staff, anyway."

I shoved the last bite of the English muffin into my mouth and tried to chew.

"Just get her to school," Neil said, staring down his son. "I don't think she'll have any trouble making friends."

Xander snorted and gave me a once-over.

"I'm sure," he said with a sneer.

I tugged at the hem of my thermal shirt self-consciously. I didn't want to ask Xander for fashion advice, but we were the only ones left. And he looked…well, he looked damn sexy. Maybe he wasn't a fashionista like Peyton, but in his combat boots, fitted jeans, and black leather jacket, he definitely knew how to put himself together.

"What's wrong with this?" I asked, gesturing to my jeans, tennis shoes, and shirt.

I instantly regretted my question. I'd given him the opening, the power, to cut me down. His eyes traveled over me more slowly this time, and my heart began to pound. I knew he was going to give me a scathing critique, tell me how my jeans weren't the right wash and my shirt was stretched out and dingy, and my tennis shoes were obviously second-hand. I'd invited it.

A venomous smile twisted his full lips. "Nothing," he said, his voice dripping with cruelty. "It's perfect."

"He's right," Mom said. "You look nice."

Before I could answer, or run upstairs and change, Xander held out his hand, the keys in his fist.

"Don't put yourself out for me," I said, a bit of bitterness creeping into my words. If the others were my friends, he was the enemy. His words might have fooled our parents, but I knew they were anything but kind.

"Do you want a ride or not?" he asked, snatching my hand from where it hung at my side. He plunked the keys into my palm and closed my fingers around them, squeezing just hard enough that they bit into my palm. He shoved his backpack against my chest until my arms closed around it. "If you want a ride, go wait by my bike," he said, enunciating each word as if talking to someone slow. "And don't even think about touching it."

"Don't feel like you have to," I said. "I'd hate to drag you away from your busy day of sulking and terrorizing the town."

"I'm going that way anyway," he said, throwing up his hands in disgust. He turned and stalked out of the kitchen before I could answer.

"Mom?" I turned to the table.

"Have a good day, Gwen," Mom said with a dreamy smile. "It's all coming together now. Don't fight it. It's destiny."

"Go to school," Neil said, turning me towards the door. "You're the child here. Stop worrying and go be a kid."

After a second's hesitation—I wasn't sure I wanted to go anywhere with Xander, even when Mom was at her best—I sighed and trudged out to the garage. I thought about wheeling the bike out the door just to spite Xander, but I was afraid it would squash me flat if I tried. Still, after I slipped his backpack on my back, I reached out and ran my fingers along the sleek side of it. I wiped my hands on my jeans and licked my lips, glancing nervously at the door as it opened.

Xander trotted down the steps and handed me a helmet. "Put it on."

"Yes, sir," I said in a slightly mocking tone.

He glowered as I secured the helmet and smiled at him. I wasn't going to let him intimidate me—or at least I wasn't going to let him know that he already had.

He stepped closer and hooked his finger into the strap under my chin, gently tugging my face up. My heart stammered in my chest when my gaze met his. His eyes were a clear, dark grey like the ocean under a stormy sky, fringed with long, thick, dark lashes that made me mad with envy. As his gaze lingered on my face, my breath stuck in my throat.

"That'll do, pig," he whispered. "Now get on." He nodded at the bike while I tried to decide whether to hurl an insult back. *Pig?* What the hell.

"Don't order me around," I said instead. "I'm not your servant."

"Too bad," he said. "If you were, I could fire you."

I climbed on the bike, shooting him a withering look. He ignored it, grabbed the backpack with one hand and flattened his hand on my belly with the other. Instinctively, I tensed as his hand pressed tightly against me, sliding me back on the seat. Heat surged through my body, and I was glad he swung his leg over the bike and climbed on in front of me before he could see the flush climbing my neck.

"Hold onto me," he said. "I don't want to have to scrape you up off the side of the road."

"I'm good," I said, clutching the seat on either side of my hips.

"Suit yourself," he said. "But don't expect me to stop for you when you fall into incoming traffic."

With that he switched on the bike, twisted the throttle, and the bike roared to life. He gunned the engine a few times, then stopped to secure his own helmet before gassing it.

The bike leapt forward, and an involuntary yelp burst through my lips. I swayed dangerously, squeezing my knees tight around his hips and grabbing onto his jacket to keep from toppling off. But I would not give him the satisfaction of wrapping my arms around him.

We bounced along the sandy gravel drive to the bottom of the hill, where the driveway ended and the narrow, sandy road began. When we pulled out onto the flat stretch, I relaxed a little and resumed my original stance, with my hands on the seat beside my hips. I tried to get the hang of moving with the bike, which wasn't hard since there were no turns or hills and we were barely going fast enough to stay upright.

The salty tang in the morning air kissed my cheeks as we puttered along the road to a slight incline. There, we rolled to a stop before Xander gunned the engine and swung us out onto a paved road. My arms automatically shot forward and clutched his shoulders. The bike tilted, and I had to lean into Xander's back to stifle my shriek. I could feel him laughing, though the sound was drowned out in the wind and noise of the engine.

We crested a slight rise and then the road dipped, and my stomach dropped out. I clenched my teeth, determined not to scream. After only a minute, we pulled up to another stop sign, this one at the bottom of an incline, and I let go of him and held onto the seat again. Above me, I saw a raven in the pines, but I ignored it. I wasn't going to be as crazy as Mom. I was going to be normal now, go to school and make friends and not even notice ravens or boys who rode motorcycles.

Xander pulled the bike to a full stop at the stop sign. Setting his feet down, he twisted around, grabbed my hand, and pulled it forward, wrapping it around his body. He pressed my palm against his hard, flat stomach, then turned and did the same with my other hand.

"Jesus Christ, would you stop being an asshole and just hold on? I'm not going to be the one to tell my father I killed his new toy."

He accelerated, turning right this time. When the bike tilted, I was already wrapped around Xander, so I leaned with him. This time, the bike didn't wobble from my clumsy riding. I was one with the bike—and with Xander.

The thought was oddly satisfying, somehow *right.*

I pushed that unsettling feeling aside and comforted myself with the knowledge that this ride would end shortly. I didn't have to like Xander just because I was riding his motorcycle. Just because I was holding onto him, that didn't make us friends. I could go back to hating him the moment my feet were on solid ground.

It was unfortunate that the first person I'd ever embraced besides my mom was Xander. I'd rather it have been any of his brothers, or even Peyton. Definitely Peyton. If I was going to wrap my arms around a boy, press my cheek between his broad shoulders to block the wind, flatten my hands against his warm body so low I could feel his belt buckle under my fingers, well, I would have liked it to be a different guy. The problem was, I didn't think I'd ever wanted to be this close to a guy. Not in any conscious way.

Even my strange compulsion to touch his brothers hadn't extended this far, to having his body between my legs, my arms wrapped around him. Just the thought made me hot all over, despite the cold.

Whether I'd imagined it or not, it was happening, and it was agony. My body felt more alive than it had ever felt. The wind raced along my arms, raising chill bumps even as my hands were toasty warm under the edge of Xander's jacket. My thighs were tight around his hips, and every movement he made on the bike made me keenly aware of the fact. The vibration and roar of the engine purred in my chest and in my veins. My heart pounded against his back, my arms clinging like he was an anchor to this world, and I would float off into one of Mom's fantasies if I let go.

I never wanted to let go. I wanted to stay stuck to him like a vine growing up the side of a house. I wanted to get closer to him, to burrow inside him like roots, wrapping around his bones so he could never rip me out.

He nudged me with his elbow, and I lifted my head reluctantly. We'd crested a small swell, and the road dropped down from there. Xander gunned the engine, and with a burst of speed, we dropped down the hill. This time, I let myself scream out loud, laughing as my stomach bottomed out. I could feel Xander's laughter vibrating through his whole body, this time laughing with me, not at me.

I whooped, urging him to go faster as we reached the bottom of the hill and the road flattened out. We sped through the tiny town, with most of the shops boarded up for winter, zipped around a corner, and skidded to a stop in a parking lot where a few dozen cars were parked.

Xander kicked down the kickstand, swung his

leg over the bike, and hopped off. With a grin that made the corners of his mouth twist upwards and my pulse flutter, he unbuckled his helmet and pulled it off. Shaking his head, he let his thick hair fall in waves around his ears. He held out a hand and hauled me off the bike so fast I fell against him, still grinning like a loon, still buzzing with the thrill of the ride.

He quirked an eyebrow at me. "You like the feel of all that power between your legs, don't you?"

The smile on my face answered for me. Riding the bike had been exhilarating, and even though we couldn't talk over the noise, it had been unexpectedly intimate, too. Despite my promise to myself, I didn't hate him the moment my feet were back on solid ground. And since he didn't look like he hated me anymore, either, I wasn't going to ruin our tentative connection by playing it cool. "Yeah," I said through a wide grin.

Xander dropped his voice to a conspiratorial whisper. "Get used to it," he said. "You're a woman. You always have all the power between your legs."

I pulled back, my face blazing with heat. But when I looked behind him, I forgot his rude comments. My stomach dropped out for a whole new reason. A long, low building sat at the edge of the cracked asphalt lot, a depressing air hanging around its brick exterior. Students milled in and out, and even though there couldn't have been more than a dozen hanging around front doors, butterflies exploded in my stomach.

School. I was finally going to set foot inside the legendary place I'd read about in hundreds of books. I couldn't wait to get inside, to see where I fit, to be among my classmates, my peers. To be one of them.

If I could even hope for that. I'd spent so long not being normal, I wasn't sure I could learn even with the Keens as my guides. "Walk me in?" I asked Xander, trying not to sound as nervous as I felt.

"Sorry, little girl, gotta run," he said, pocketing his keys. His earlier laughter was gone, replaced by cool indifference.

"But—you said you'd make sure I got to my class."

A group of rough-looking kids hanging around the back of a dented pickup truck eyed us openly. A girl with bleach-blonde hair, dark eyeliner, and ample cleavage on display despite the cold gave a lazy wave before taking a drag on her cigarette. Xander flipped the collar of his leather jacket and gave me an Elvis-worthy sneer. "It's the smallest school on the planet. I don't think you'll get lost."

"Aren't you going in?"

"I learn more under the bleachers than in class," he said. "Catch ya later, babe."

With that, he turned and strolled over to join the smokers behind the truck. I stood there feeling like I'd woken up on a raft in the middle of the ocean without a paddle. I thought about strolling over to join Xander, but he'd made it clear he was ditching me. All my nice feelings about him vanished as I saw some of the guys punching his shoulders and slapping his back, laughing and shooting significant looks my way. Xander played along, laughing and slapping them low-fives.

I didn't know exactly what those looks meant, but the tone was clear enough. They were laughing at me, and not in a fun way. I hadn't even stepped through the doors, and I'd already messed up. The worst part was, I didn't know what I'd done wrong. I hadn't expected Xander to hold my hand and walk me through the whole day, but I'd thought he'd at least get me started and not turn on me at the first opportunity.

But he hadn't. I was on my own.

Stupid raven. Maybe they really are bad luck.

Nothing to do now but pretend Xander didn't exist, that he wasn't standing there with his friends watching and waiting for me to fall apart. I wasn't about to give him the satisfaction. Taking a deep breath, I channeled my inner Scarlet O'Hara and marched towards the ugly building with my nose in the air.

CHAPTER EIGHTEEN

Xander

I knew I shouldn't have left Gwen by herself, and not for some bullshit reason like I felt sorry for her, because I didn't. The girl was way too sheltered, and I wouldn't be doing her any favors by stepping in and doing the hard stuff for her. If I walked her into the office, they'd take one look at us and think she was already tainted by my evil ways. And so would everyone else.

The school was too small to risk making the wrong first impression. Besides, I didn't like the way she was smiling at me. I'd seen that starry-eyed look on too many faces around here, and I'd learned the hard way what it meant. But I was a quick learner, and I hadn't fallen into that trap yet, even though one ride on the crotch rocket had all the girls wanting to ride me next.

It was fun making them want what they could

never have.

So I ditched the new girl after one ride, before she could start thinking she had feelings for me that went beyond lusting after my bike. That would be bad news and not just because her mother had married my father. There was something weird going on between us, not just the usual high of riding, and I needed to put a stop to it before it went any further.

To be honest, it scared the shit out of me. I read people like Eliot read computer code—not just for fun but because I could. I didn't think Gwen was any different from any other chick. It wasn't her, and it wasn't me, but some freaky alien shit happened when we were together, like a chemical reaction.

Halfway to my friends, I started to regret ditching her. I wasn't second-guessing my decision. No, I regretted it because my friends were looking way too interested.

"Damn, bro, you always find the hotties," Doug said. "I need to get a bike, so I can pick up chicks like that."

"Shut up," I said.

"Did you already tap that ass, and now you're leaving her high and dry?" Kent said, slapping my back. "Classic Keen."

"Don't call me that."

Chelsea handed me a cigarette. "So what's the scoop, then?" she asked, blowing smoke out the corner of her mouth. "Who is she? She looks lost."

I shrugged and leaned on the tailgate of

Kent's truck. "She's no one. Some new chick. I gave her a ride, that's all."

"A ride on your tip," Doug said, cracking up.

"Shut up, asshole," Chelsea said. We'd had a thing for like, two minutes, but she'd been with Doug so long she was like a sister to me now.

Gwen cut past a row of cars so she wouldn't have to walk by us, which was smart of her. I figured the guys would rib me about her a couple more minutes and let it go, but instead, Doug whistled at her.

A vicious streak of anger flared up inside me, and I slugged his shoulder, my knuckles punishing his muscle. "Ow, dude," he said, grabbing his shoulder. "That actually hurt, you asshole."

"It was meant to," I said. I knew I'd overreacted, I just didn't know why. But it was too late to go back now. Xander Keen didn't do apologies.

"I thought you had her whipped," Kent said. "Not the other way around."

"Xander's in *lo-ove*," Chelsea mocked.

"Are you jealous?" I said, snagging her cigarette. "I'll give you a ride later, for old time's sake."

"Don't even think about it," Doug said, putting an arm around her.

"Come on," I said. "Let's ditch this sad pile of bricks before they make us actually go to class."

I couldn't shake the picture of Gwen's sweet

little dismayed face in my mind, though. I almost wanted to go to class just to walk by her classroom and make sure she'd gotten there okay. That was definitely not a Xander move.

CHAPTER NINETEEN

Gwen

So Xander was a pig. No surprise there. If the fading bruise on his cheek and the fact that he was home the day we'd arrived while everyone else was at school hadn't convinced me that he was trouble, that was my mistake. Just because he'd gotten a thrill out of going fast on his bike, that didn't mean we were cool.

As I approached the building, students stepped back to let me enter, but to my relief, I didn't get any nasty comments. Just curious looks as the other students measured up the new girl. I realized too late that I was still wearing Xander's backpack, but I didn't want to turn around and bring it to him. If he couldn't be bothered to get it, I'd just have to walk in with it. I did my best to smile mysteriously, though I wasn't sure what that looked like, so I probably looked like I had a toothache. No one knew me, so I'd just have to hope I was a mystery to them.

Why was the new girl starting in the middle of October?

I could make up a cool backstory, since *crazy mother* wasn't very high up the list of mysterious pasts. Maybe I'd gotten kicked out of my last school for having an affair with a teacher. But if that was the case, I'd probably need to hang out with Xander's crowd, so I moved on to other possibilities.

Genius who had a mental breakdown?

Too close to a sensitive topic.

Girl in the witness protection program?

Too close to the truth.

Girl whose parents won the lottery and bought a house on the Cape?

Also close to the truth, which wasn't bad in this case, but too easily disproven.

The next thing I knew, I was stepping through the doors into the school. I'd made it. A smile formed on my lips as relief flooded through me. Automatically, I turned to my left, something pulling me like gravity towards...the men's restroom?

Okay, this is a little weird.

I stopped outside the door just as it swung open and Eliot stepped out. "Gwen," he said, looking surprised but pleased. "You made it. Awesome. Let me help you get your schedule. I'll walk you to your classes before first period so you know where they all are."

I almost threw my arms around him with gratitude. "Thanks," I said instead, hooking my fingers through the straps of Xander's backpack and trying to play it cool. I'd made the mistake of showing my feelings to Xander, and it had backfired, so I wasn't going to do that again. At least not yet.

"Where's Xander?" Eliot asked, resting his fingers lightly on my back and guiding me down the hall towards the entrance.

"In the parking lot," I said with a shrug. "He says he's too smart for school."

"Sounds like Xander," Eliot said with a shake of his head.

Just then a cute stranger intercepted our path. He was medium height and build, with a fringe of blonde hair falling across one eye. "Whassup, playa?" he asked, his blue eyes crinkling at the corners as he held up a hand to high-five Eliot. And then, as if performing some sort of ritual, he stuck out the longest, pointiest tongue I'd ever seen in my life, unfurling it like a flag. I recoiled from the obscenity of the thing.

Eliot shot me a slightly embarrassed look, then reluctantly held up a hand and let the guy slap it. "Hey, Joaquin."

"And what do we have here?" Joaquin said, fixing his sloppy grin on me. He pulled back and made a big show of examining me from my feet to my face. Then he leaned in until his nose grazed my shoulder and made a slinky movement, drawing his nose up my neck to my ear.

I leaned away, laughing uneasily. "Did you just

smell me?"

"Yeah, baby," he said, sniffing loudly. "And you smell like...fresh meat."

"Come on, man, step off," Eliot said, putting a palm on Joaquin's chest and pushing him away. He maneuvered himself between me and Joaquin, but Joaquin just bounded around him, bouncing on his toes.

"I'll see you later, you delicious dish," he said to me, pointing both index fingers at me and clicking his tongue.

"Wow," I said when he'd bounded off down the hall, calling to someone else he knew. "Just...wow."

"Yeah, you really don't want to get mixed up with guys like that," Eliot said, opening the door to the office.

"There are more guys like that?" I asked, glancing back over my shoulder.

Inside the office, we got my schedule without a problem, though my head was spinning after listening to my list of classes. I didn't know how I'd keep them all straight and remember where they were all located. But Eliot didn't seem concerned. He held the door open for me, and I ducked out under his arm, resisting the urge to curl up against him and let him take care of me.

You wanted to be here, I reminded myself.

The hallway was teaming with students when we stepped out of the office. A loud, shrill buzzing went off above us. My first school bell!

We could barely move in the crowd of students, most of whom were pushing to go the same way we were, away from the office. One person was trying to go towards the office, being jostled by the crowd. My tension melted when I saw his familiar face.

"It's like swimming upstream," Zeke said, finally reaching us. "How you doing, Gwen? Eliot treating you okay?"

"It's not me you should be worried about," Eliot said, putting a protective arm around my shoulders. I leaned into him, thankful for the support.

"You're the one I'm most worried about, bro," Zeke said, taking his place on my other side and slipping an arm around my waist. "Come on, let's get you to class before the giants show up."

"Who?"

He gave me a blank look and then laughed. "I meant the douchebags," he said, shaking his head. "I don't know why I said giants. I must have been thinking about football."

I nodded, pretending that made sense. I was too distracted by the day ahead to worry about football teams, or the fact that my mom's hallucinations might be spreading.

"This school is tiny, so it should be pretty easy to learn your way around," Eliot said, looking at my schedule and pointing to my first period class.

It didn't feel tiny to me, but I nodded anyway.

The whole thing was overwhelming, and by the time they showed me my last class, I'd forgotten where my first class was. Zeke smiled and slapped hands with just about every guy we saw, saying hello and calling everyone by name, guys and girls. When we finally arrived back at my first class, the halls were nearly empty.

"Gwen," Peyton yelled, bouncing out of the room and throwing her arms around me. "I was hoping we'd get some classes together. Come on, I'll show you where to sit."

Turning back, I mouthed "thank you" to the guys before Peyton led me to a seat on one side of the classroom about halfway back. The school had been anxious to get me into classes and had put me in regular classes right away, though they said I'd have to test and probably do a lot of extra tutoring to get caught up, since I'd missed the last nine years of school.

Classes went okay all morning. Peyton walked me to second period art, which I didn't have with any of the Keens. Finn had art third period, though, and when he saw me walking out, he walked me to my next class. I barely made it to my next class before the bell, only to find the room empty except for a teacher eating a sandwich and reading a paperback.

"It's time for your lunch," he said without looking up.

Lunch. Shit. I'd forgotten all about lunch, and apparently so had my mom. Of course she had. She'd been busy worrying about the world going up in flames, and I'd been busy worrying about her. As usual I didn't have any money, and the rest of the Keens were probably so used to having money that they'd never thought someone wouldn't have pocket change. But the teacher didn't invite me to sit in his room, so I couldn't just hang around.

Besides, this was my chance to see the social order I'd read about in books. My chance to find a place in it, to blend in and be one of them. My heart pounded with excitement as I headed in the direction of loud voices and smells. In the entranceway, I froze. The tables were crowded with a sea of faces I didn't recognize. I'd gotten some questions from other students in my earlier periods, mostly where I was from and why I was there, but I hadn't made any friends.

Still, I wouldn't let that stop me. School was the dream I'd never dared to hope could come true, and here it was, laid out in front of me. This was the real test. I knew from the books I'd read that the cafeteria would make or break me. There, I would be judged and either found worthy, or...decimated by social stigmas. Usually, cafeterias had cool but foreboding nicknames, like *the gauntlet* or *hell*.

I slipped in at a table near the door and pulled out my schedule to see if I still remembered how to get to my remaining classes. A minute later, someone slid in beside me, and I looked up to see Finn. Today, his hair was pulled back in a low ponytail, and his green eyes caught mine and held on for a second.

My heart fluttered.

"Hey," he said, giving me a shy smile.

"Hi," I said.

"You're not eating?"

"I forgot my lunch," I admitted. "But I'm not really hungry. What about you? Where do you normally sit?"

"I usually eat in the art room," he said. "I just came down here to...I don't know why, actually. I just wanted to, I guess."

"I'm glad you did," I said.

"Let me get you something," he said, digging in the pocket of his light-washed jeans. They had a slit on his thigh, and I found myself staring at the strip of exposed skin. I swallowed and pulled my eyes away. "What do you want?"

Not to find all four of my stepbrothers so damn attractive?

I glanced around, my eyes catching on the next table, where Joaquin was chomping into a burger. He caught my eye and gave me an exaggerated wink.

"Fries would be good," I said, my stomach knotting with hunger when I saw the untouched pile of fries on his tray.

"Fries it is," Finn said, heading for the food line at the front of the cafeteria.

While he was gone, I studied the room. People were still trickling in or arriving in small groups, finding their friends, and squeezing in beside them at the long, grey tables. I wanted to see how it all worked, so I was content to sit on the outskirts and observe. I was especially curious about my siblings' places in all of it. I already knew Zeke and Peyton were part of the *in crowd*.

"Hey, baby," Joaquin called from the next table, his voice edged with taunting. "You look lonely. Why don't you come over here and sit? I got a seat with your name all over it." He scooted back and gestured at his lap, wiggling his eyebrows at me.

I shook my head, biting back a smile at just how ridiculous he was. Did that actually work for him?

He shook his floppy, blonde surfer hair out of his eyes and tried again. "I got the motion of the ocean," he coaxed, lifting his hips and gyrating in the air. After a few seconds, he got a little carried away, thrusting his hips against the edge of the table. A carton of milk toppled over, splashing across his tray.

Stifling my laughter, I turned away, covering my mouth so he wouldn't see me cracking up at his antics. My gaze landed on Zeke, sitting at a table in the middle of the room. The moment I spotted him, his eyes swept across the entire cafeteria and landed on me. A huge smile broke across his face, and he waved, motioning for me to join him.

I lifted my hand just above the edge of the table and gave him a tiny shake of my head. I might want to brave that table tomorrow, when I'd dressed nicer. Maybe I'd be popular, too. In books and movies, that was the goal of high school, even more important than graduating. I knew popularity must be something wonderful. Today, though, I didn't want the pressure of meeting all those people and trying to figure out exactly what popularity was. I just wanted to watch.

I spotted Peyton standing on the other side of Zeke's table, her back towards me, leaning her hip against a girl's shoulder while she talked. The girl had her arm around Peyton's legs, and it sunk in that she'd mentioned having a girlfriend a few times. With all the new information I'd had to absorb, I'd glossed over her comment. I hadn't realized she meant she had a *girlfriend*, the kind that was more than a friend.

My thoughts were interrupted when Zeke stood and ambled over to my table, carrying his lunch. He slid in beside me. "Hey, Gwen," he said. "Why are you over here by yourself?"

"Just, uh, getting the lay of the land."

"Cool," he said, chomping into his burger. "Let me be your tour guide?"

I smiled and nodded, feeling my face warm slightly when I noticed half his table looking at us, leaning in to talk to each other.

"I guess that's the popular table," I said.

"Yup." Not a trace of humbleness entered his words. I appreciated his straightforwardness. I needed it. I wasn't the best at reading subtext.

"I don't see Eliot," I said. "Does he eat in the

library or computer lab or something?"

Zeke sat up straight and surveyed the cafeteria. "There," he said, pointing with a French fry. To my surprise, Eliot wasn't sitting at the nerd table at all. There were no scrawny dorks with glasses and bad skin at his table, no overweight guys with greasy hair and Superhero shirts clutching Mountain Dew bottles in one hand and monster cards in the other. His laptop was nowhere in sight, and his nose wasn't buried in a book. In fact, he was buried in...girls.

A girl with long blond hair was draped over him, so close she was halfway on his lap, and she looked like she was intent on making it all the way on before lunch was over. A brunette was kneeling in the chair opposite him with her butt in the air so she could lean across the table and share a pair of hot pink earbuds with him. A black girl was seated on his other side, gripping his bicep and whispering in his other ear.

"What's going on there?" I asked. "I figured he'd never talked to a girl in his life."

Zeke laughed at that. "Are you kidding? Dude is a total chick magnet. He gets more action than me."

"Really?"

With a guilty look, Zeke swallowed a mouthful of burger. "I mean, not that I get a lot of action. I'm not a player or anything. I totally respect chicks."

I laughed and shook my head. Again, I'd assumed and gotten it all wrong. I had to stop doing that. It was just that books were all I had to go on. I had to make sense of these people somehow or I'd get so overwhelmed with trying to figure them all out at once that I'd curl into a ball and never come out. Or go all zombie-eyed and disappear inside myself like Mom after her major episodes.

I swallowed my confusion, trying to make sense of this new Eliot. For some reason, I felt slightly betrayed by his failure to conform to my image of him, as if he'd misled me. He'd told me he'd been on a date, not that he had three at once every day.

Finn walked by his table, and though he didn't say a word to his brother, Eliot's eyes zoomed in on Finn's target with laser focus. Our eyes met, and a wave of tingles swept across me, raising goosebumps all over my body. I stared back at him, refusing to be embarrassed. I wasn't doing anything wrong.

Neither is he, a little voice inside reminded me. But I still felt like he was.

He must have thought so, too, because he sat bolt upright and his face went bright red. Without a word to his fan club, he plucked the earbud out, detangled himself from several pairs of arms, and followed Finn.

Finn plopped down across from me with a heaping plate of steaming fries, and I almost moaned in relief. I felt better just seeing them, and his presence was as reassuring as the food. "I got enough for everyone," he said. "Hope you don't mind sharing."

"Not at all," I said. "Thanks."

Eliot slid in at my empty side. "Sorry about that," he said, looking shame-faced.

"About what?" I asked, reaching for a fry while Finn emptied ketchup packets into a pool at one edge of the plate.

"Those girls," he said. "I wasn't thinking."

"It's okay," I said. "You don't have to sit with me."

Yes, you do, I told him silently.

"I don't?" He glanced around at the others, confusion creasing his brow.

"You could always sit at a table across the cafeteria and make a scene by staring intently at me."

My stepbrothers blinked at me in unison, like synchronized owls.

"That's what always happens to the new girl in books," I said, stifling a giggle. A mysterious charge had built inside me, almost unbearable. I thought I might actually lose it, Mom-style, in the middle of the cafeteria.

"I want to sit with you," Eliot said gently, his hand brushing my thigh under the table. "If that's okay."

I almost gasped out loud at the pull of his touch, as if he'd pinched me instead of barely brushing my leg. But the overwhelming buzz inside me dissipated with his touch, as if I'd passed some of the energy to him.

"Are you okay?" Finn asked, looking up from the plate.

"Yeah," I said, reaching for another fry. My fingers brushed his, and an involuntary twitch went through them. It was all I could do to grab a fry instead of his hand. As Zeke and Eliot reached in for a fry at the same moment, all our fingers brushed together, pausing instead of pulling back. None of us spoke, as if afraid to break the spell of this intimate moment between us.

"You guys will not believe this," Peyton said, plopping down beside Finn.

We all pulled back at once. I was so flustered I couldn't meet any of their eyes. I'd heard of raging hormones, I just didn't think they would happen to me. And here I was, not even sure which guy I wanted them to rage at. Every time a guy walked into my life, my need grew stronger.

"I was telling everyone about that freaking tsunami wave, and they wouldn't believe me," Peyton said.

"You told someone about that?" Zeke asked, frowning.

I was just relieved that she'd interrupted, although somehow, I was simultaneously disappointed.

"Well, yeah," she said. "Alejandra's my girlfriend. I tell her everything. But she said her mom takes the dogs for a run on the beach every day, and she didn't see anything."

"Maybe it was just that beach," Finn said, not looking up from the fries.

"A tsunami would hit every beach," Eliot said. "That wasn't a tsunami. It was just a really big wave."

"Yeah, I know, a real tsunami would have washed all the houses off the Cape, but still," Peyton insisted. She reached in for a fry, and a spark darted between her finger and mine like a static shock. For a minute, we all ate in silence, our fingers bumping and slipping against each other. Something built inside me like my own tsunami. That energy, that charge that left me breathless and wanting. Every time my fingers touched theirs, a spring inside me coiled a little tighter. My insides felt hot and liquid, and I wanted more, and more, and more.

Suddenly, I realized how fast we were all eating, licking ketchup and oil and salt off our fingers, reaching in together so our hands would touch again and again. I didn't taste the food at all, only waited for the next hand to go in so I could push mine in next to it. My breath came faster, my body electric with a need I'd never felt before. I'd gone from never having a crush on a single person in my life to being inexplicably drawn to every single one of my stepbrothers.

"Exactly what is going on here?" demanded a high, grating voice. A surge of anger drove up my chest like a fist. How dare an outsider interrupt this? Couldn't she see we were sharing something special?

"Go away, Barb," Eliot said, barely glancing at

her.

Barb. That's how she felt. A thorn needling her way into this sacred ritual.

"Go away?" she asked, thrusting out one hip and planting her hand on it. She swung her long brunette hair behind her shoulder, and I recognized her as the girl who had been leaning across the table in front of Eliot, sharing her earbuds. "You can't tell me to go away, Eliot. I'm not a dog."

"I don't have time for this right now."

She pursed her lips and narrowed her eyes, glaring at me. "And who is this?"

"Gwen," Eliot said, turned my name into something that sounded like a sigh of anguished longing. If Zeke had made my name sound like someone fun, Eliot made it sound like someone beautiful and ethereal, a girl who wore filmy white dresses and stood at the window looking up at the moon every night.

My chest throbbed when I met his eyes.

Barb must have noticed something in the look that passed between us. "Oh, really?" she asked. "And what's so special about *Gwen* that she can get all the Keens together in one place?"

If Eliot had made my name sound beautiful, she'd made it sound like a squashed bug.

Three things happened simultaneously then. I realized we weren't all together. Xander stepped through the door. And all the windows in the cafeteria shattered.

CHAPTER TWENTY

Eliot

The cafeteria had erupted like a nuclear explosion, except instead of mutating my classmates' DNA, it immediately turned them into hooting, cheering, shrieking maniacs.

One girl screamed, "I don't want to die!"

All her friends laughed, but I wasn't sure she'd been joking.

"Please exit the cafeteria in an orderly manner," one of the lunchroom monitors said through a bullhorn.

No one paid him the slightest attention. Two lacrosse players jostled against the end of our table, pumping their fists in the air and high-fiving Zeke as they passed.

"School's out...for-ever," one of them sang at the top of his lungs.

"Our fine education system, ladies and

gentlemen," I muttered as a chorus of *MOOs* broke out at the back of the line.

"What the fuck is going on?" Xander demanded, ignoring the crowd and glowering at us. "Who called me?"

None of us had moved. While Zeke and Gwen looked at him blankly, I checked my phone. With all the weird stuff that had been going on lately, I wouldn't have been surprised to see that my phone had started calling people at random. But I didn't have any pocket dials.

Finn seemed to share my thought, but after checking his phone, he shook his head.

"Well? Somebody called me," Xander said, snatching his phone from his pocket and thumbing it on.

"So? Which one of us was it?" Peyton asked.

Xander swore under his breath and shoved his phone back in his pocket, but he looked more subdued. "No missed calls," he said quietly.

"Let's go out to the field," Zeke said, standing from the table. "It's time to talk about what's been going on."

I nodded and stood with him. Zeke and I butted heads a lot, which didn't really make sense because I was obviously the brains in the family while he was the brawns. We shouldn't have been in competition, but we always seemed to be. This time, though, we were in full agreement.

The other students filed out, instructed by a

couple increasingly-hysterical lunch monitors who obviously thought it was much more serious than the students. Not surprising. Most people in a town this small thought school was a joke, and nearly as many thought life was one. Just another reason I'd started applying to prep schools for next year. When I applied for Harvard, I wanted more on my resume than what Wellfleet could offer.

We all rose from the table and ducked out, waiting at the doors while Finn dumped our trash. When he joined us, we walked out the side doors without a word.

"You think they'll dismiss us for the day?" Peyton asked as we walked across the back lot towards the football field. It wasn't much, since Wellfleet's team was about as small as you could get and still qualify to play.

"They'll probably say it was something ridiculous, like a sudden change in air pressure," I said.

"But we all know different," Xander said, shooting Gwen an angry look, as if this were her fault. I was a little surprised he'd agreed to go to the football field at all, since he had an unhealthy hatred of sports in general and football in particular. If he ever came out here, it was to skip class and smoke cigarettes under the bleachers with his fellow truants. His self-destructive tendencies made no logical sense to me, since they went against human survival instincts.

"Up top," Zeke said, and we all fell in behind him as he jogged up the bleachers, scaring off a raven that was perched on the railing. The rest of us arrived at the top approximately five seconds later, since we weren't used to running bleachers. We all gathered around, Zeke on the top step with the girls on either side of him, me and Finn on the next step, and Xander standing at the railing with his elbows resting on it.

"Does this kind of stuff happen around here a lot?" Gwen asked.

"No," Xander growled.

"Sometimes," I said. "But not as...severe."

My family glanced at me for explanation. "Little things," I said. "The fuses blow in our house a lot, even though Dad's had a bunch of electricians out to check the wiring and breaker boxes. Sometimes stuff happens at school, too. The auditorium lights go out during assemblies and stuff. But nothing like this."

"Only since *she* showed up," Xander said, glowering at Gwen again.

"I do feel like I've always known you," Finn said, darting a look at Gwen. "But it's more than that."

"I heard a voice in the bathroom the night you and your mom got here," Zeke said.

"What did it say?" Gwen asked.

"I was looking in the mirror after I took a shower, and this voice said *wake up*."

Peyton laughed. "Are you sure you weren't getting ready for school and talking to yourself?"

"No, dude, it wasn't me. And there was no one in the bathroom. It freaked me out, bro."

"So you think I was standing outside the bathroom talking to you?" Gwen asked, crossing her arms. "You're all blaming me?"

"I'm saying this shit didn't start until you showed up," Xander said.

"The windows blew out of the cafeteria when *you* showed up," Gwen pointed out.

"Um, hello, what about the fact that when we first met, there was a mini earthquake?" Peyton said. "I think that qualifies as more important than anyone's weird feelings. And you were all A-okay with Dad's explanation of that."

"Okay, so there's a few little things," Zeke said. "And then, yeah, there was the earthquake that was definitely not the heater going on. Sorry, Dad." He added the last part while looking up, as if Dad were in the clouds, listening.

"And there was the monster wave and then the windows," I said. "Anyone else notice the common denominator?"

"Yeah," Xander said. "Her."

"Stop being an asshole," Zeke said. "What's the numerator, Eliot?"

I shook my head. I'd been studying this problem from all angles and trying to find answers online. The cafeteria incident had confirmed my theory.

"Not her," I said. *"Us."*

"What do you mean?" Zeke asked.

"It's not just Gwen. She's part of it. But I have deduced that we're all part of it. Those three things happened when we were all together, either in one room or standing close together at the beach."

There was a short silence as everyone did their own theorizing.

"So what do we do about it?" Peyton said after thirty seconds. "Not eat dinner in the same room?"

"Fine by me," Xander said. "Count me out."

"For one, I don't think we should tell anyone," Finn said.

"Too late," Peyton said. "I told Alejandra about the wave."

"Your airhead girlfriend doesn't have the capacity to comprehend whatever you told her," Xander said.

"At least she's not braindead from huffing glue like yours," Peyton shot back.

"Okay, chill," Zeke said, holding up a hand and turning to me. "Eliot. Any ideas?"

Before I could answer, Gwen shifted around on her seat and sandwiched her hands between her knees. "Something weird happened to me, too," she said. "When I almost drowned."

"Did you see a light at the end of a tunnel?" Xander asked.

"Shut up," Peyton and Zeke said in unison. Sometimes, they seemed more in sync than me and Finn.

Gwen hunched her shoulders against the wind, a strand of hair sweeping across her face. Zeke put his arm around her, and the whole metal bleachers buzzed as if an electric current was running through them.

"I don't know if that's a good idea," I said, nodding to his arm.

He scooted away from her, peeled off his hoodie, and handed it to Gwen. I wished I had a hoodie I could have given to her. I didn't play lacrosse or football, and I usually thought the fangirls who wore the players' hoodies or letterman jackets looked silly. But Gwen looked adorable huddling into his oversized hoodie.

"So what'd you see, Gwen?" he asked.

"I'm not sure," she said, biting her lip.

"That's helpful," Xander said.

Zeke shot him a warning look, and he glowered down at the field like he wanted to blow up the whole thing. He probably did. Not that I blamed him. The guy had been through a lot in the past few years, and the football field was a bitter reminder of that.

"It was like a light," Gwen said, then added quickly, "a person made of light. Or a form. I don't know, maybe an angel. It said we were pieces of the same, um, thing. And now that we were joined as one, she was complete."

"What does that mean?" Peyton asked.

"That's not much to go on," Zeke agreed. "You sure it didn't say anything else?"

"She said something about another world," Gwen said. "Midgard, I think?"

That word sounded familiar, like one I'd heard before, but my memory was having a failure of retrieval moment. I pulled out my phone and tapped it into the search bar. "No," I said. "That's this world, according to Norse mythology."

Gwen went a little pale.

"What is it?" Finn asked before I could.

"I'm sure it's nothing," Gwen said, shaking her head.

"Tell us," Peyton said as Finn reached up to take Gwen's hand.

The vibration started again, but I left it alone.

"My mom," Gwen said slowly. "She has nightmares about this giant wolf called Fenrir."

"Like from the comic book?" I asked, and then it clicked. Like Thor, Fenrir was a comic book character based on Norse mythology.

"You know who's an expert on Norse mythology," Zeke said, standing and stretching, making a show of flexing his muscles.

I stood and reached out a hand for Gwen, but I reconsidered and pulled back. I hadn't sufficiently reasoned through the possibilities of what would happen if I touched her at the same time as my brother.

"Who?" Gwen asked, looking from one of us to the next.

"I think it's time we had a little talk with Daddy-O," Xander said, starting down the bleachers.

There were too many variables to call this an equation, and talking to Dad did seem the next logical step to solving some of this. Still, we all looked to Zeke for confirmation before following Xander, who wasn't known for being reliable or making wise decisions. When Zeke gave us the nod, we all got up and followed Xander off the field.

CHAPTER TWENTY-ONE

Gwen

When we walked into the kitchen, Mom and Neil were both sitting at the table, as if waiting for us. At least someone had been expecting this. I sure hadn't expected to skip half of my first day of school.

"You're home early," Neil said. "What happened?"

"The windows in the cafeteria blew out, that's what happened," Zeke said.

Neil nodded, a frown furrowing his brow. "I was afraid of something like that."

"You could have given us a heads up," Peyton said, crossing her arms and frowning for maybe the first time in her life.

"What the fuck is going on?" Xander demanded, pacing the kitchen like a caged animal about to go ballistic.

"Sit down," Neil said, taking Mom's hand.

"Let's talk."

The twins sat, and a second later, Peyton joined them. Zeke put a reassuring hand on my back, but the buzz it sent through me did anything but settle my rattled nerves. I felt a little like Xander looked right now, like I was about to explode, too. I slipped in at the table next to Mom, and Zeke sat beside me.

Xander hovered in the doorway, glaring.

Neil sighed and leaned back in his chair, crossing his arms across his broad chest. "I guess I should start at the beginning," he said, looking at my mom. "When we met."

My eyes moved back and forth between them while I absorbed this information. "You knew each other?" I asked at last.

"No," Mom said quickly. "We only met once."

Neil cleared his throat and shifted in his seat. "At the hospital. The night you were born, which also happens to be the night both of your mothers went into labor," he said, turning to the twins.

Zeke took my hand under the table. And even though I only had to watch this horrible truth sink in, I was glad for the support his grip offered.

The twins looked at each other, then turned to their father.

"Our...mothers?" Eliot asked. "More than one?"

"You're not twins," Neil admitted. "You have

the same birthday, that's all. You're not related by blood at all."

While they studied each other, Xander took a turn around the kitchen, cursing under his breath. At last, he stopped and faced Neil. "Anything else we should know? Like maybe I'm adopted? You lied to all of them, so now it's time for the truth. Let's have it, *Dad.* I wouldn't mind getting the fuck out of here if this isn't my real family."

"It's your family," Neil said quietly. "Blood isn't what makes them your brothers."

"Neither are you," Xander shot back.

Neil nodded. "Maybe I should have told you earlier. But something happened that night at the hospital, something I didn't fully understand, even though Olivia told me. I saw her have one of her visions that night."

"Visions?" I asked Mom. "Is that what you told him they are?"

She nodded, her fingers worrying at the sleeve of her sweater.

"She told me what happened," Neil said. "That something had ripped through from another world into this one. A fire giant, to be exact."

"Other things followed," Mom said. "Gods, monsters…"

"I thought she was…unstable," Neil said. "I didn't put much thought into it. But it put me on edge all night. When I went back to talk to her the next morning, she'd checked out and left against the hospital's orders."

"With Dad?" I asked Mom.

She nodded. "That's right. I didn't know they'd be coming for us. Your father…he died fighting a fire giant. Holding it off so that we could get away."

I'd heard that before, so I only nodded. At least she hadn't kept the kind of secrets from me that Neil had kept from his kids.

"I tried to find her, but she's good at hiding," Neil said, smiling at my mother in admiration.

"I noticed," I said. "We've been on the run my whole life. I just didn't know we were running from you."

"Money could only get me so far," Neil said. "And it was never far enough. Thankfully, one of my sons is a computer genius."

"Are we your sons?" Finn asked.

"Of course you are," Neil said. "You'll always be my sons."

"Adopted sons," Finn clarified.

Neil hesitated, then nodded. If he'd been carrying this weight on his shoulders, getting it off wasn't helping. He looked ten years older than when we walked in.

"So what does this have to do with us?" Xander asked. "Let me guess. You think I'm the demon that came through from this 'other world' that a crazy woman saw."

"Mom's not crazy," I said through clenched

teeth.

He gave me a look that said, *Oh, please.*

"Xander, you're not a demon. And Olivia's not crazy. She has a rare gift. The gift of Baldur."

"That's what you call it?" I asked.

"The gift of sight, if you'd rather," Neil said. "She sees things that are to come, as well as things that happen in other worlds besides this one."

"You lost me at other worlds," Zeke said, speaking for the first time.

"We live in this world, Midgard. Over the centuries, we've been so caught up in our own lives that we've forgotten a time when the gods mingled and interfered in human affairs," Neil said. "Humans may only live on this world, but there are other worlds besides this one. And they aren't always content to stay contained within their borders as we are."

"Can we get through this rip into the other worlds?" Eliot asked, even more gorgeous with curiosity and excitement lighting up his eyes.

Neil hesitated before answering. "As far as I know, no one ever has."

"Which means if someone did, they didn't come back," Eliot said. "Doesn't mean it can't be done."

I shivered and held tighter to Zeke's hand.

"Okay," I said slowly. "So the night we were born, something came through into this world, and my mother saw it. But if you're not the twins' father, why were you at the hospital?"

Neil gave a small smile. "Xander broke his arm," he said. "He's always been reckless, even back then."

Xander scowled. "I'm not reckless."

"We were all at the hospital that night," Neil said. "Everyone in this room."

"Yeah, but there must have been a lot more people, too," Peyton said. "Where are they?"

"We don't know how many other beings came through that night, gods and giants and other things. But we know that when they did, six kids flat-lined at once."

The six of us looked around at each other.

"Us?" Zeke asked.

"You."

"I knew it," Xander said. "You think we're possessed by demons."

"We don't know what it is," Neil said. "But we think you're hosting something."

CHAPTER TWENTY-TWO

Zeke

Xander snort-laughed so hard I thought he might give himself kidney stones, but it made perfect sense to me. I couldn't speak for the others, but I'd always felt like a god, so I figured that's what was inside me. Sweet. Who wouldn't want to find out they were hosting a god? I mean, it was a lot better than some of the other things people could host. Like tapeworms. Nobody wanted to host a tapeworm.

"Are you sure?" Gwen asked. "I mean, are you sure we *all* are?"

I caught her doubtful look at Xander, who was still honking like a goose. Pretty sure he caught the look, too, though he'd never give it away. But let's just say if I picked up on something, it was a pretty sure bet all my siblings had already picked up on it, like, yesterday.

"We're not sure of anything," Neil said.

"Except the facts. We were all at the hospital that night. The six of you flat-lined at once for inexplicable reasons that were never medically explained. You all survived. And your families...didn't. We don't know how long the rip was there beforehand, or what else came through after that night. But Olivia is accurate in her predictions, and she says something powerful came through that night."

"So it was all true?" Gwen asked, looking at her mom like she'd just found out *she* was adopted. "You weren't sick all that time, you were just selfish?"

"I was protecting you," Olivia said.

"From what? All this?" Gwen asked, gesturing around at our sweet house. "From being rich? From being a normal person capable of carrying on a conversation with a normal human being?"

"From the giants," Olivia said.

"And yet, Neil's done a fine job protecting all his kids without living out of a dumpster."

I wanted to squeeze her hand, to calm her down and tell her it was all okay. But it didn't sound like her life had been okay at all.

"I should have known I could never have a normal life," Gwen said. "Not even for a week."

"I told you what I saw," Olivia said. "I didn't lie to you. You always knew what we were up against."

"And I'm supposed to be happy about that? Why? What did these people miss out on by not knowing? They got a house, and family, and friends. I got a lifetime of running and loneliness."

"We ran together," Olivia said. "We had each other."

"No," Gwen said, gripping the edge of the table. "We ran for you. None of that was for me. If you'd wanted to do what was best for me, you would have come here a long time ago."

Gwen's face had gone all pink with anger, and I had to say, she did look pretty hot when she was mad. But Peyton had told me never to say that to a girl, and I didn't figure I should interrupt their argument, anyway.

"That's not important now," Dad said firmly. "You're with us now, and we can't change the past."

"But what about all the other things you said you saw?" Gwen asked her mom, ignoring Dad. "The monsters and wolves and giants. Things coming after us. Ravens spying on us. What about Fenrir and the end of the world?"

"I told you what I saw," Olivia said.

"It can't be true," Gwen said. "It just can't. There's only one world. This one." She stopped talking, her breath coming fast.

I squeezed her hand. The urge to be near her was like an itch, and touching her was the only way to scratch it. Besides, the chick looked like she was about to have a panic attack, and it was my job to make things okay for her. I didn't know why, but it was.

"How can you know that?" Eliot asked. "Just because it's all you've ever known and experienced, that doesn't mean it's all there is."

"Yeah, I've never been to space, but I believe in aliens," I pointed out.

"I don't think that's helping his case," Peyton said, rolling her eyes.

But I knew I'd helped, because Gwen's hand relaxed in mine.

"What's real to you, Mom, isn't real for other people," Gwen said, more gently this time.

"Before last week, you'd never eaten lobster, or stood by an outdoor fireplace, or been in a mansion," Olivia said. "I know you've had a small life up until now, and I'm sorry that you're upset about it. But these things are real, Gwen. They may not be real in this world, but they're out there. And they're coming."

"And that's a bad thing?" Eliot asked.

"Yes," Dad said. "We believe you were sent here to stop them, somehow. I've been trying to bring you all together for the past ten years to see if you can stop them."

"Why?" I asked. "What's so wrong with them being here?"

"I think they're the reason so many of you are without parents," Dad said, looking around at us. "Everyone here has lost someone."

I looked around. We'd lost Mom. Olivia and Gwen had lost Gwen's dad. And I guess the twins had lost another family, although I didn't see how that could come as a shock to them. I mean, I'd always wondered because twins were supposed to look exactly alike, and no one could confuse my brothers unless they were super dumb. They didn't look alike at all. I always figured Mom must have had an affair, since Finn didn't look anything like Dad. At least Eliot had the same hair color.

"What about us?" Peyton asked, interrupting us as we all looked at each other, weighing our losses against the others'.

Dad's shoulders slumped.

"You said that Xander broke his arm," Peyton said. "And Finn, Eliot, and Gwen were all born within hours of each other. What about me and Zeke?"

"Also adopted," Dad said. "But you are brother and sister. The night this happened, you were in the NICU, Peyton. You were premature, so you'd been staying there. On her way to visit you, your mother was in an accident. She and Zeke were being treated for injuries."

I figured I should have seen that coming. I mean, if I was part god, that meant one of my parents was a god, and I didn't think Dad was very godlike. And obviously a god wouldn't die, so that ruled out Mom.

"Great," Xander said, slumping against the doorframe. "I'm the only one related to you?"

The not-twins glared at him.

"I don't care, you're still Dad to me," I said. "And you guys are all my brothers."

"Agreed," Peyton said.

I meant it, but I won't lie, I did feel a little closer to Peyton now. Maybe it was just because she was sitting beside me.

"Is anyone really surprised by this?" Xander snarled, like we were all stupid. We actually were, compared to him. Dude was too smart for his own good.

"I am," Peyton said bluntly.

Xander scowled. "I'm six months older than Zeke," he said. "Didn't you ever wonder about that?"

"No, I didn't," Peyton said, straightening and flipping her ponytail like she was about to lay the smackdown on one of her bitchy friends. Our school was too small to have more than one popular clique, so there was always some backstabbing going on, which I usually heard about from both sides. Of course I always took Peyton's side. She was my sister. But also because she could throw shade like a lesbian cheerleader from hell.

Or as it turned out, lesbian cheerleader goddess. Because if I was part god, that meant she was, too. I was pretty sure, at least.

"I knew," Eliot said quietly after a minute of watching Peyton and Xander stare each other down. Eliot shrugged, looking uncomfortable when we turned his way. "I knew Mom couldn't be both of your mothers. I figured Xander was Dad's son with some old girlfriend or something."

"Why me?" Xander asked, throwing up his hands. Everyone in the room gave him an incredulous look. I didn't really understand, so I tried to psychically convey that I was with Xander on this one, in case that was one of my god abilities.

"Because...it's obvious," Gwen said at last.

"Why don't you shut up," Xander growled. "You don't even belong here, let alone need to witness a fucked up moment in this fucked up family."

I watched Gwen shrink beside me, and I put my arm around her shoulders, regretting my momentary feeling of camaraderie with Xander. "Dude," I said. "Not cool. Leave her alone."

"She belongs here as much as all of you," Dad said.

"As far as I can see, I'm the only one who belongs here," Xander said. "Lucky me."

"To be honest, I thought that's who I was tracking down," Eliot said, nodding at Olivia. "I thought you were trying to find your ex-girlfriend who dumped her son on you."

"Too bad that's not how it happened," Xander said. "I'm sure Dad would love to ditch me on some stranger if he could."

"You know that's not true," Dad said, frowning at Xander.

"As much as I'd love to stick around and listen to you all bicker, I have to admit, you're right,"

Gwen said. "I don't belong in this conversation."

"So go," Xander snarled at her. "No one wants you here, and you're only making yourself look like an asshole."

"Fine," she said, standing with a lot of poise for such a little girl. "While you figure out your family drama, I'll be taking a nap. You're all crazy, anyway. There's nothing inside us but blood and guts, just like everyone else."

Gwen turned, and I started to rise to go after her. Then I realized what I was doing and sat back down, but just being away from her for a minute had started to twist my gut. Like I had to be with her twenty-four seven, or I'd explode. The girl was seriously messing with my mojo. I couldn't get enough of her.

"Give her some time to process," Olivia said to me. "She's not used to so much commotion and conflict."

I nodded, figuring she was right. I couldn't imagine being the only kid in this house, without all my brothers and Peyton. It would be like walking around with half my body missing. That would make walking around really hard.

Peyton turned to Dad. "How could you not tell us?"

"I'm sorry," Dad said. "I knew the day would come when I had to tell you. I just didn't want it to come so soon."

"Dad, I'm almost eighteen," I said. "How

long were you going to wait?"

"Until I found the key to all this," he said, nodding to where Gwen had disappeared up the stairs.

"What if you hadn't found her?" Peyton asked.

"I was confident I would," Dad said, taking Olivia's hand. "And if I hadn't... I would have told you children about her and sent you to find her when you graduated."

"When who graduated?" Xander asked.

"One of you," Dad said. I figured I had a better chance of graduating this year than Xander, so he must have meant me. Which was cool because I seemed to be taking this better than everyone else. Dad had always been our dad, and he still was. We hadn't found out anything surprising, like that Dad was really a demon. That would have been hard to believe.

"So tell us how you ended up with all these kids," Olivia said.

"Yeah, Dad, why don't you tell them," Xander said. "And in case anyone's wondering, yes, I already knew that none of you were Dad's kids, but he wouldn't let me tell you." He shot Dad a withering glare.

I figured the guy had a right to be pissed. We may have had our differences, but we'd always been family, always had each other's backs. We'd stuck with Xander even when he made psycho friends, got arrested, or punched some idiot at school. It must have killed him that he couldn't tell us something like this. He'd never stopped treating us like his family, so I wasn't pissed at him for not telling us. Knowing Dad, he'd held something massive over Xander's head to keep his mouth shut. Probably yet another reason Xander and Dad had the shittiest relationship of any of us.

"Sure," Dad said, raking his hand through his dark hair. "After you had your vision at the hospital, Olivia, I didn't really put too much into it, but it disturbed me. So I did some research, and I found out all about the gods and monsters you saw."

"Giants," Olivia corrected.

"Right," Dad said. "I was curious about what had happened to Xander, and soon after I found out about the other kids whose hearts had stopped at the same moment. With a little help from a nurse in financial need, I was able to get their names."

"Nice," I said, because Dad knew how to work people when he needed to, but I knew he really had helped that nurse. He probably paid her a lot more than she'd asked for that information.

Dad turned to me and Peyton, his face all sad and grim. "Right away, I looked them up and found out that your mother hadn't made it. She'd seemed fine, and they were about to release her, but when they went to wake her, she had passed."

"Oh, wow," Peyton said, her eyes all wide and shiny. "I...I wish I'd had a chance to meet her."

"Someone tried to check you out of the hospital that day, saying he was your father, but when they asked for ID, he refused to provide it. Security escorted him out when he caused a scene. Whether or not he was your real father, he never came back for you. They contacted the number on file for your father, and he said he couldn't take care of two kids all by himself." Dad took Peyton's hand. "He was grief-stricken over the loss of his wife."

"Maybe there's more to it," Eliot said quietly.

"We'll never know," Dad said. "When I found this out from the nurse, you were both still in the hospital. We went in and took you both home, and you were ours by Christmas that year."

I figured that was another thing money could do, one I'd never thought of—get your adoption paperwork pushed through faster. I did the math in my head. I would have been three. Peyton was zero. No wonder we didn't remember our birth parents...or did I? Maybe those weird memories that didn't fit were real after all, like walking with Mom at the duck pond, or Dad telling me that when I lost my helium balloon that it had gone up to heaven.

"Did he ever come looking for us?" I asked.

Dad shook his head. "I looked him up when you were a little older, when your mother...when my wife got sick. I thought maybe instead of watching us go through that, maybe you had a father out there looking for you, one who regretted a decision made in grief. That maybe he'd want to spend a weekend with you now and then, give you a break from life here. I thought you deserved to know your birth father. All I found was his obituary."

"I guess that ends that," Peyton said, slumping in her chair. "We don't have another family, then."

Dad shook his head, looking kind of miserable. I felt bad for the dude, having to tell us all this at once. It was kind of his fault for waiting until he had to tell us all together. Except Xander, who had probably figured it out himself and confronted Dad. Didn't sound like our biological dad was a winner anyway, and I knew Dad was a total winner. All you had to do was look around to see that.

"And us?" Finn asked.

Dad looked uncomfortable, which I figured was something he'd never let any of his board members see. But he was being real with us. "Finn," he said with a sigh. "Your birth mother was never married. She was apparently an addict, and when you were eighteen months old, the neighbors called child services on her for trying to give you to them. She said you were talking in tongues."

"Um…has she ever heard a baby talk?" Peyton asked.

"She was charged with neglect several times before the state stepped in and took custody. You were in bad shape, and you ended up in the hospital. The nurse who had talked to me before happened to remember your name, so she looked up your file. I hadn't followed up on the other kids since adopting Zeke and Peyton, but the nurse called me. That got me interested in it again. It seemed a strange coincidence that you were abandoned as well. And it was almost too easy to take custody. Like divine intervention."

Dad offered a weak smile, but Finn looked green. I could imagine the dude who loved church didn't really want to hear that his mom was a drug addict sinner. He took it in without comment, though.

Eliot looked positively fascinated by the stories. He was leaning forward in his geeky, intense way, like he was solving the world's toughest equation and it gave him a woody.

"And how'd you wind up with me?" he asked.

Dad gave a quick nod. "I started following you and Gwen both, as well as I could, from what I could find online. I was curious, mostly. When you were two, your mother checked herself into an institution. She said she wasn't safe to be around you anymore. Your father was away on business. After a few days, your mother seemed stable and said she missed you. She tested clean for drugs, and she'd voluntarily committed herself, so they released her. Shortly thereafter, she took her own life."

There was a silence around the table. Eliot didn't look upset, just interested. "How'd my biological father die?" he asked.

I didn't know how he'd figured out that part,

but Dad confirmed it with a sad smile. "Heart attack in his car on the way home after his trip."

Finn spoke at last, all quiet and slow. "So we're infested by some kind of force that killed all our parents to bring us to you?"

"I don't think they were trying to bring you to me," Dad said. "And I don't think that what you're hosting killed your parents. I think there's something else out there. And it's trying to get to whatever's inside you."

CHAPTER TWENTY-THREE

Gwen

In my room, I buried my face in my pillow and screamed. I was so, so angry at my mother for the way we'd lived and at myself for not believing her all those years. On top of that, I was beyond frustrated that I couldn't seem to control my greed for physical contact. Even when I was in the middle of yelling at my mother, I was simultaneously forcing myself not to turn around and grope Zeke's muscular shoulders as he sat beside me. My body was alive with the sensations of being touched, another thing I hadn't experienced thanks to Mom's choice of lifestyle.

When I wore myself out from screaming, I flopped onto my back and stared at the ceiling, remembering Xander's harsh words. I was pissed at him for treating me like a child having a meltdown, as if it were irrational to be angry at my mother. It was bad enough that he hadn't wanted us here when we first showed up. Now that my mother had married Neil, we were family, but he hadn't become more accepting. If anything, he hated me even more now.

I wished I could hate him back, but no matter how hard I tried, I couldn't make those flutters go away when he walked into a room. To my stupid body, Xander was just as attractive as the others. Every time they were near, my skin ached with the desire to be touched by one of them. After a while, holding hands with Zeke had been overwhelming, both too much to bear and not enough.

As I lay on the bed, I glanced at the door, listening for their footsteps on the stairs. In books, boys always ran after girls. I hadn't run away for attention—almost the opposite. I'd been overwhelmed, and yet, as soon as I was away from them, I wanted to be with them again. I wanted one of them to knock on the door and ask if I was okay.

I also wanted Mom to come up and tell me Neil was kidding. He had to be kidding. This couldn't be real. I'd spent my whole life knowing it wasn't real. Of course that had worried me constantly, knowing my mother wasn't well. But that explanation made sense. The other one, the new one...it just didn't.

Staring up at the ceiling, I tried to wrap my brain around it. If there was a god in the area, of course it would choose the Keens. This was where a god should live. Not in a car with a license plate stolen off an abandoned vehicle. I must be the giant, then. The Keens certainly looked like gods. They were all unbelievably beautiful in their own way. Not that I was ugly, but...come on. I could barely hold a conversation, let alone a god. I'd probably hosted more than my share of fleas in my life, but a goddess?

I rolled onto my side and lay my cheek on my hands. No one came to check on me, and I started to think all the romance novels I'd read weren't as good research as I'd originally assumed. Turned out, my stepbrothers were more interested in their adoption than what I was doing, which actually made a lot of sense. Stupid romance novels.

Having barely slept the night before, I fell asleep while they hashed out their family drama. When I woke, the house was quiet. I felt different somehow. Not because I believed I was a giant or some sort of supernatural creature, which was ridiculous. If I'd been infested all this time, wouldn't I have superpowers or something? At the very least, I should have been able to have a home.

Neil hadn't said what we were. He'd said we were *hosting something*. Like it had possessed us the same way a demon would. Were we demons? What was a fire giant, anyway?

Giant or not, I wasn't going to let my chance at normalcy slip through my fingers that easily. I'd gotten to go to school for exactly one-half a day, and it wasn't nearly enough. I hadn't figured out how anything worked, let alone how to socialize with fellow teenaged humans. I wanted to scream at the unfairness of it, no matter how many times my mother had told me life wasn't fair. But this time, I'd put my foot down. She wasn't going to deny me the school experience any longer. No one ever said giants weren't allowed in school.

Not that I actually believed I was a giant. But if there really was something inside me, I wasn't going to let it run my life a moment longer than it already had. My life was mine, and I'd make my own destiny.

It was barely getting light, but I didn't want to risk going back to sleep and missing a ride in the car that day. No way was I getting on a motorcycle with Xander again. If one of us was a demon that had come through, my money was on him.

I crept downstairs, planning to go to the library. A strip of light from under a doorway down the hall distracted me, though. It was the room Eliot had said was Finn's studio. Remembering his promise to show me some of his art, I tiptoed down and tapped on the door.

No answer.

"Finn?" I whispered. After a minute, I said his name a little louder. I didn't want to wake Neil, so I kept it pretty quiet. When he still didn't answer, I had to admit to myself that maybe I was being nosy and that he didn't want to talk to me. Or maybe he just hadn't heard me. I didn't want to risk calling louder, so I slipped down the stairs and headed towards the pool room, meaning to go sit on the deck.

Just as I reached the door, I heard soft splashes inside, the sound bouncing off the walls like a strange echo chamber. I stopped and flattened my palm against the glass, not sure I wanted to interrupt. For a minute, I watched the form streak through the water, up and down the pool relentlessly, furiously. His movements were sure and swift, almost desperate, as if trying to outswim a demon.

Or as if he were possessed by one.

I stepped back from the door. Even without seeing his face, I knew who it was. And I didn't want to bear the brunt of his rage one more time. Part of me knew that I couldn't be the real target of it—he didn't know me well enough to hate me. Still, I was tired of putting up with it, of telling myself it wasn't meant for me. Whatever reason he had for treating me like shit, it didn't change the fact that he was doing it.

Moving silently down the hall, I stepped into the living room, expecting someone there, too. I didn't know if all families were like this or if the Keens were vampires who never slept, but it seemed like every time I left my room, one of them was already waiting in whatever place I ended up.

The living room was empty. I crept out the French doors onto the deck, hoping to catch the sunrise. The sky lit up with pale pink in the west over the bay. A lone gull swooped by overhead, and the smell of the ocean was strong and damp around me. I curled up in a chaise longue under a blanket someone had left out and waited for the rest of the house to wake up.

Half an hour later, the doors slid open behind me. I turned to see Finn, his hair damp and curled around his ears. I tried not to stare as he stepped out, wearing loose jeans and a white T-shirt, but god, he was cute.

He held a travel mug in each hand. "You like coffee?" he asked, sinking onto the bottom section of the chaise longue.

"Thank you," I said, reaching for a cup. It was a ceramic mug with a scene of Paris on the side, and I had a flash of how far I'd come. I was usually drinking coffee from a Styrofoam cup, filling it with as many packets of creamer as I could so the calories would go farther, fill me up longer.

Finn smiled with his lips closed. "Cool."

"I knocked on your studio door earlier," I admitted. "I was hoping I could see some of your work, but you didn't answer."

"I'm so sorry, Gwen," he said. "I always work with headphones on. I wish I'd heard you."

"It's okay," I said, scooting down the chair to sit beside him. He looked so regretful I wished I hadn't told him. My eyes moved over his strong jaw, his long lashes that curled against his cheek as he looked down, his dark lips that looked so soft...

I had that overwhelming desire to touch him again. It was weird how quickly I had grown to yearn for their touch after not being touched by anyone but my mom for most of my life. But now that I'd had it, I couldn't get enough.

I was bursting with desire, emotion, and pent up feelings that I'd never had before. Now I had so many I thought I'd burst. I'd never experienced these things, and I didn't know how to deal with them, how to get rid of them.

I didn't dare put a hand on Finn's knee, but I pushed my leg against his for a second, resisting the urge to sigh and close my eyes with pleasure at that simple gesture.

Finn cleared his throat, and I jerked my leg back. Before my brain could come up with a good excuse, my mouth opened and a word burst out. "Itchy!"

Finn's brow furrowed in confusion. "Huh?"

"I said itchy," I mumbled, staring into my coffee. "My leg. I mean, my knee. That's why I was rubbing it on your knee. I was…itching."

"Okay…"

"Sorry."

"It's okay."

"I don't have bugs or anything," I said. "Like fleas. Nothing weird that would make me itchy. It was just a regular, ordinary itch."

"It's okay, Gwen. Really."

I exhaled, cursing myself for being such a complete social failure. Finn didn't really seem to care though. He was even smiling. I didn't want to force a smile, though, because I was pretty sure I'd look like a scary clown. Instead, I distracted myself with questions. "So…did I miss anything yesterday?" I asked. "Anything I should know?"

"Dad thinks whatever came through that hole killed all our parents. Except yours, I guess."

He didn't sound bitter, just tired.

"I'm sorry about your parents," I said. "I know I'm lucky I still have my mom, but it wasn't easy. We were surviving all that time, but we never really got to stop and live."

Finn's hand closed around mine, and he leaned his head on my shoulder. I rested my cheek against his head, breathing in the subtle vanilla scent of his shampoo. My body was in agony for more, screaming at me to turn my head and bury my nose in his hair and inhale it until my lungs were full of hairballs. He didn't even seem scared of catching bugs from me after my weird comments. His head was right there on my shoulder, so close I could have kissed it.

I really wanted to kiss it.

Maybe I could kiss him without him noticing…

Is that super creepy?

Probably. I had to restrain myself.

We were still sitting like that, Finn seemingly peaceful while my insides tied themselves in knots, when Peyton opened the door and told us to hurry up if we wanted to ride with Zeke.

Finn stood, offering me a shy smile and a hand up. I put my hand in his, enjoying the contact more than I should. "Come on," he said. "Let's go live a little."

CHAPTER TWENTY-FOUR

Gwen

"Oh, my God, Jen. What is she wearing?"

I looked up from my locker to see three girls looking me up and down, identical expressions of disgust, incredulity, and scorn on their faces. They scanned me from my used Converse to my jeans to my hoodie. I shrank inside. Where had I gone wrong?

I'd seen the movies and TV shows. I'd read the books. I was ready to join my fellow humans in high school, to forget the craziness of my past—and the night before—and leave that life behind. I was tired of crazy. I wanted, needed, normalcy. Peyton had given me hope that I could join the girl herd, gossip about boys and makeup, lie on the bed and read magazines and worry about the things other girls worried about.

Not gods and giant wolves and raven spies.

At last, I was encountering the species I had studied numerous times, wondering that they could be the same animal as me. Apparently, they were wondering the same thing. Though they didn't look exactly like the girls in the TV shows, even I could tell they were important. I recognized one from yesterday—Barb. Another girl had sleek chin-length hair with a dyed stripe and the height and cheekbones of a model. The last girl in the group was just as pretty. They all had freshly glossed lips, lush eyelashes, and manicured eyebrows. They wore pretty much the same thing I did.

"Wasn't she wearing that yesterday?" asked the tall girl, the one they'd called Jen. She blew a bubble with her gum before sucking it back into her mouth. I was standing not three feet away, but they weren't talking to me. They were talking to each other, like they didn't know I could hear them as I pulled out my books for second period.

"I heard she's living with the Keens," Barb said. "You'd think she could afford to dress a little nicer if she's trying to impress one of those boys." She said *those boys* with a degree of reverence Peyton reserved for Starbucks' seasonal flavors.

"Like any of them would look at her," the third girl said. "Those jeans were lame ten years ago."

"Speaking of Keens, I've got work to do if I'm going to get Xander to go out with me," Jen said. "Let's go."

They twirled on their heels in unison and strutted off down the hall, their swinging hips clad in the *right* jeans. It seemed to bring them the right kind of attention, because I saw several guys turn to check out their butts as they went.

Eyes stinging, I bowed my head and turned back to my locker, my pulse pounding and my face flaming. I'd failed. Shame ran through me—not just because I'd worn something that was apparently a fail, but because I hadn't stood up to them. When I'd seen movies with girls like that, I always thought I'd be so tough if they acted like that to me. I'd never let them pick on me like that.

But when it had happened to me, I'd frozen. It felt worse than I'd ever imagined. Worse than someone telling me to get my crazy mom off their doorstep. Worse than someone yelling at us and telling us they'd call the cops, worse than the man who had thrown dirty dish water out the back of his restaurant onto us. Those people saw us as nameless, faceless, homeless people. They didn't hate us for being us, but for crashing on their doorstep.

This was personal. They saw me, and they didn't want me.

And it hurt.

I knew it shouldn't. I should hold my head high like Scarlet O'Hara and not care what they thought. I didn't know them or like them, so they shouldn't be able to hurt me. But they had.

I felt sick as I walked to my next class, my head down, hoping no one noticed that I was wearing jeans that weren't even cool in the decade when they were made. Hoping no one noticed that I'd pulled on the same hoodie I'd worn the day before over a clean T-shirt.

Slipping into my seat, I breathed a sigh of relief. I'd been excited to go to school this morning. While everyone moaned about another school day, I couldn't wait to experience all high school had to offer. I wasn't going to let a few broken windows and more crazy talk ruin my dream. I'd heard all that for years, the Norse beings, the giants that killed my father. I didn't blame the Keens for being upset about the adoption revelations, but none of that was new to me. High school was new. I just wanted to be a part of it.

Obviously, I needed to be more specific in my wishes.

This morning when Zeke had pulled his BMW into the parking lot, I'd walked in with the Keens. I'd been right in the middle, with Zeke and Peyton on one side, Eliot and Finn on the other. As we walked towards the school, I imagined we were walking in slow motion, like in all those movies where the badass crew does a slo-mo walk into battle with a rockin' soundtrack. People had turned to watch us walk by. I'd felt cool as hell.

This was the part where the needle scratched

and the fantasy ended.

I slouched down in my seat, careful not to look at anyone. Why hadn't I asked Peyton to take me shopping? She always looked cool. And why hadn't one of the guys thought to take me? Yesterday, Xander had said I looked perfect, but obviously he'd been setting me up for this moment. If I knew anything about high school, it was that people would crush anything that didn't fit the status quo, viciously and without mercy. And I didn't fit yet. How could I? I'd lived most of my life in a second-hand vehicle.

Something landed on my desk, and I nearly jumped out of my seat. An elaborately folded square of paper lay there like a bomb about to go off. What now? Was someone else going to make fun of me?

Slowly, I turned in my seat. The blonde from Xander's group bugged her eyes at me and nodded towards my desk, where the note lay untouched.

Great. If she was Xander's friend, she was probably going to tell me I looked homeless and crazy, not just outdated. Not that she looked super awesome. Her blonde hair was stringy, like she hadn't bothered to comb it, and her roots were growing out about an inch long before the bleached blonde started.

I turned back to my desk and slowly unfolded the note, still treating it like an explosive. Her words were scrawled across it in big, sloppy handwriting.

Do you really live with Xander?

I glanced back at her and shrugged.

She mouthed, "Watch out."

I turned to face forward again. What did that mean—watch out for Xander or for her? Was she pissed that I lived with her boyfriend?

The thought made me strangely ill. I knew I had no claim on any of the guys—and they were my stepbrothers on top of that, so I couldn't claim them even if I wanted to. Not in the way she and Jen apparently wanted to. And to be honest, the way I wanted to.

But knowing it couldn't happen didn't make me any less attracted to them. It didn't make me any less jealous when another girl wanted them.

When the bell rang, I hurried out of class, anxious to get away before the girl could talk to me. I walked out and ran smack into Eliot.

"Hey, you okay?" he asked, putting his hands on my shoulders and holding me at arm's length, studying my face. Though his touch was light, I suddenly felt as relaxed as if he'd given me an hour long massage.

I gave him my most grateful smile. "I'm okay now," I said, before I thought it through.

Eliot grinned and bit his lip, his dimple on full display. My heart skipped. "Well, then," he said slowly. "Let me walk you to class?"

I opened my mouth, but every thought seemed to have deserted my brain when he smiled at me, so I

233

only nodded mutely.

"Can I get your number?" Eliot asked. "I mean, I know that sounds super weird, but I just...I don't know...I got this feeling right before class started that you needed me. I know, I told you it's weird. And then I realized I couldn't text you."

"I don't have a phone," I admitted, hugging my books to my chest.

"What? Seriously?" he blurted out.

I shrunk another size inside my clothes. I wanted to disappear, to rewind this day and start over.

"Dude, why are you making Gwen look like that?" Zeke asked, falling into step on my other side. "She's all...droopy."

"I'm sorry," Eliot said quickly. "I didn't mean to make you feel bad, Gwen. Of course you don't have a phone. I'm taking you to get one right after school."

"You don't have to—."

"I want to," he said, holding up both hands. "Chalk it up to my massive anxiety. I just like to know everyone's okay. Please let me?"

I smiled, trying to imagine Eliot as I'd thought he was when I met him. Shy, awkward, without friends. That Eliot would have anxiety. This Eliot had...

Barb.

She strode up behind him and slid an arm around his waist, smiling up at him. "Hey, stranger," she said, her voice light and flirtatious. Now Eliot looked like the guy I'd bumped into on the stairs my first day. Flustered, embarrassed, out of his element.

I expected Barb to shoot me a smug smile or a warning look so I'd back off. Instead, she ignored me as completely as if I didn't exist.

"We'll just leave you two alone for now," Zeke said, holding out an elbow like he was about to escort me into a dance. I slipped my hand into the crook, and he pressed it to his side, smiling down at me as we left Eliot and Barb to themselves. I tried not to think about them. A minute ago, I'd gotten my hackles up over Xander and his girl. Now, I was burning with jealousy over Eliot. As if it weren't enough that I had a thing for one of my stepbrothers, I seemed to have a thing for all of them.

"What was that all about?" I asked, unable to keep my curiosity to myself.

"Eliot's a weird dude," Zeke said. "He thinks he's got it all figured out. He just tells all the girls he doesn't believe in monogamy, and then he gets all of them at once."

"Wow," I said, wishing I hadn't asked. "I might have expected that with Xander, but not him."

"Nah, dude," Zeke said. "Xander's philosophy is the opposite. He's a lone wolf. Can't be tamed."

"How's that different?" I asked.

"He won't let anyone have him, so all the girls want him. You know, because all the girls are keen on the Keens."

I laughed and shook my head. "Why am I not surprised?"

"What do you mean by that, Gwen?" he asked, a teasing spark in his eye.

My face warmed. "Just...I mean, for high school guys...you have cars and money and you look how you do..."

"How's that?" His smile got wider. Behind him, I saw Jen and the other girl who dissed me before class. They were heading our way, their eyes locked on Zeke.

I knew they were about to swoop in, and my hand tightened possessively around his arm, pulling him closer to me. Before they could get his attention, I found my fighting spirit. Zeke deserved better than a bitchy girlfriend. Though my knees were quaking, I smiled up at him and said, "Don't act like you don't know you're hot."

There. I'd just admitted it. I winced, regretting the words already. What if it weirded him out, or he thought I was desperate, or laughed in my face.

Instead of laughing at me, Zeke bit back a smile. He leaned down, his lips brushing my ear. Shivers raced down my entire body. "Then don't act like *you* don't know it."

He released my arm at the door to the classroom, and I must have walked into class and sat down, though I couldn't seem to feel my legs. Did

Zeke think I was hot? Or was he telling me that he knew I found him hot?

My thoughts were in a jumble all through class. Did all girls feel like this when a boy smiled at them the way Zeke smiled at me, or were we really connected in some weird, supernatural way? Whatever the answer, I knew that my attraction to them was real, not just the product of a bond we had no control over.

When I walked out of class, still in a daze, someone slammed into me, hard. My books flew out of my hands and scattered on the floor.

"Oops," Barb said, stepping around me. To think that the day before I had actually thought I might end up being popular.

"Bitch," her little friend muttered as they strutted off down the hall.

And there it was. The record-scratch of reality stopping my fantasy once again.

CHAPTER TWENTY-FIVE

Eliot

I was planning to spend lunch practicing with the mathletes team, but I couldn't stop thinking about Gwen. I couldn't stand the thought of missing out on time with her while my brothers were soaking up her smile. Halfway to the classroom, I veered down the hall towards the cafeteria. I wasn't getting any weird intuition about her needing me, and I was glad my brothers were there to protect her. But I wanted to protect her, too. She and I shared something special, and I didn't want to let her down by failing to show.

When I walked in, Barb glided over, smacking her glossy lips together, and took hold of my arm. As I looked around for the Keens, she led me towards our usual table. Spotting Gwen's blonde head lowered over her tray, I balked, realizing I'd let Barb tow me along like a fish on a line.

"What's wrong?" Barb asked, looking up at

me with those big eyes of hers. I'd always liked her best of the girls I was seeing. She'd take selfies of us and send them to me with little hearts drawn on them. It was cute, and we looked cute together. But it was like I'd always been waiting for something else, something real. Until Gwen, I'd never known what that was.

"I think I'm going to sit over there today," I said, raising my arm to pull free of Barb's grip.

Her wide eyes narrowed, and she pursed her lips. "Where?"

"With my family," I said, nodding at them. After Dad's revelations, I wanted to be near them. I wanted to figure out what we all were, and I wasn't going to find out in Barb's company, no matter how cute she and her friends were.

"Since when do the Keens sit together at lunch?" she asked. "Your brothers usually don't even eat in the cafeteria. Is that…Xander?" Her eyes bugged at seeing him there. He probably hadn't eaten in here all year.

It didn't surprise me. I shrugged. "I guess we all wanted to sit with our family today."

"With *her?*" she asked.

"Yeah." I could have made excuses, but it felt like a sacrilege to deny Gwen's influence. Besides, I needed to figure out the meaning of what Dad had said. I wanted to ask Xander if he knew anything about my birth parents or the chance of gods and monsters coming through rips in the fabric of our world.

Instead, I was dealing with girl drama. The girls I hung out with didn't really care about little things like Armageddon. They were more concerned about competition.

"I can't believe this," Barb huffed. "You walked out on me yesterday, brushed me off like I was nothing, and now you're doing it again? And you're not even going to apologize?"

I opened my mouth to protest, but then I realized that wasn't fair. She wasn't nothing, but almost overnight she'd begun to mean nothing to me. Last week I would have fought for her. I'd honestly cared about her and the others, too. But now, I just wanted to be done with the drama. Suddenly, all the relationships I'd had felt superficial, meaningless.

"I am sorry," I said honestly. "I didn't mean to hurt your feelings."

"But you're still going to do it, even knowing it hurts me, aren't you?"

Barb may have been a lot of things, but she wasn't stupid. We'd had a good time together. Now, it was time to move on, and though I didn't owe her an explanation, I wanted to give it to her. She'd always known I would never give her what she wanted. At least I could give her the truth.

"I'm sorry," I said again. "But I need to do this."

"Are you breaking up with me?" she asked, her voice going shrill. A few people at nearby tables turned to stare. Others dropped their voices and whispered, pretending not to stare.

"If you want to call it that, then I guess I am," I said. "I need to focus on my family right now." That was an understatement. Not only had I just found out I was adopted and not related to anyone in my family, but I didn't even know if I was human.

Or if any of my brothers were. For all I knew, we were the key to stopping Ragnarok. Or hell, maybe we were the ones who were going to start it. Whatever the case, I wasn't content to go on like nothing had happened the night before.

"What's going on with your family?" Barb asked, her tone verging on desperate, though I could tell she was trying for supportive. "You can talk to me about anything, Eliot. I...I love you."

I winced at her words. She'd always known I wasn't going to settle down with her. We were teenagers, for god's sake. We were still in high school. I'd always planned to go to Harvard, and I'd made it clear all along that we weren't actually dating, so there would be no messy breakup.

And yet, here we were.

"I hope you can find a guy who gives you what you deserve," I said. "But it's not me. It never was."

"I can't believe you," she said, rage burning in her gaze. "You're pathetic, Eliot Keen. You're going to regret this. And don't come crawling back to me when your own sister won't give it up for you."

With that, she whirled and headed for the door. I tried to shrug off her words and the stares of the crowd. She was probably right. What did I think I was doing? I couldn't actually expect anything to happen with Gwen. I could like her—I had some kind of weird, supernatural connection with her—but in the real world, these things didn't happen. We couldn't be together.

But I didn't care. I just wanted to be near her, even if nothing could happen. I wanted to see her sweet little face, those plush lips, her eyelashes that curled so shyly against her cheeks when she looked down. And the spark in her eyes when she got excited or riled up about something—that was just as sexy.

I followed Barb towards the exit but only because my siblings were gathered at a table near the door. But when Barb reached the table, she didn't blow by with her nose in the air. She stopped, and I came to a halt right behind her.

"This is your fault, skank," she hissed at Gwen. "And you're going to pay for it."

"What's my fault?" Gwen asked, looking up from her spaghetti with a startled expression.

Barb snatched up Gwen's tray and smashed it into her face.

CHAPTER TWENTY-SIX

Gwen

As chunks of spaghetti slid down my face and plopped into my lap, I had the most inappropriate urge to laugh. I'd just been officially initiated. I'd seen this in so many movies. The food fights, the mean girl throwing a drink in someone's face. But if this was the way to gain acceptance, I would rather my lunch had been something more…dry. A hamburger would have just fallen to the floor without leaving more than a ketchup stain on my shirt.

For better or worse, I was officially part of public school now.

I was so frozen with shock that it took me a second to register the chaos erupting around me. I groped at the table, searching for a napkin to wipe the spaghetti out of my eye sockets. Strong arms circled my waist and pulled me back, chair and all.

Pulling up the hem of my T-shirt, I wiped

spaghetti away from my eyes, not wanting the acidic sauce to burn them. At last, I could see. Xander had Barb shoved up against the wall, one hand pressing into her upper back to pin her there and the other holding her wrists like handcuffs. Her eyes were bulging, and she was whimpering to be released. Zeke was trying to drag Xander off, yelling at him. Girls started screaming, chairs scraping back as other students dove in to join the fight, or scooted away, or jumped up to huddle against the wall.

I started shaking so hard I felt sick. Not just at the realization that I'd been attacked, but at seeing Xander attack her. Somehow, through all the noise and melee, I heard his voice, deadly quiet and smooth as velvet. "Don't fucking touch my family."

Zeke pulled him back, and he slowly let go, dropping Barb like he was dumping a bag of trash at the curb.

I realized that Peyton was beside me, waiting for an answer. A second later, my brain backtracked to find the question from the millions of voices around me.

"I—I'm okay," I said. "Gross, but okay."

"Your nose is a little red, and not just from tomatoes. Must be where the plate hit you." She studied me a second, then nodded. "Come on, let's go clean up."

My senses seemed to drop back into place one at a time, as if they'd disappeared with the instinctive clench of fear upon seeing a fight. First sight had arrived, then sound, and now I realized Finn's arms were still around me. A swell of emotion rose inside me. He'd pulled me away from the fight so no one would crash into me, and kept his arms around me to shield me if anyone came this way. Turning in his arms, I stood on tiptoes and gave his cheek a quick kiss before pulling away. "Thanks," I whispered.

I stepped back to join Peyton, then turned to say something to Xander. But he was already gone.

***

In the bathroom, Peyton started rolling out a long train of crappy brown paper towels while I stood over the sink, splashing my face with warm water. Now that the disturbance was over, another sense had come back to me—smell. My whole face smelled like greasy spaghetti and parmesan cheese. I must have gotten some smashed up my nose, but even when I blew it, the scent lingered.

I didn't know much about perfume, but I was pretty sure none advertised hints of cheese and subtle notes of garlic. It wasn't my first choice, but when Peyton asked if I wanted to go home, I shook my head.

"I've only been here for two days, and I already skipped half of yesterday," I said.

"Yeah, you better watch out, or you'll get a reputation like Xander," she said, grinning as our eyes met in the mirror.

"Oh, you mean a guy who goes psycho when anyone messes with him?" I asked, throwing a wad of soggy towels in the trash.

"I'm not going to say he should have done that, but that girl had it coming," Peyton said. "I mean, she hit you in the face with a tray!"

"I didn't ask him to do that." I'd seen bums fight and it gave me the same feeling. Terrified, sick, stunned. I'd seen how easy someone could snap over nothing, and there was always the chance they'd turn on me next.

This time, someone had been attacked *because* of me. Xander had snapped in a way that even my mother never did. She might not be mentally stable, but this was a different kind of crazy. Even when she was seeing things and hearing voices, Mom had never been like that. She'd never hurt me. She'd never hurt anyone. My mother was afraid. Xander was someone to be afraid of.

"Look, I'm not going to pretend it's hard having what we have," Peyton said, looking me over. "If we lived in some crappy little shack, I'd probably get hell for being gay. Now, I might get some bitchy comments, sure. Bitches be jealous of all this." She gestured from her pink hair to her Uggs.

"I can see why."

She laughed and gestured at me. "Lose the hoodie, and I think you'll be fine for the rest of the day."

Hands still shaking, I attempted to peel it off over my head, but it was smeared with oily sauce, and I didn't want to smash the spaghetti all over my face again. I ended up having to kneel down and let Peyton ease it up and over my shoulders without turning it inside out. We were in the middle of wrestling it off when the door opened and two sets of feet appeared in my vision, which was mostly obscured by the sweatshirt.

"God, Peyton, get a room," said a familiar, cutting voice. Jen.

"That's just nasty," said another. "You could at least use a stall to scissor your girlfriend."

Cruel laughter filled the bathroom as they banged noisily into two stalls.

"Ignore them," Peyton said, tugging the sleeves off my arms. "It's my favorite pastime."

At last, I pulled free of the shirt. I still had some spaghetti sauce in my hair and on the neck of my t-shirt, but there wasn't much I could do about that.

"Can we get out of here?" I whispered.

We left the bathroom, still echoing with Jen's mean laughter.

"What's with those girls?" I asked, relaxing as we headed down the hall.

Peyton shrugged. "They're just being themselves," she said. "You know. Bitches."

"You'll have to introduce me to this girlfriend of yours," I said, cutting my eyes sideways at her. I wanted to ask her more about that, but I didn't know how to say it without sounding completely ignorant.

"Of course," she said. "I can't waste this

fabulousness being celibate my whole life just because it's a small town."

"That must be hard," I said. For some reason, I felt weird about her revelation. I'd never actually met a gay person before, but I didn't think that was it. It was more that I didn't want her spending time with someone else.

"Oh, no," she said. "That wasn't the point I was about to make before we were interrupted. I know we're lucky in a million ways. I'm not even comparing it to what you grew up with. And there's people even worse off. We're so privileged, Gwen. But sometimes it has down sides. Like when people want to use you, or destroy your dad's company, or break up your family. Xander, he was the oldest, and he got it the worst."

She tugged on my sleeve, leading me into the little lobby off the gym. I'd passed through it on my way to PE, but Peyton pulled me over to a trophy case and pointed to a picture behind a trophy. "Can you believe that's him?"

I squinted at the picture, trying to make my eyes see what she was seeing. And then I spotted him in the second row of the football team's picture. He was almost unrecognizable, with short, neat hair and a huge smile, his eyes crinkling and a dimple the size of the Grand Canyon in his cheek. He was smaller and younger looking, too, but the smile was the big thing. That and the fact that Xander, the delinquent who skipped class to smoke cigarettes and do god-knows-what under the bleachers with his three stoner friends, used to play football surrounded by dozens of friends.

I probably would have stood there staring at that picture for another hour if the bell hadn't rung. Peyton took me by the shoulders and turned me to face her. "You sure you're okay? Because I will find that hussy and bitch-slap her into Helheim if you say the word."

"Say what word?"

Time seemed to hiccup as she reached for my face. Slowly, her soft fingers skimmed my cheek as she tucked a strand of stiff, crunchy hair behind my ear. "Never mind," she said, for once unsmiling.

I swallowed hard, suddenly tumbling with a million conflicting sensations. Alice must have felt like this as she was tumbling into Wonderland.

The sound of footsteps in the hall broke the spell, and Peyton dropped her hand, laughing nervously. "I'll see you after school," she said, quickly turning away. "And this weekend, we can go into Boston and go shopping. Get you some new clothes. Unless, you know, you want to check out holes in the fabric of the universe."

I shook my head. I didn't want anything to do with that. All those years, I'd thought we were running for Mom's sake. But now I wondered if I hadn't benefited from it, too. Now that we were settling in one place, I didn't know how to get away from the things I didn't want to think about—my mother's condition, the insanity of what our parents had said, the weird things that happened when I was in the same room with my new siblings. Even, apparently, Peyton. If I couldn't hop in the car with Mom, how could I escape it?

And then I saw Jen's friend walking by, texting as she went, and it came clear in my mind. There were distractions all around me. New clothes. A new phone. A new life. If I refused to acknowledge the thing living inside me, maybe it would go away. I wasn't going to let something else control me the way Mom's illness had. It was time for me to make my life my own. I didn't want any part of being a god. I just wanted to be a teenager.

CHAPTER TWENTY-SEVEN

Gwen

That afternoon Peyton and Zeke had practice, and Xander went off with his friends. Finn and Eliot gave me a ride home. Finn disappeared into his art studio while Eliot helped me find a phone to order online. I tried not to let his nearness distract me, but it was hard. My fingers ached to reach out and touch that soft, dark hair at the nape of his neck. Curling my hands into fists, I tried to push away the overwhelming impulse. It was like something had been sleeping inside me all my life, and now it had been awakened.

Maybe that was how it happened. The thing that came through from the other world had been unlocked when it came in contact with the others.

After ordering a phone, I escaped to my room and lost myself in a book. When the house had been silent too long, I climbed off the bed and meandered downstairs. The sun had finally come out, and it fell across the gleaming wood floors and brightened the whole house. Looking around, I marveled at the vaulted ceilings, the windows that stretched all the way to the roof, the sparkle of the sun off the gentle ripples in the water below. A boat bobbed in the water, and far off I could see the strip of land that hemmed in the bay.

Suddenly, a raven landed on the windowsill. I jerked back, stifling a cry. I didn't actually think they signaled evil, but I'd spent my life looking for them. A few times, I'd kept sightings of them from my mother, not wanting to pack up and leave yet again. But we always left, raven or no raven.

Glancing around, I tried to slow my beating heart. She wasn't here to freak out. She'd gone into town with Rosa to shop for groceries.

The thought of leaving made panic clutch at my heart, though. I had gotten used to the luxury of good food and comfortable beds with startling rapidity. Not to mention the company of people my age.

I turned down the back hallway and hurried in that direction, away from the raven. Without intention, I found myself standing at the glass door to the long, rectangular pool room. One long side of the room was made entirely of glass, while the opposite long wall backed the rest of the house and was made of slick white and blue tile. One of the two short walls that formed the ends of the room featured huge windows and a set of French doors that opened onto the deck. Opposite that was the door I was standing before.

I stepped through, my eyes immediately drawn to the left, where clouds of steam billowed from a showerhead against the long tile wall. For a second, the clouds were so thick they obscured the person standing there. A wetsuit hugged his bottom half, but he'd unzipped it and peeled it off the top of his body. His head was back, hot water pouring from the showerhead and cascading over his tan body.

Now *he* looked like a god. I knew I should say something, but I couldn't break the spell. I'd never really seen a male body before, and it was different than I'd imagined. Angular as I'd heard it described in books, but the curves of his muscles under the skin were more graceful than I'd expected, more delicate.

I stood there for a second, rapt by the strangeness of this body, before he slid his thumbs into the wetsuit clinging to his hips and peeled it down to his feet. I gasped in shock. It had happened so fast. I didn't have a chance to warn him that I was there before he snapped back upright. He threw a shock of blonde hair back, and I had a second to think that wasn't right, that no one in this house had hair like that.

He met my eyes, a grin splitting his face in two. That familiar smile, slightly too big for his face.

Joaquin.

He reached back to slide both hands through

his hair, standing unashamed in all his full-frontal glory. As always, instinct told me to run, but the shock held me rooted in place. Still grinning, Joaquin ran his hands from his hair down his body, over his chest, his abs. He grabbed himself, grinning like a hyena all the while.

Before I could turn and run, the door flew open behind me.

"What the fuck," Zeke yelled, leaping past me.

Finn grabbed my shoulder and spun me around, and I clung to him as if he'd saved me. Even though he was wet and sandy and also wearing a wetsuit, his embrace comforted me more than anyone else's would have. I was relieved beyond measure that someone had interrupted, that it had been Finn rather than Xander or even Eliot. Finn was the only person I would have touched in that moment.

"Thank you," I whispered into his shoulder. Conflicting emotions raced through me—shame, curiosity, elation, excitement, fear.

Zeke and Joaquin were yelling at each other behind me. "I was just taking a shower," Joaquin said, his voice a mixture of whining and laughter. "She's the one who wanted to watch."

"Dude, that's my sister," Zeke yelled.

"For like a day," Joaquin protested.

"I'm sorry," Finn murmured into my hair.

Zeke's voice spoke before I could. "Have fun out in the cold, asshole." A cool breeze swept through the damp pool room, and I heard the glass door slide open and then closed.

"Hey," Joaquin yelled, pounding on the glass. "Give me back my clothes!"

"Let's go," Finn said, detaching himself and pulling me into the hallway.

I couldn't look at him. I felt like I'd been caught doing something shameful, something I wished he hadn't seen. I didn't want him to think of me differently because I'd been watching Joaquin. But I had been. Now, I followed Finn, trying not to notice how tightly the wetsuit clung to his body. His shoulders were broader than I'd noticed before, his muscles defined through the clinging material. When he wasn't standing next to Zeke, who was built like a football player, he looked bigger and stronger than he had before.

But now that I'd seen Joaquin, my mind didn't stop there. I couldn't stop myself from wondering if Finn looked like that under his wetsuit. I couldn't help but know that he was probably not wearing much—if anything—under it. I couldn't help but wish it had been him under that shower when I walked in.

Finn led me upstairs and into his room. While Zeke's bedroom had been strewn with a few clothes, with some shoes randomly kicked under the bed, and a messy desk and shelves, Finn's was so neat and sparse it looked like no one lived there at all. If he hadn't told me he was taking me to his room, I would have thought he'd taken me to a guest room.

"This is yours?" I looked around, hoping to catch a glimpse of his artwork, to see some comics on his desk. But his desk was bare except for a little stand with a few pens and pencils in it. Instead of his own art, the walls had the same kind of beachy watercolor paintings as the room Mom and I had been sharing.

Finn nodded, his wet hair pulled back in a ponytail. "I'm sorry about Joaquin," he said. "He surfs with us, so he usually rinses off here before heading home. I didn't know—I'll make sure that doesn't happen again."

"Okay," I said, concentrating on breathing deeply.

Finn looked as uncomfortable as I felt. "I—I might rinse off," he said. "If you want to hang out here, or…"

"Or join you?" I squeaked, my jaw dropping open.

"No!" Finn practically shouted. Dark red swept over his face like he'd flipped a switch. My own blush must have matched his. Because, well, now my stepbrother thought I was a sex-crazed weirdo, which was quite possibly true, but beyond the point.

"Or go back to your room," he said, more gently this time.

"I knew that." The tension was so thick the air nearly hummed with it, and I fled in humiliation. As soon as I was in the hall, I breathed a sigh of relief. But it didn't last long. In a house with five kids, it seemed I was never alone. Peyton came skipping down the hall in a pair of pink Ugg boots, black leggings, and a slouchy white sweater with a pink scarf over it. The girl I'd seen with her in the cafeteria ambled along the hallway behind her.

"Hey, I was looking for you," Peyton said, grabbing both my hands in hers. "I wanted to introduce you to my girlfriend. Alejandra."

Heat crackled up my arms.

"Uh, okay," I said. "Hey, Alejandra."

The girl behind Peyton stepped up and slid her arm around Peyton's waist. Her black hair was cut in an edgy pixie style, and her eyes were lined with heavy kohl liner, but my eyes kept returning to that hand sitting so casually, so possessively, on Peyton's hip.

"It's great to meet you," Alejandra said, giving me a wide smile.

"Are you okay?" Peyton asked, her brow furrowing. "You seem…"

"I kind of walked in on Joaquin showering," I blurted out, because I couldn't exactly tell her I'd just accidentally propositioned her brother.

"Oh, man, I'm so sorry," Alejandra said, eyes widening.

"Can we call him Teeny Joaquin-y?" Peyton asked, holding up her pinky finger.

For some reason, her joke made the panicky feeling in my stomach melt, and I found myself laughing with the other girls.

257

"Just take my word on this, whatever's in his pants, you don't want it," Alejandra said.

After agreeing, Peyton said they were hanging in her room if I wanted to join, but I'd had enough company for the day. My head was still in a whirl over all that had happened at school and since then, so I excused myself and escaped to the library. The room was empty and quiet, and a sense of reverence fell over me when I entered. I collapsed into a chair, feeling drained.

I wasn't used to so many people, so much going on. My life with Mom had always been chaotic, but I'd never had to worry about anyone but her. And even though I wanted to be alone, I found myself thinking about the others. About Peyton hanging out with her girlfriend. Eliot and Xander off somewhere, maybe with their girlfriends. Finn in the shower. Zeke had also been in a wetsuit after surfing. Was he showering in the pool room where I'd interrupted Joaquin?

I got up and perused the library, trying to forget my worries. Instead, I found myself drawn to a section with a bunch of mythology books. All day, I'd avoided thinking about the stories of gods and monsters, of giants and death. But it had nagged at me, and as soon as I was alone with no distractions, it came raging back. What if Neil was right? What if there really was something living inside me, inside all of us? If it had been there all along, then maybe my mom wasn't really crazy at all.

Afraid to let myself believe it, I ran my fingers along the spines, looking for one about Norse gods. When I found it, I tugged it out and opened it. If there was something powerful inside me, and if it had even the slightest chance of helping my mother, I couldn't ignore it. I had to find out what it was and what it could do.

CHAPTER TWENTY-EIGHT

Finn

"Fuck. God dammit, son of a fucking bitch."

I stood in the hot shower, muttering curses under my breath. I couldn't get the picture of Gwen out of my mind. How shocked she'd looked. How naked Joaquin had been. How she was now tainted, her purity smirched by *my* friend. I'd invited him to go surfing. I'd invited him to come hang out. I'd done it out of charity, but what had it gotten me? I'd violated my stepsister.

What did it matter if I added swearing to my list of sins?

The thought of Gwen made my body stiffen.

"Fuuuuuuck." I rested my forehead against the wall and looked down at my growing hard-on. What was happening to me? She was legally my sister, for God's sake.

God. Ha. Probably another fucking lie I'd

been told my whole life.

Doubt—add that to my list of sins, too. I was full of them.

So what did it matter if I gave in to the sick and twisted desires in my mind? Lust was just one more deadly sin to check off the list.

And what did it matter if I let that burning seed of anger blaze up, like Xander did every day. I wasn't better than him. I was a sinner like everyone else. Wrath—I had it in spades. Towards my lying father, towards my dead mother, towards my brothers, all of them. Towards Joaquin for being the one she walked in on. I wanted to fucking kill him.

A month ago, I hadn't been like this. A month ago, I had been good. Not blameless—no mere mortal could be perfect. But I'd been a good person.

Now, I was jerking off in the shower, thinking about my stepsister. Her flawless ivory skin. Her flowing blonde locks. Her sweet, innocent eyes. And I was corrupting her. Was it worse or better if I pictured her as an angel while I took her innocence?

This was how far I had fallen.

My life was a crumbling pile of dog shit. From the day I was born, it had been one big fucking lie. I was a bastard, destined to hell from the moment I was conceived. Why even try to be good?

A month ago, I'd had this tidy little life. I did my silly little comics, I surfed, I kept my head down, and my nose to the grindstone. I didn't let myself get distracted by parties and girls. I went to church three times a week. I prayed every night and every morning. Sure, I sometimes "woke" to find some pretty weird scenes painted on the walls or canvases of the studio Dad had put in for me. They weren't sinful things, though, just unexplainable. That's why I kept it locked, where even Dad wouldn't see them.

Though the "dad" part was a joke. I wasn't his son at all. I wasn't the twin brother of Eliot the Lady Killing Genius, as he'd called himself when we played knights and sandcastles on the beach as kids. I wasn't the shy one of the Keen family. I didn't have a family. I was the bastard orphan son of a junkie whore.

Not the mother I'd known. Not the one whose bed I had sat by, whose hand I had held in her worst moments, moments not even my brothers had witnessed. Moments when she'd done and said things only a dying woman could, things that made me grey with shame for her. I'd believed her when she called me her son. We'd stood by her through the breakdowns and the valiant moments of bravery and strength, when she thought she could overcome. I'd stood with my brothers behind her, like an army, always having her back.

And what had it all been for?

She'd told me I was her son. She had lied, and now, she was burning in hell right beside my whoring real mother. She was dead, and I hated her for it because now I couldn't properly hate her for lying to me. I couldn't be angry at her the way I was angry at Dad. The way I was angry at Xander for knowing all along and not telling us. We were supposed to tell each other everything.

I was angry at Eliot for noticing that Zeke wasn't our brother and not telling me. I was angry at Peyton and Zeke for being real siblings. For being so cheerful about the whole world, when they were going to hell right beside the rest of us—Peyton for loving her girlfriend, Zeke for acting on the love for his girlfriends. I was angry at the Bible for saying something so stupid could make you go to hell.

Basically, I was just pissed at everyone and everything in the world. I cleaned up the shower, dressed, and headed down to the studio. Checking the hall, I unlocked the door and slipped inside.

An apocalyptic scene greeted me. An abandoned baby carriage holding an infant, its cheeks sunken and eyes glassy, a fly sitting on its forehead. Conjoined twins stood nearby, stabbing each other with knives. Dead animals lay in the street behind them. Flames licked up from the city on the horizon. In the background, a giant humanoid shape lumbered towards the city.

Had I done this? Hands shaking, I grabbed a can of white paint, sloshed it into a paint tray, grabbed a roller stiffened with too many coats of paint, and began to slap it over the horrifying scene. How many times had I done this now? They just kept coming back.

Sometimes, I still had trouble believing this came from my hand, from my mind. If it weren't for the paint all over my clothes, I might believe someone else had done it just to make me think I was losing my mind. I might believe that if I hadn't been interrupted by a knock at the door or a phone call on occasion, only to look down and find a pallet beside me and a brush in one hand, poised over a still-wet, half-finished portrait of a screaming woman lying in a doorway, a needle protruding from her arm and feral cats feasting on her innards while a man stood over her watching.

My fake dad's words echoed in my head. Giants. Possession. People being stalked and killed, driven mad. Maybe I was the demon they were looking for. Maybe I'd come through the gate that night—the gate to hell. Maybe my real mother was right about me, but no one had listened. If I could do this with no memory of it, in some kind of fugue state, then maybe I could also drive my mother mad and make people hang themselves.

I'd just finished covering the wall with a sloppy coat of paint when my phone chimed. It was time for dinner with the family. Time to pretend that I was totally fine with the fact that I'd been lied to my whole life. Everyone else seemed okey-dokey with it. If I was the crazy one, how come I was the only one having a normal reaction to that news?

CHAPTER TWENTY-NINE

Eliot

After dinner I called a hot tub meeting. We used to do those a lot when Mom was getting worse towards the end. We'd go out and sit there pretending nothing was happening in the house, so we wouldn't have to hear her crying. We'd talk about anything but her and Dad. Other times, we'd discuss only them, trying to figure out what to do.

She and Dad had brought us together by adopting us, but in a sick way, her illness was what kept us close all those years. When it was in the house, her illness had acted as bond between us, a shared secret. Our united front had kept it from prying eyes and inquiring minds. Our family fought it as one, until the end.

Once she was gone, though, her shadow became a trap, clinging and claustrophobic. We'd each done what we could to escape it. We'd grown apart, each of us grieving in our own way, alone or with other friends. Since she died, we hadn't met like this. But now we had a reason to.

Gwen was bringing us back together, whether she knew it or not.

I climbed in the hot tub and waited. The day had been a little warmer than usual, but the temperature was dropping again now that it was dark. A minute later, Zeke trotted out and hopped in, making a wave roll through the tub.

"At least there's not enough water to almost drown one of us," he said with a grin. "What's up?"

"Let's wait for the others," I said just as Xander slinked out and slid into the tub.

I was wary about having all six of us in such close proximity. As each of my siblings arrived, the particles in the air moved faster, growing more and more excited. There had always been a little bit of this when we got together. It made us buoyant, exuberant, reckless. Sometimes, it was hard to remember that we weren't invincible. But now that we'd been blowing out windows and making waves, I didn't know what to expect.

Peyton and Gwen arrived together, clutching robes around them. Peyton tossed hers in a chair and slid into the tub, winding her ponytail into a bun so it wouldn't get wet. Gwen stood beside the hot tub, looking uncertain but so cute I wanted to reach out and take her hand and pull her into my arms. I had a feeling that telling her all the things I told most girls wouldn't work on her, though. She probably wouldn't even know flirting when she saw it.

"Come on in, water's great," Zeke said with an easy grin, leaning back and laying his arms along the rim of the hot tub.

"Yeah, don't stand out there, you'll freeze," Peyton said, scooting over towards Zeke. The hot tub would have fit a dozen people, though, so there was plenty of room. Steam rose in plumes from the water bubbling gently around us. Gwen stood there for a few seconds longer, like she didn't know how to get into a hot tub. She probably didn't. From what I knew of her life so far, she hadn't been in a lot of hot tubs.

"Oh, for fuck's sake," Xander said, standing and stepping from the tub. I glanced sideways at Gwen, observing whether she noticed the way he looked with his tattoos showing and water cascading over his body. She definitely had.

I was going to have to hit the weights harder if I wanted to keep up.

Xander scooped Gwen up in his arms and stepped into the hot tub, ignoring her cry of surprise. Releasing her with a smirk, he sat down and leaned back, mirroring Zeke's casual position. On him, it looked more like gloating.

Gwen's robe billowed out around her, floating on top of the water. I swear the temperature in the water went up about ten degrees until it was almost painful.

I caught Gwen's bewildered, desperate expression and chose that moment to divert attention from her. "Where's Finn?"

Peyton twisted around to check the door, and Zeke leaned over the side of the tub to snag his phone from the glass table nearby. Gwen shot me a quick, relieved smile and struggled out of her robe. I barely caught a glimpse of her slim, feminine form, clad in a loose white T-shirt over one of Peyton's swimsuits. She quickly slipped under the water's surface, seating herself halfway between me and Zeke.

Now that we were all here, I turned my attention to my phone. I'd been so busy waiting for Gwen to peel off her robe that I'd barely realized my scatterbrained twin was absent.

Not twin, I reminded myself. He wasn't even biologically my brother, but I knew better than to think that meant anything. The sixteen years we'd spent sharing our every thought with each other mattered. We would always be brothers, even if we didn't share a single strand of DNA.

"He's on his way," Zeke said, setting down his phone. "What do we do when he gets here?"

"Don't get too close?" Peyton asked.

"I've been reading up on Norse mythology," Gwen said quietly.

"I don't know if we can call it mythology if it's real," I said. Then I cursed myself for sounding like a pedantic asshat. She didn't want a lecture. She had information to share. I was all about solving this puzzle, so I shut my mouth and waited for her to go on.

A minute later, Finn came shuffling out in a pair of swim trunks and slid into the hot tub. The temperature immediately spiked, and the jets began churning the water. I stood, ready to hop out if it got hotter, but after a minute, I started to adjust to the new heat.

"So tell us what you found out, Gwen," Zeke said, turning the dial to shut off the jets. Nothing happened, but none of us moved to do anything more about it. We had bigger concerns tonight.

Gwen took a breath. "Okay, so there's this world, the human world, which is called Midgard. And there's eight other worlds, all connected in this giant tree of life." She stopped speaking and looked around at us, as if expecting someone to stop her or maybe laugh. I noticed her eyes dropped before meeting Xander's, and I made sure to offer her my most encouraging smile. I wasn't sure what had happened between them, but I didn't like the way she shrank back from him.

We were all in this together.

"Go on," Zeke said, moving closer to her. I couldn't tell for sure, but I thought he'd taken her hand. I should have given her support first.

"According to this, the whole thing will end when this giant wolf named Fenrir breaks free of his chains and destroys the gods in what we'd probably call the apocalypse. They called it Ragnarok."

I'd done a little reading myself, and I knew she was giving us the basics, but I didn't want to stop her. For once she seemed to have found her stride, her uncertainty melting away. When she spoke about what she'd read, her whole face changed, and her body language grew more confident and assertive. It was like watching a bud open, the leaves unfurling from inside and knowing exactly which direction to grow.

"I don't know a lot," Gwen admitted, glancing at the house. "I tried asking my mom, but she just said we had to join together as one."

"Like sex?" Zeke blurted out.

Color washed over Gwen's cheeks, and she extricated her hand from his. "I don't think so," she said. "I don't think our parents would have gotten married if that's what we were supposed to do. She said she'd done her job by marrying your dad. But I can ask again when she's more...lucid."

"They don't know what we're supposed to do," Xander said quietly from his end of the tub. "They told us all they know. It's up to us to figure it out."

Gwen took a breath as if gathering strength to go on. "I think that whatever I saw on the beach was part of it. I think we need to complete her somehow."

Zeke opened his mouth, and I just knew he was going to say "like sex" again, so I spoke before he could. "What do you have in mind, Gwen?"

"She said something about joining to

complete a circle. Maybe it's really that simple. Join hands and make a circle."

Xander muttered something about witchy nonsense.

"We could at least try it," Gwen said. "If everyone wants to."

Peyton perked up. "I used to do stuff like that in middle school," she said, scooting towards Zeke and reaching for his hand. "I was sure I was a witch. Maybe I am. I'm down to find out."

"I'm down for anything," Zeke said, taking Gwen's hand again.

When I saw the discomfort that gave Gwen after his earlier comment, I knew I had to make her feel better in whatever way I could. It was a compulsion beyond my control. Before I knew it, I was sliding along the bench seat and gathering Gwen's small hand in mine.

"We've never all touched at the same time," I said. "But after seeing what happened when we were in the same room, it's got to do something. I just hope we don't boil ourselves to death."

"Yeah, maybe we should get out of the hot tub," Finn said, his shoulders hunched.

"Whatever's going to happen will happen," Xander said, gliding through the water towards us. "If we don't boil in here, we'll be thrown to our deaths or some shit. Let's just get it over with."

He found his spot on Peyton's other side, and I knew something was going to happen. Even before

Finn joined the circle, the vibration in the air was almost painful. Sparks of electricity seemed to cling to the hair on my legs, even though they were submerged in water.

Looking around at my siblings, I knew we were all in the right place. Somehow, we'd always fallen into this pattern, and Gwen fit perfectly into the circle. Zeke was always the center, and now, between the only two girls, he seemed like a king holding court. Peyton was at his side, Xander there to protect her and Finn when Zeke wasn't. Finn's hand waited to connect with mine, twins no matter what. And on my other side, Gwen formed the link that had always been missing between me and Zeke, calming the competitive waters between us.

"What'll it hurt to try?" I said, holding out my hand to my cautious brother. In truth, I had no idea if it would hurt one or all of us. But I knew something was going to happen. It was building, brewing like a storm. I could almost smell the ozone in the air.

"He doesn't have to," Gwen said, squeezing my other hand. She turned to Finn. "It was just an idea. You don't have to do it if you don't want."

"He's one of us," Zeke said.

Finn nodded, his eyes on Gwen. Somehow, she was the catalyst that had set all this off. I didn't know how, and it was killing me that I couldn't figure it out. If this gave us answers, it was worth a few scorched leg hairs.

"Zeke's right," Finn said. "Like it or not,

we're all part of whatever's going on. I guess I'm in. Let's see what happens."

With that, he took hold of my hand, completing the circle.

CHAPTER THIRTY

Gwen

An invisible force gripped me and held me in place, as if I'd been caught in an inescapable current of electricity. A tiny tornado seemed to spiral in the center of the circle we made, pulling up the water. As it spun, it became taller and taller, until a ten-foot water spout whirled in the center of the hot tub. Suddenly, it exploded in a gust of wind that blasted in every direction, whipping our hair back. Hot water blasted into our faces and across the deck.

Panic flooded through me, but my hands refused to unclench from those of my new family. We were plugged into something beyond us, and it wasn't ready to release us. The hot water left churning around us went still, the surface flat Kansas corn country, and the air around us fell still. I shot a look around the group, only then realizing they were experiencing the same sensations I was. Their wide eyes mirrored my own surprise and fear.

Suddenly, from the steam rising from the water, a figure began to form. Our faces turned up as it rose, shining from the center of our circle. The light nearly blinded me, and I had to squint to keep my eyes open. It was the figure of a man with a golden beard that matched his hair. And when I say golden, I don't mean blonde. I mean it was like twenty-four carat gold that radiated light. He didn't really have a face, just a blinding white orb as bright as the sun.

"My pieces are assembling," he said. It wasn't exactly a voice we heard with our ears, but one that was felt as truth, that came from around us and inside us. Somehow, we'd made it together by joining hands.

"You did not make me, silly humans," the voice said, and I jolted at the realization he'd seen my thoughts. "I fathered many races in your world, but you cannot make a god. I am the son of Odin."

"Are you here to destroy us?" Peyton asked.

"If I destroyed you, I would be destroying myself," the god said. "For it is I that you have been hosting."

"Not demons?" Finn asked. Strangely, I wasn't sure if he'd spoken either. His voice had the same anchorless effect as the god's, so I didn't know if we were all now reading each other's minds.

"You have been hosting a god," the voice said. "I came into the world of Midgard the night you were born. I used to wander this land, but the bridge has weakened, and gods no longer enter this world as freely."

"Which one of us is hosting you?" asked Zeke's voice. "It's me, right? Because I totally feel like a god sometimes."

"All of you," the god said. "A mere mortal could not withstand the presence of a god, so we have to divide ourselves among several. The more of my pieces join together, the more easily I can speak to you. One of you holds the central part of me. You humans might call it…the stomach. The life force."

"One of us is god guts," Zeke said.

"Perhaps God Essence is a better word. The mortal with my Essence must be present for me to speak to you."

"You're speaking to us now," I said. "That means she's here now, right?"

"That is right, mortal."

"Who are you?" Eliot asked.

"I am Heimdall," the god answered. "The gatekeeper of the worlds and guardian of Bifrost."

"Bifrost?" Eliot asked. The intention behind his question came through to me like a shadow following the words. He wanted to know why this god was here, what it needed.

"Bifrost is the bridge in the sky," Heimdall said. "It connects your world with the world of the gods. It is my job to keep giants from crossing the bridge into Asgard."

"You want *us* to stop giants?" I asked.

"First, you must assemble the rest of my

pieces. Only when you are all together am I complete. There are nine human hosts, just as I am born of nine mothers."

I wanted to point out two very valid concerns. First of all, there were only six of us, and second of all, you couldn't actually be born from more than one mother. But hey, maybe the gods had different rules about things like logic and, you know, counting. Who was I to argue?

Apparently, Zeke had no such reservations.

"Wait, where's the nine?" he asked. "Even if you count our parents, it's only eight. Right?" He looked around the circle at us, as if he might have done the math wrong.

"My Essence calls to all my parts," Heimdall said. "She is like the trunk of a tree, and the rest are the branches. She must summon all nine to complete the journey across the bridge."

"Who's the center?" Peyton asked. "It's not me, right? It's Gwen."

I shrank back. If my weeks on the road were any indication, I sure didn't have this *eau de god*. "Me?" I asked. "Why me?"

"It's you," Xander's voice said, an edge of accusation to it.

"How do you know?"

"Because it's obvious," he said, his tone mocking the one I'd used when I'd said those words about him being Neil's biological son.

"He's right," Peyton said. "This all started

when you joined us."

"How do we find the other three hosts?" Eliot asked.

"You must find the fire giant first," Heimdall said. "Cast out the giant from your midst. That is your first task."

I wanted to look around, but my body seemed bound in an immobile, limbo state. Still, I could feel the presence of each of my stepsiblings around me. I did not, however, sense any fiery giants from hell.

My money was on Xander.

"Who's the demon?" Finn asked. "Or fire giant, or whatever it's called."

"It has been trying to destroy me since I arrived in Midgard," Heimdall said. "It draws near even now. You must rid yourself of it before you leave Midgard, or it will follow you onto the bridge and destroy it."

"And that's bad," Zeke said.

"Your world and everything in it will be destroyed if the gods cannot cross Bifrost to fight the giants at Ragnarok."

Heimdall began to spin in the air, his reflection shimmering on the water around us even when he moved so fast he was only a blur. "Find my final pieces and prepare yourself for Bifrost. When you need me again, you know how to call forth my form."

"You're leaving?" Peyton asked, her voice filled with the anguish that gripped me at the same moment.

"I am a part of you," Heimdall said. "I chose you. I cannot leave. When you are together, you will feel whole as I become whole. But be wary of those who would come between you and divide you. You must stay united as long as you can. You will lose a part of me in another world, even as you gain yet one more. One will betray the others, and one will fall prey to the trickster."

Suddenly, he wavered in the air, then shrank to the size of one blinding pinprick of light. After a second, rays of golden light shot out in every direction, and then he blinked out. The same impossible blast of wind that had started the vision exploded from the center of the hot tub again, like a mini bomb blast that knocked us all backwards. My hands slipped from my brothers' and clutched at empty water.

I looked around at my new family. They all appeared as shaken as I felt. Even Xander's usual surly scowl had been replaced by a stunned blankness.

My heart hammered in my chest, and my head spun with all I'd just seen and heard. Fantastical things. I wanted to pinch myself to see if I was dreaming, but the hot water bubbling around me, the cool breeze drifting across the deck, and the raven perched on the roof told me that it was real. I knew now that the ravens were sent here to watch us by Odin, the Norse father god. I had read that in the books in Neil's library. I knew about Heimdall, too. It was impossible, yes, but not a dream.

And not a hallucination, either. The others had seen it, too. I wasn't going crazy. I wasn't losing my sanity. It had happened. And unlike my mother, I was surrounded by people who believed me. People who had shared my experience. More than anything, I wanted to go to my mother, to tell her how very sorry I was that I'd never believed her. To beg forgiveness for judging her the way everyone else had. She wasn't crazy, and yet her own daughter had dismissed her as easily as a stranger—more easily than a stranger.

As a stranger on the internet, Neil had believed. At last, I understood what had puzzled me for so long. She hadn't known Neil well enough to love him when they got married, but she'd found the one person in the world who gave her what she needed, the one thing I hadn't given her all those years. Validation. After all those years, she'd probably started doubting her own sanity. I understood why she'd grabbed on so tight, held so fast, to the one person who told her that not only was she sane, she was important and gifted. If only I'd known...

"I'm going to talk to my mom," I said, standing and stepping out of the tub. My earlier insecurity about taking off my clothes in front of the group seemed ridiculous now. It was just a body. They'd all seen my boob at the beach, anyway. Now, none of it mattered. It was just skin. Everyone had it.

"Anyone else think we should visit the hospital where that thing came through to begin with?" Peyton asked behind me, but I didn't stay for the answers. I grabbed her robe and ducked inside, running up the winding stairs to the second story.

Mom wasn't in our bedroom. A snake of panic wound around my spinal column as I raced down the hall, calling her name. There were a lot of rooms up here. Our room, another guest room, the bathroom shared by the two rooms. Zeke's room, Peyton's, Finn's, Eliot's, Xander's. I didn't think about their privacy, just opened each door. I knew they were all down in the hot tub, anyway.

I'd been in most of the rooms already. When I opened Eliot's door, his room looked just like I imagined it would be, and that comforted me somehow. He wasn't the way I imagined when I met him, with all those girls. But his room was like a fancy computer lab. Three huge monitors sat at an angle on his desk, so he could see all three at once when seated in the ergonomic black leather chair. The buttons and gadgets on the desk below the monitors looked like something you'd find in the cockpit of a spaceship.

The only thing unexpected was his bed. It was king-sized and unmade, with wine-colored sheets tangled up in a tan comforter at the foot of the bed. It gave me a second's pause, the maturity of that bedding. Those were adult sheets, and I suddenly wondered how many girls he'd brought here to do adult things under those sheets. I didn't know what I expected—*Star Wars* sheets?—but it was not this. Seeing them made me feel young and insufficient somehow. Shame twisted in my belly, and I turned away and hurried down the hall, not surprised to try Xander's knob and find his door locked.

On the next floor, I ran down the hall, opening all the rooms except the studio, which was locked. I found my mother in the library, lying on a brown leather couch with a book open in her lap.

"Mom," I said, rushing to her side and wedging myself onto the sliver of couch beside her.

"Hi, Gwen," she said, flipping a page.

"I'm sorry," I said, a sob choking my words.

"For what?" she asked, setting her book across her lap and smiling up at me.

"For not listening to you," I said. "For not believing. I'm sorry that all along, I thought you were seeing things that weren't there. You must have felt so helpless and alone. I can't even imagine. I'm so sorry, Mom."

Mom marked her place in the book with a finger and closed it. "What's all this about?"

"I believe you," I whispered. "I just wanted you to know that."

"I thought you always believed. That's why you came with me when it was time to run. To keep the world from ending."

Shame closed off my throat, and I shook my head. Somehow, she'd never realized that I didn't believe her. I must have been a better actor than I thought because I always went along to appease her, so she wouldn't have a screaming freak-out in the parking lot of a Taco Bell. Not because I believed there were giants chasing us.

"Why else would you have come with me?" she asked, a frown creasing her forehead.

Knowing that she believed in me all that time, all those years, when I didn't believe in her, was worse than the alternative. It was one thing for her to go through life knowing the world around her thought she was crazy. The last thing she needed was to know her daughter had also thought that. I couldn't unburden myself and ask forgiveness if it would hurt her more. This was my shame to bear.

"Because I love you." It was the simple truth that had never wavered.

CHAPTER THIRTY-ONE

Gwen

Heimdall's words echoed through my mind as I rejoined the rest of my family, of myself. One of them would be lost. One of them would betray me.

The thought gnawed at me as I returned to the back deck. I had a pretty good idea of which one would betray me. It was harder not to trust him than I expected, though. He was an ass, but...still. It was hard to hate someone you knew. It was hard to stop myself from trusting him as I got to know him.

And what if it wasn't Xander? I stepped through the sliding doors onto the back deck. The night was warmer than recent one. A gentle salt breeze stirred my hair, and the distant lapping of gentle waves soothed my frayed nerves. The others were all there, deep in conversation. My eyes moved from one of them to the next.

Sweet, shy, warm Finn would never betray

me. He didn't have it in him.

Fun, protective, easygoing Zeke had saved my life at the beach that day.

Peyton wouldn't believe in deceit. She was accepting of everyone and straightforward about who she was.

My eyes fell on Eliot. He was unpredictable. More unpredictable than Xander.

Yes, Xander was a total pig ninety percent of the time, but I could count on him to be that way. I knew not to trust him, but some part of me did, anyway. And that part was growing all the time. Maybe that was my downfall. I would be betrayed even knowing better, because I couldn't help but feel I was beginning to understand him.

But Eliot, with his rumpled sheets and his secret smiles, his intense eyes and logical mind...I just didn't know. He might be persuaded that something else made sense. Hosting gods didn't seem like something he'd easily accept and wrap his mind around.

"Do I need to carry you to the tub again, your highness?" Xander asked, his stormy grey eyes fixing on mine as he swung around. "Or are you going to run away again?"

"You're one to talk," I said, moving across the deck towards the edge of the wooden hot tub. This time, it didn't feel like nothing, as it had after seeing the god. But it was easier than the first time, even with all their eyes on me. I could do it. They were all undressed, too.

Xander snorted. "I'm still here. Where were you just a minute ago? Or when Dad was telling us about our fucked up family?"

His words hit me like ice water.

"You told me to leave."

"And you did," he said. "There's no reason to come back now. Run away, little girl. Just like your mommy. We got this."

Forcing my lip not to tremble, I peeled off my robe and discarded it in a nearby chair. My t-shirt clung to my body, and I was sure they could see the abnormal darkness beneath the clinging, wet fabric. They fell silent, all of them watching as I climbed the three wooden steps that matched the hot tub's siding. I knew what he wanted, what he expected. But I wasn't going to give it to him.

If Hester Prynn could bear her scarlet letter, I could bear my scarlet scars.

I wouldn't cower inside a robe or slip into the tub quickly to hide under the water. They thought I was a coward. They didn't know what the fire giant had already cost me. Taking a deep breath, I grabbed the edge of my T-shirt and peeled it over my head, dropped it to the deck behind me, and stood exposed for all to see.

My eyes locked on Xander's, and I spread out my arms. "Here I am," I said, the words snapping off my tongue like cracking ice. "Take your best shot. What do you have to say about me now? I'm deformed, I'm scared, I'm a pig? What else you got?"

"Gwen..." Peyton whispered, her fingertips covering her perfect lips.

I pinched the skin around my waist, forever mottled with red, angry splotches. "I know, right? It's disgusting. So maybe I'm not perfect like all of you. You think you're so tough, Xander? You've got all the money in the world, a powerful father, and a team of siblings to have your back. Maybe I am stupid and naïve. But I fight my own battles, and I'm not running away. I've already survived a fire giant. So let's have it." I gestured for him to throw his worst at me.

No one spoke. For a moment, I was unbreakable. Whatever he said, I could take it.

Xander's eyes didn't accept the invitation to critique my body. Instead, they stayed locked on mine. My stomach trembled at the intensity of his stare. That gaze penetrated farther than clothes, farther than scars and flesh, into my bones, my soul. It said more than his words ever could. It said I was nothing but a little girl throwing a tantrum. That I wasn't worth fighting.

He chuckled softly, then lifted his hands from the water and began a slow clap.

My anger had crested like a wave, and now it came crashing down. I forced myself to stay upright, not to race for the house, run up to my room, and hide my face in the pillow. My eyes stung. My throat ached. But I would rather cry in front of him than hide. I'd been hiding all my life, and I was done. I'd challenged him, and as much as I might regret it, I wasn't going to back out now.

"Thank you," I said through clenched teeth, and I bowed at the waist, even though it made my stomach roil, as if I were about to hurl into their luxury hot tub.

Trying to salvage what little dignity I had left, I stepped slowly into the tub, feeling both defeated and relieved to drop his gaze. When I'd slid into the water, I could breathe again.

Peyton gave me a sympathetic, encouraging smile, and Finn gave me a slight approving nod. That was worse than judgment. If I hadn't broken down from Xander's cruelty, I might under the weight of their kindness. Their pity made me feel small.

My eyes met Zeke's, and a shock went through me. He didn't look scornful or disgusted to have seen my imperfect body. He looked ravenous.

My breath caught, and I pulled my eyes away. I found myself turning last to Eliot, waiting for his response. His eyes were bright with curiosity.

"What happened?" he asked.

"I was burned in a fire," I said flatly.

"Your mom mentioned that," he said. "That your dad died fighting a fire giant."

"I was supposed to die with him, but I lived," I said, turning to the others, but especially Xander. "So don't tell me I can't fight a giant with you. Because I've already won once."

"You didn't win. You escaped," Xander said with a smirk. "Hey, look at that. Another time you ran away."

"Dude, shut up," Zeke said. He turned to me, his blue eyes serious for once. His hands found my shoulders and turned me towards him, holding onto me with that steady, strong grip that made me feel safer than anything in the world. "We're not going anywhere without you."

Xander snorted.

"I'd hate to give you another black eye when you're just getting over the last one," Zeke said, glowering at his brother as he sat back, pulling me in close beside him. I could feel the hardness of his muscled body, his bare skin against mine, and I couldn't breathe.

"You gave him that?" I asked when I'd caught my breath.

"What? No," Zeke said with a crooked smile. "I'd never hit my brother."

Peyton started giggling, and a second later, I did, too. Zeke joined in and then the twins. And for a second, it was okay. It was okay that I didn't know how to talk to people, that I'd lost this fight to Xander, that he didn't laugh with us. It was okay that my mother had married Neil, making me related to these boys whose touch made me breathless. It was even okay that a god was stuck inside us, that a giant was trying to roast us to death. We had each other, and for a moment, it felt like enough.

CHAPTER THIRTY-TWO

Gwen

It seemed strange to go back to school the next day. Did fractured gods attend human school? Did they shrink from mean girls, wear thrift store clothes, and plan shopping trips to Boston that weekend to stock up on cuter outfits? Did fragments of gods roam the halls of every school or just ours? Did other dads collect their broken pieces like archeologists unearthing shards of ancient pottery, trying to fit them back together?

Wednesday passed in a blur. I tried to focus in class, but my mind oscillated between fearfulness at the dire prophecies, suspicions about my own siblings, and denial that any of it was real. A giant wolf that was going to eat the gods? Other worlds?

Now that we were aware of what we were housing, we didn't seem to be causing any miniature natural disasters, which was good. Xander had ditched, so we were one short at lunch, anyway. I'd just about let out my breath when Joaquin came swaggering in. I choked on my milk, my face igniting with heat. Crap. I'd almost forgotten I'd have to see him at school every day. After seeing him as I had, it was hard to look him in the eye.

"Hey, Gwennie," he said, strolling over to our table and dropping into an empty seat across from me. He flipped his floppy blonde hair back and wiggled his eyebrows at me. "How's my favorite little voyeur?"

I stared at my meatloaf as if I might find actual meat in it.

"Dude, don't even," Zeke said, sliding an arm possessively around my shoulders.

"Hey, chill," Joaquin said, holding up both hands. "No judgement here. I enjoy a little peep show as much as the next person."

Eliot sighed. "Go away, Joaquin."

"Hey, I'm just saying," Joaquin said. "I think Gwen owes me a little peek at the goods, don't you? I mean, she got to see mine. It's only fair, dude."

Zeke's body stiffened. "Walk away now," he said, his voice low and harder than I'd ever heard it.

"Okay, okay, I'm going," Joaquin said, standing. "You may have them all fooled because you look like a sweet little angel, Gwen, but I know you liked what you saw."

He grabbed his crotch and stuck out his obscenely long tongue, wagging it at me and winking before he sauntered off to harass Eliot's abandoned lady-friends.

"You okay?" Zeke asked, his arm still around me.

"Fine," I said, my face still burning. I barely knew Joaquin, but I had to admit, I had been admiring him under the shower. He wasn't all big and brawny like Zeke, but he was built like a surfer. He looked good.

But there was no way in hell he was ever seeing my "goods."

After school I rode home with Eliot and Finn. My phone arrived in the mail, and Eliot helped me activate it. Then we did homework and discussed how we could recognize, summon, or diagnose a giant among us. That night at dinner, Zeke invited me to watch him play football on Friday.

"You'll get to see me cheer, too," Peyton said, shooting me an oddly shy smile.

Finn had gone to church, and Xander was off with his friends again, so at least I was spared his cutting remarks.

After dinner Peyton dragged me up to her room, where she insisted I take some of her clothes to wear the next day. She was curvier than me, but not enough to make a huge difference when it came to stretchy yoga pants and baggy sweaters. I stood in front of the mirror, staring at myself.

"I don't look like me anymore," I said.

"You look amazing," Peyton assured me,

arranging my giant bundle of hair over a scarf she'd draped around me.

"I look like…you."

"Like I said, amazing," Peyton said. "Now I have a serious question."

Our eyes met in the mirror, and my stomach fluttered. "What's that?" I whispered.

"Have you ever had a haircut in your life?"

I relaxed as she maneuvered me into a chair before the mirror and began to unfasten my hair. I'd expected a different question.

Pulling out my hair ties, she arranged my hair over my shoulders and down my back. "Your hair is awesome," she said, her eyes meeting mine in the mirror. "You should wear it down sometime." Her fingers combed through my hair, quickly at first, then more slowly.

Tingles began to run from the crown of my head through my entire body with each stroke. What was happening to me? Was it just because we shared a g od? Or was that like shared blood, and it made my attraction to her even creepier? I wanted to pull away, to run out of the room and escape this confusion, but it felt so good, too good, to have her fingers in my hair. We stayed that way for a minute, two, three. As her fingers slid through my hair from roots to tips, I closed my eyes, sighing with pleasure.

Suddenly, Peyton gave a nervous laugh and turned away, grabbing a big brush with her school picture decoupaged onto the back. She pulled out her own high ponytail and began brushing her baby-pink hair in quick, even strokes, her eyes locked on her own reflection.

"I'll just...thanks for letting me borrow these," I said, scooting out of her chair and grabbing up the extra shirts she'd given me. I hurried from the room, not sure what had just happened or what to think of it.

That was the question I'd expected her to ask—something about us. If I'd ever been attracted to a girl before, if I was attracted to her. I didn't know how to answer the first question. I hadn't been attracted to another girl, but I'd never really known another girl, so how did I know if I liked them?

I crept into my own room, where I'd elected to stay with Mom. She and Neil seemed to be making no pretense of wanting to be married in the traditional sense, and I felt better knowing exactly where she was. Maybe she felt the same about me. It was a hard habit to break.

The next day when I walked into school, I tried not to be self-conscious about what I was wearing. After all, no one had ever seen me in the clothes Peyton had given me. It didn't matter if they didn't look like me. I had no image at this school yet—I could be anyone. I didn't particularly want to be pegged as the girl with outdated, garage-sale style.

A voice raked over my skin like a strand of barbed wire. "Have you ever seen something so pathetic?"

I gave my outfit a quick glance—tan Ugg boots, black leggings, a baggy cream-colored sweater, and a navy scarf. Maybe the tan and cream were too close together in color? I looked up from my locker with dread, already knowing who had stopped by to gawk at me. But again, not knowing why.

"Oh my god, is she actually wearing Peyton's clothes?" Jen asked.

"That is so sad," their other friend gushed. She burst into shrill giggles, which drew the attention of a couple other people in the hall.

"Here I thought she was trying to get in Xander's pants," Jen said.

"I thought it was Eliot," Barb said.

"But it turns out it's Peyton," their friend shrieked. "Literally!"

They all started honking with laughter. I decided I really didn't need my books that bad after all, and I turned and fled. If anything, I was less brave now than the first time they'd made fun of me. I couldn't even find my inner Scarlet O'Hara. No doubt she'd abandoned me in disgust.

But then I remembered. I didn't need Scarlet. I had a freaking god renting space inside me. Suddenly, I felt silly for running. And just like that, I stopped caring what they thought. For the rest of the day, I was bulletproof. It didn't matter if I didn't understand why Heimdall had chosen me, or if I was worthy or not. The fact was, he had chosen me. Only I could make myself worthy.

But until we went to Boston to look for the giant, I had to keep pretending to be normal. I'd dreamed of it so many times, but in reality, I'd never be normal. Pretending was as close as I could get. So I went to my classes, and after school, I went to the office to get the address of the library, where I was supposed to go for tutoring two evenings a week for the rest of the year. Between that and the help I was going to get from Eliot, I figured I'd be on a seventh grade level in math by the end of the year. But hey, at least I was on track in my lit classes.

Zeke and Peyton had practice after school, and Eliot was taking Finn to church. "Don't make me ride with Xander," I pleaded when Eliot broke the news to me.

He shook his head. "I know you guys got off on the wrong foot, but you and him are going to have to work things out. We're all part of each other, Gwen. He's a smart guy. He knows this doesn't work without all of us."

"What if he's the demon?" I asked. "The giant that's trying to get us?"

"He's not a demon," Eliot said, turning me to face him.

"How do you know?"

"Because he's my brother." Eliot searched my eyes. "Even though he already knew we weren't related by blood, he never treated us as less than brothers or less than him. He may be a big man on campus, but he's no giant. He would never hurt any of us."

I swallowed hard, resisting the urge to beg him to stay, to beg for him to protect me. "And me?" I whispered.

"And you…" Eliot's hands softened on my shoulders, and he ran them down my upper arms to my elbows, pulling me in. My head swam, my heart suddenly fluttering in my throat. My eyes dropped to his lips, and I swallowed again. He was going to kiss me. I could feel it. I knew I should stop it as surely as I knew that I wouldn't.

He licked his lips nervously. "Just work things out with him, okay? He may be a bit jaded about life, but he's not going to bring about the end of the world."

The spell holding me broke, and I realized where we were. That to the school, I was Eliot's sister. If it wasn't enough that we were related by law, now we were parts of the same god. Like with Peyton the night before, it gave me a weird incesty feeling to think about it like that. I used that squeamishness to drag myself out of my stupor of desire.

The hall was emptying out after school, and as much as I loved Eliot's hands on me, I didn't think we should be touching in a two-mile radius of Barb, anyway, wherever she was. If the monster wasn't Xander, it had to be Barb or one of her minions. I figured I should break that news to Eliot before they reconciled, but I didn't know how that would come across.

Hey, so, no offense but your ex is probably the demon who killed all our parents.

Just a tad crazy and jealous, perhaps?

"You'll be fine," Eliot promised, his gaze firm as it met mine. "I promise. If Xander was out to get you, he wouldn't have pulled you out of the ocean that day."

"That was Zeke," I reminded him.

"No," Eliot said slowly. "Xander did. He didn't tell you that?"

I shook my head. Of course not. Xander never told me anything about himself, even the nice things, apparently. The thought of him saving me was unsettling. Between that and defending me from Barb, it was almost like he cared.

"You're going to miss tutoring," Eliot said. "I already told him you needed a ride, so he's waiting for you."

"I still don't like needing anything from him," I said, slumping against Eliot.

Eliot pulled me in and gave me a quick hug. "Don't let him intimidate you. His bark is worse than his bite."

I didn't know about that. His bark could be pretty biting. But I trudged off towards the parking lot to get a ride from him—if he hadn't already taken off and left me to walk home by myself. When I got there, most of the lot was already empty, but I spotted Xander and his bike on the far side of the lot, where he always parked.

He was seated on his bike, leaned way back, in a position that made it impossible for my eyes not to drop straight to his crotch. Apparently, I wasn't the only one with that thought because he was being fawned over by a tall, slender girl with a sleek, dark bob.

Shit. Jen.

She was standing so close she was brushing against his thigh, pushing his shoulder in a playful, sexy way. He barely moved, his body relaxed, a lazy smile on his face.

In a glance, I read the scene like it was written in one of my garage sale paperbacks. She wanted him, and he sure as hell knew it. He was definitely enjoying it, but he was also waiting for me. He didn't intend for anything to come of it. He looked flattered but not terribly interested. She was obviously trying to change that, maybe asking if he'd take her for a spin or inviting him to a party. He was probably giving her some asshole answer like, "Maybe." Then he'd leave her hanging.

I wasn't sure if I should interrupt or wait until she left. Cautiously, I started across the parking lot, my bag on my shoulder. Halfway across, Xander's penetrating gaze locked on mine, and my stomach lurched. Of all the guys, he was the only one who could make me feel small, and naked, and vulnerable with just one look.

As if to prove me wrong about my earlier assumptions, to prove that I knew nothing about human beings and couldn't read people for shit, Xander snaked his arm around Jen's waist and pulled her close, looking up at her from his seated position. She smiled down at him, her fingers brushing his cheek.

My stomach twisted again and I slowed. It was one thing to interrupt a conversation, another to interrupt an embrace. Some ugly, bitchy part of me really didn't like that she was all over my stepbrother, but I didn't want to bring his wrath down upon myself if I didn't have to. So I hung back, letting the scene before me unfold.

Xander said something to Jen, and she pulled away just enough to step over the bike and straddle it, facing Xander. While she was climbing on, his eyes locked on mine, a challenge burning there. His mouth twisted into a smirk when he saw whatever was written across my face. I'd never learned to hide my emotions, and I'm sure the storm of jealousy inside me was reflected outside for all the world to see.

When Jen was standing straddling the bike, Xander grabbed her hips. Eyes on mine, he let his tongue barely skim his top lip as he eased her forward and down onto his waiting lap. I had to swallow hard, forcing my eyes to stay on his, not to drop to where they were joined. She wrapped her legs around him and threw her head back, but Xander didn't seem to notice. He was still watching me, daring me.

I couldn't move. My heart was a jackrabbit in my chest, racing, racing. Screaming at my body to turn and run, to flee. My mind was stubborn as a bull, though, refusing to budge.

I would die if I saw what came next. I just knew it. But I had accepted his challenge, and if he'd kill me to prove his point, then that's the way this was going to be. He'd know then that whatever he did, I'd survive it. I wasn't going anywhere, no matter how much he hurt me.

When I didn't drop his gaze, Xander slid his arms around Jen and grabbed her ass with both hands, squeezing her butt and grinding her against his crotch.

She slid her arms around his neck, and they started making out furiously, with no further warning. My throat constricted, and my knees buckled. I grabbed onto the car I was standing beside, forcing myself not to look away. My whole body felt numb with shock, like when I witnessed a fight.

I'd never seen two people kissing like that. It was different in real life, when I was standing right there, than when I'd seen it in movies. I could see how deep their kiss was, both of their mouths open, their heads tilted sideways to lock their jaws together. There was something predatory about it, like watching a snake devour its prey.

I stood there, about ten paces from the bike, just waiting. I'd spent my whole life waiting. A few more minutes wouldn't kill me, despite the feeling in my chest that said otherwise. I wouldn't let Xander scare me off with a little parking lot grope session. I was part of a freaking golden god, and what was Jen? At most, an evil giantess.

So I crossed my arms and leaned against the car, studying my nails and trying to look bored as they did their thing. After a minute, Xander pulled away and smiled at me. His lips were wet and shiny. I wanted to find him repulsive, with her spit all over his face, but he still looked like a god.

"Waiting in line for your turn?" he asked with a sneer.

Jen twisted around and saw me at last. She was pretty, her striking features highlighted by her cropped hair, which had a wide stripe of purple on each side, framing her narrow face. Her jeans hugged her long legs like they were made for her, not handed down from a sister with a different sense of style. Though it was chilly, she was wearing a tank top that showed off a tattoo on one shoulder.

Suddenly, I felt smaller and more stupid than Xander alone could make me feel. Usually, I could hold my own against him. But today, he'd employed a weapon.

"It'll be a while," she said, arching one perfectly-plucked brow.

After seeing her shove her tongue down Xander's throat, I thought I might throw up all over her if I opened my mouth to speak.

"Get lost, why don't you?" she said when I didn't speak.

Say something…Don't just stand there staring like a

pervert.

"I am lost," I said, grabbing the sticky note the office had given me and holding it up with both hands like a shield. "I don't know how to get to the library."

Xander snorted back a laugh. I hardened myself for his response, which would no doubt be cutting and unlike mine, actually make sense.

"Is she serious?" Jen asked Xander. Then she twisted around towards me again. "Ask someone else, loser. Xander's taking me home today. I won't be done with him for a long time. What I have planned might take all...night...long." She ran her claws slowly down his chest, smiling up at him as she said the last few words.

"Don't count on it," Xander said, grabbing her waist and heaving her off the bike.

She stumbled, hopping to catch her balance. "What the fuck?" she yelled, color rising to her cheeks. "You're going to kiss me like that, and the minute this bitch comes along, you're ditching me?"

Xander's lids dropped, and he raised his chin, his eyes hard. "Watch who you're calling a bitch," he said, then added, "bitch."

He dragged himself along the seat slowly, and again, my eyes couldn't leave his hips. There was something about seeing him straddling that machine, his jeans creased at his hips, his black motorcycle boots skimming the pavement, the angle of his hips, his black leather jacket, his hips, his hips...God, I could not stop staring.

"Get on, little girl," he said, sliding on a pair of shades and jerking his chin at me.

I was about to turn to jelly, seeing him astride that thing, but his voice was hard as flint. It steeled me a bit, and I collected myself enough to obey, though I was hyperaware of my body as I walked past Jen. I was sure she was going to jump on me the second my back was turned. My hands felt strangely detached from the rest of me, floating uselessly at my sides until I reached the bike. After handing Xander the note with the address, I clambered onto the bike and slid forward, clamping my knees around his hips.

"Have fun fucking your bitch sister," Jen said, turning away as Xander twisted the throttle. The bike leapt forward, and I clung to Xander's hips. I could feel every breath I took, the coldness of his leather jacket under my palms, the warmth of the seat, the wind against my cheeks and in my hair. He was shaking, but it was different from the last time, when I'd felt him laughing.

This time, neither of us laughed. I didn't know what was wrong with him. I'd been so smug about reading his interaction with Jen, only to find out I had it all wrong...and then, it seemed, to find out I'd had it right all along. My head was whirling with confusion. I didn't want to think that had all been a show for my benefit—I wasn't that arrogant, to think he'd do anything for me. But it was hard to find another meaning behind what had just happened.

Unlike the last time we rode, I knew enough to lean into the turns with Xander, to match his body with my own. I waited for each one, determined not to mess up. But I didn't want to press up tight against him like I had the last time. Even having him between my legs felt different now, more meaningful than it had the first time.

Xander didn't pull my arms around him, and for that, I was relieved. I didn't want my hands pressing into the warmth of his body, feeling his abs through his shirt, his belt buckle above his zipper. I had looked at it. I was like some high school version of Pandora. I'd opened the box, I'd peaked. I'd looked at the bulge in his jeans, and now I couldn't stop thinking about it. Was he aroused inside his jeans? Would I be able to tell? And if he was, had Jen done it, or had I?

Even holding onto his hips took on another meaning. I could feel them shifting with the movement of the bike, could feel the rhythm of them rocking each time we hit a bump. Part of me wanted to pull away, but another part wanted to keep going, for the ride to last forever. It was like when I'd seen Joaquin, and I knew I should leave, but I hadn't.

By the time Xander pulled over on the side of a tiny street, I felt sort of dirty and cheap for having held onto him and having those thoughts after seeing him make out with another girl. He skidded to a stop and jumped off the bike, spinning to face me. His hair was a windswept mess, his features twisted with rage.

"Why'd you make me do that?" he yelled, yanking his sunglasses off and hurling them to the cracked pavement.

"Make you do what?" I asked, my voice calm but wary. If my crappy life had taught me anything, it was how to talk to unreasonable people.

"You know what," Xander growled, closing the distance between us with one stride. He slid right up against me, staring down at me with undisguised hatred.

My own anger rose to meet his, along with some instinct to fight back, to defend myself. "Are you talking about making out with that girl or treating her like shit afterwards?" I asked. "Because I'm sure you can come up with a better excuse than saying I made you do it."

"Stop fucking with my head," Xander yelled, grabbing his head with both hands like he was about to rip out handfuls of that gorgeous chestnut hair.

I had a ridiculous urge to stop him, but I caught myself. Instead, I did the more sensible thing, taking the opportunity to climb off the far side of the bike, just in case he decided to drag me off, too.

"I'm not in your head any more than you're in mine," I hissed. "It's not my fault we're tied together. Do you think I'd pick *you* to be part of a god with me?"

"What if I don't want to be part of your stupid god?" His voice was low but deadly, his eyes still blazing. "Why'd you come here and fuck up our lives? We were fine before you came."

"Really?" I asked. "Were you? Because I kind of got the feeling that wasn't the first time you'd treated a girl that way."

His gaze turned icy cold "What does that have to do with anything?"

"I'm just saying, it didn't look hard for you."

"You don't know fuck-all about my life."

"Don't I?" I asked. "Let me guess. I just don't understand how hard your life is. You grew up in a freaking mansion on the beach, with everything you could ever dream of handed to you on a silver platter. That must be so hard for you, Xander. Sure, your pillows are made of money, you hit the genetic jackpot in the looks department, and every girl in school wants to take a tumble between your sheets. But go ahead. Cry to me because Daddy didn't buy you a yacht."

Xander's hand shot out, grabbing my jacket and hauling me forward until I was leaning over his bike, my toes barely scraping the ground. I braced my hands on the seat, trying to push away from him, but he was too strong. He closed his eyes and took a deep breath, as if inhaling my scent, before dragging his nose across mine. His eyes opened into slits, as black as the deadliest storm. "You don't know shit, little girl," he whispered, so close I could feel the heat of his breath against my lips.

"I know that maybe there's a reason the god chose us," I said. "Maybe there's something we're supposed to learn from each other."

"I'm supposed to learn from you?" he purred, his smirking lips caressing mine as he spoke. "You're a joke. You think you can be part of me or my family? You'll never be anything to us except our father's latest toy. I don't even know your name. You're not a god. You're nothing."

"Stop," I said, my voice shaking. My legs threatened to give way, and tears ached behind my eyes. Gripping his wrist, I tried to twist away, desperate to get free before he saw me cry. He held on another second, pulling me so close that I was dangling from his hold. Then he pushed me back and let go, as if he were disposing of something he was glad to be rid of. Without a backwards glance, he threw his leg over his bike, twisted the throttle, and roared away, leaving me standing alone in the empty street.

CHAPTER THIRTY-THREE

Gwen

For a minute, I stood in the small cloud of dust from Xander's bike, letting the tears sting my eyes and run down my cheeks. I had no idea where I was, but I sure as hell didn't want to go home and face him right now, if ever. Was this the betrayal Heimdall had warned me about? Could Xander actually refuse to take part in this?

He was supposed to drop me off at the library, but when I looked around, all I saw were small buildings and houses. I sighed and picked up his shades. They'd probably cost as much as my mother's car, and he'd left them lying in the street.

"Lovers' quarrel?"

I spun towards the voice, only to find Joaquin standing against the side of a small building with the same grey shingles and white trim as most of the houses in the area. He had a skateboard propped up against the wall beside him and his backpack slung over one shoulder.

I quickly turned away to wipe my eyes, though he must have been standing there for a while if he'd seen my fight with Xander. A dart of panic went through me at the thought. Had he heard us talking about our god?

Then I remembered that until a few days ago, I thought my own mother was delusional. Even if he'd heard us, he wouldn't believe it.

"Come on, let's ditch this place," Joaquin said, skating to join me in the middle of the empty street.

"I'm supposed to be meeting my tutor," I said. "Do you know where the library is?"

Joaquin cruised along on his board, and without thought, I started walking beside him so we could talk. "Library," he said, pointing to the building on the corner where he'd been standing. Then he poked a finger to his chest. "Tutor."

"You're not my tutor," I said, stopping in the middle of the street.

He held up both hands. "I know, I know, it's hard to believe a dude as smokin' hot as me is also a brainiac." He swiveled his board around so he was skating backwards in front of me. "I'm the whole package, baby."

He leaned to one side, making a ridiculous gesture up and down his body that I guessed was supposed to demonstrate that he was, indeed, the whole package. Then he lost his balance and lurched off his board, which shot off down the street.

I couldn't help but smile as he chased it down, even though I still felt a little sick and shaky from my fight with Xander. His words still echoed in my head like an endless feedback loop.

> *Little girl*
> *You're a joke*
> *I don't even know your name*
> *You're nothing*

I had overstepped, too, lost my own temper. I'd said nasty things to him, too. And the truth was, I didn't know shit about his life. Had my words hurt him as much as his hurt me?

If I was nothing to him, they couldn't have. But he was something to me. Despite my every effort to be as cold and cruel as him, I wasn't. I had never learned to close off my heart. His words cut me to the bone, wormed their way into my deepest insecurities.

My mother and I had always had each other and only each other. How many nights had I lain awake with the nightmare anxiety eating away at me, wondering what would happen if I couldn't save her? I would be alone in the world, without even proof of my name.

Why should Xander remember my name, when I couldn't even prove it was real?

Only my mother knew the truth. It had never made me sad before, but now that Xander had pointed it out, I felt empty and worthless. I had never mattered to anyone but my own mother. For all the world was concerned, I didn't exist. I was nothing.

"You're not going to cry again, are you?" Joaquin said, cruising back to me on his board.

"No."

"You've got that look on your face," he said. "The one you had just before you busted out crying."

"It's nothing," I said, hooking my fingers into my backpack straps.

"Didn't look like nothing to be," Joaquin said. "Tell you what. First you can tell me what happened, and then we'll study. Besides the big brains and the smokin' hot bod, I'm also a good listener."

I swallowed hard, remembering the last time we'd been alone together, when I'd walked in and seen him showering.

"Why would you want to listen to that?" I asked finally.

"I told you, I'm a good listener. Besides, you can't focus when your mind is on your bad-boy brother."

"It's not."

"Dude, don't lie," he said. "I'm being nice here, and not even trying to get in your pants."

"That's a first."

"I know," he crowed like he was super proud of himself.

"Do you need a gold star?"

Joaquin grinned and circled me on his board. "Hey, my house is literally right there," he said, gesturing to a row of apartments with some small houses beyond them. "We can put our stuff down, and you can tell me what Xander did this time, and I can tell you why, and then we'll study."

"Why what?"

"Dude, I've lived here my whole life," he said. "I know all the Keens. Everyone here knows everyone else. You're not the first girl I've seen crying over Xander."

With that, he started gliding down the street.

Reluctantly, I followed. "Again…why are you being nice to me?"

"I'm nice to everyone," he said. "Have you ever seen me being a dick? Come on, not everyone here is as messed up as your brother. I get it that you're new here and everyone wants a piece of you, but I'm just after the tutoring paycheck. Besides, maybe you could use a friend who isn't, you know, living in the same house as you."

He was right. I'd never seen the guy stop smiling. He was more goofy than creepy. Now that we were alone, he was less hyper and ridiculous, too. Maybe without the pressure of living up to whatever image he had at school, he'd be less of a cartoon. After all the weirdness at home, I appreciated his straightforwardness. I really could use a friend who was just a normal kid, who wasn't at risk of bursting into flame if I accidentally touched him.

I didn't know anyone here except my stepsiblings and their various partners, and somehow, I didn't think their evil girlfriends would go out of their way to make my life easier. Besides all that, Joaquin was volunteering information about Xander that no one else had. Maybe if I knew the real reason he didn't want me around, I'd be on a more level playing field. I could talk to him about it, come to an understanding even if I couldn't change his mind.

"This is me," Joaquin said, hopping the curb and zipping along a short walkway to the row of tiny, ugly apartments.

My thoughts were quickly overtaken by the stark contrast between this shabby one-story building, hidden away a block behind the library, and the mansion thrusting out over the bay, obscene in its opulence.

No wonder Joaquin liked to go shower over there. I didn't blame him. His apartment building was depressing and run-down, reminiscent of some of the storage lockers I'd lived in. He pushed open the door, and the stuffy smell of mildewed carpet greeted us as we stepped inside. Joaquin flipped on the light, which didn't do much to dispel the gloom. It was a studio apartment, with a futon bed against one wall, a TV against another, and a kitchen that wasn't much more than a stove, refrigerator, and microwave.

I'd lived in places like this a few times. Some part of me wanted Joaquin to know that I understood, so he wouldn't feel ashamed of his humble family. Not everyone lived like kings. Stepping into such a familiar scene again after living with the Keens made me both horrified by the conditions I'd lived in and ashamed of the gross extravagance of my new wealth.

At the same time, he didn't know anything about that girl. He knew Rich Gwen. I decided to keep it that way a little longer.

"Tell me about your fight," Joaquin said, propping his skateboard up next to the door. I spotted a surfboard against the wall in a closet-sized bathroom, a wetsuit hanging in the shower.

"Your parents are at work?" I asked.

"No parents," Joaquin said, opening a cabinet over the stove.

"You live alone?" Telling him a sob story about my fight suddenly seemed self-indulgent and hypocritical. I was living in that mansion over the sea, too, not just Xander. I had been given a lottery ticket. Not everyone was that lucky.

Joaquin chose from the collection of plastic cups with gas station logos crowded together with a stack of bowls in the cabinet. "Yeah, my parents died," he said. "I got emancipated so I can live alone. Sweet, huh?"

"I guess?"

Joaquin opened the refrigerator and poured Grape Drink from a gallon jug into the two cups he'd chosen. "Don't be shy, you can sit down," he said. "Though let me just make the bed first. You probably don't want to touch what's on those sheets."

"I'm okay, really," I said. "You don't have to do anything special for me."

I was so not sitting on his bed after that comment.

After handing the drinks to me, Joaquin pulled a faded comforter up over a grungy sheet, then plopped down on the bed and patted the spot beside him. "Sorry I don't have a table or anything," he said, looking around like he'd just noticed that. "I really don't spend any time here. I'm usually at the beach when I'm not at school."

"I can tell."

Joaquin leaned back and hooked his hands behind his head, grinning at me. "So you've been thinking about me?" he asked. "Wondering what I do after school?"

"No, I just—" I motioned at my hair. "You have that beach bum look."

"How's your drink?"

"Good," I said, then realized I was still holding his cup. I handed it to him, almost fumbling it during the handoff.

"Total surf rat," Joaquin agreed, hopping up to open a tiny door that revealed a hot water heater. He pulled out a folding chair from beside it and set it in the middle of the floor for me. "Don't worry, I won't be showering at your house again. Not after they locked me out butt-ass naked. Let me just add that it was really cold that day. In case you saw anything that wasn't impressive. Shrinkage is real, man."

I snort-laughed Grape Drink up my nose.

"It's all good," he said, setting his cup on the floor and lying back on his bed again. "We can still be friends."

"I really don't care if you shower there," I said. "Just…wear your swim trunks, or give me some warning next time."

"Cool. I totally won't make you show me yours," he said with a grin. Then he wiggled his eyebrows and stuck out that freakishly long tongue again. "Unless you want to."

I winced. "I think I'll pass."

"Maybe next time." He bounced up off his creaking futon to pace around the room, restlessly opening and closing doors at random. One of the kitchen drawers looked like it was entirely full of packets of Taco Bell sauce.

He paused to lock the door. "Sketchy neighborhood," he explained when he caught my frown.

But a weird feeling was starting in my stomach.

"My pad isn't the best babe magnet," Joaquin said. "Usually, I just take the chicks down to the beach, tell 'em I got the motion of the ocean, baby." He raised his arms and swiveled his hips.

If it weren't for the locked door, I would have laughed. He was so utterly impossible to take seriously. But I had a hard time believing there was any bad neighborhoods in this tiny beach town. Looking around his room, I couldn't even see a window big enough to squeeze out. Throughout my life, I'd absorbed some of my mother's paranoia subconsciously. I didn't like stairs, closed spaces, or my back against walls with nowhere to run. I didn't like locked doors unless I was the one locking them.

"I'm a little claustrophobic," I said, standing. "Maybe we can go back to the library."

"Aw, but we just got here," he said. "We're just getting started. Let's talk the talk, get to know each other. You can tell me anything. We're friends, right?"

I suddenly had the feeling if I answered his question wrong, my face would end up on a poster inside the grocery store. I swallowed hard, eyeing the door. Why had I come here with him? He'd seemed so harmless and silly. Inappropriate and crude, yes, but in a nonthreatening way.

Because you're such an expert judge of character?

"I think I'm just going to go," I said, reaching for my bag.

"I think you're not." Joaquin's voice was hard now, all the teasing gone. Like a clown that had removed its mask.

I dove for the door, not bothering with my bag. Slamming back the deadbolt, I grabbed the knob and twisted. Locked. Dammit.

Joaquin body-slammed me against the door. My temple bounced off the metal surface, throbbing painfully. Before I could recover, he twisted my arm behind my back. "Now that's not being a very good guest, is it?" he asked, wrenching my arm up until I yelped in pain. "Maybe your mom didn't teach you manners when you were homeless, so let me just help you out with that."

I tried to push away from the door with my other hand, but he grabbed that one, too. While he was distracted by getting that one under control, I yanked my other hand from his grip and grabbed for the little lock mechanism in the center of the cheap gold knob.

Joaquin slammed the heel of his hand against the back of mine, crushing it against the knob. The lock I'd been groping for bit into my palm, and I heard something crunch in my hand. A loud, shuddering gasp came from my lips as he jerked both my hands behind my back. Turning me around, he marched me over to the chair.

"First rule of being a good guest," he said, slightly out of breath from our scuffle. "When your host tells you we're going to sit and chat, you oblige him."

He tried to force me down into the chair. I kicked it over.

It fell sideways, the metal thudding against the cheaply carpeted floor. Joaquin's hand pinned my wrists like cuffs, but he grabbed the back of my neck with his other hand, squeezing as he marched me forward. "I guess that means you want to do this on the bed."

"No," I cried, a fresh wave of adrenaline

barreling through me. I spun towards Joaquin, ripping my hands free. My brain seemed to drain of everything but pure, instinctual terror. I slashed at him with my fingernails, my fists.

I'd caught him off guard, though he tried to grasp my flailing arms. The door behind him was like that proverbial light at the end of the tunnel. I had to get there.

I dove for the chair on the floor. It was one of those with a metal frame and a padded seat that simply folds flat. It hadn't folded in half when I kicked it over, but I grabbed two of the legs and spun in a circle, swinging it as hard as I could.

The metal clanged against Joaquin's skull, the reverberations sickeningly satisfying as they traveled up my arms. While he stumbled backwards, I dove for the door. Twisted the lock. Twisted the knob.

I had one foot literally out the door when Joaquin grabbed my goddamn hair. He dragged me backwards, and I fell, hard. Scrambling for something to hold onto, my foot hooked around the doorframe. Still gripping my hair, Joaquin heaved me farther in, kicking the door closed on his way. I grabbed at his arm, his hand, trying to end the torture happening to my scalp.

In seconds, he'd hauled me back across the room. He threw me face down on the bed and straddled my hips. When I tried to push up, he caught my hands and pulled them behind my back again. I cursed my mother for not letting me be a normal kid who worked out at the gym, or played sports, or even had PE class. I felt pathetically weak and powerless under Joaquin's muscled thighs.

Just as I was about to break down, my phone rang. I tensed. Joaquin tensed. "You're supposed to be in tutoring for two hours," he said. "Who's calling you?"

"I don't know, let me just check," I said. "Oh, wait, that would require hands."

"Fuck it. They'll think you had your phone off in the library," he said, turning his attention back to me. "Now, here's how this is going to work. See, you're not very smart, Gwen. When you freaked out about getting on the bed, you told me what you're really afraid of. If I was tutoring you, I'd make sure you didn't give away so much information."

"What do you want?" I asked, my face muffled in his pillow.

"I really didn't want to rape you," he said. "But I will if you make me."

I sucked in a shuddering breath. His pillow smelled like stale smoke and dirty hair—a scent I was all too familiar with—and boys, one with which I was sadly lacking in familiarity. If he raped me, I'd forever be marred by this experience no matter who I was with.

But if he killed me, I'd never know what it was like to kiss a boy, to revel in his scent instead of holding back a gag. I'd never know what it meant to be a true friend, to navigate high school, to go to college, to get a job, or to have a fight with someone who wasn't my mom. I'd never fly on a plane, go to a concert, or fall in love.

In the past weeks, I'd barely begun to live. Before then, I'd never held a boy's hand, or ridden on a motorcycle, or felt my heart flip when someone smiled. I was thankful for these things. But I was greedy, and I wanted more than that. I wanted so much more.

"Let's make a deal," Joaquin said. "I'm a fair guy. All I wanted was to talk. You're the one who made a big scene."

"I'm sorry," I whispered into the pillow. I remembered reading somewhere that some men will hurt you more if you fight back. Maybe he was the kind who would take pity on me if I begged. I wasn't above it. Hell, I'd begged for money on the street just so my mother could have dinner.

"That's better," Joaquin said, stroking my hair back from my cheek. "Now, we're going to have a nice little conversation for the next two hours. If you hadn't gone all psycho on me, I wouldn't even have tied you up. We could have done things nice and civil, like friends. Just like you'd talk to your stepbrothers. But no. You had to act like a complete freak, didn't you, Gwen?"

His voice was hard, but I had no trouble making mine sound quavering and pathetic. I just let out my natural fear. "Yes."

"So here's how this works," he said. "You sit

in the chair, and I tie you up. I ask you a question, and you answer. If I like your answer, you get to stay there, just as you are. If I don't like it, there will be consequences as I deem necessary."

"What kind of consequences?" I asked, my voice shaking.

"That depends," he said. "Maybe my kind of consequence. Maybe yours." He made a motion with his hips like he was riding a bull, and I shuddered, tears springing to my eyes.

"If you scream, you get to live your worst nightmare. How's that sound?"

I nodded, a tear leaking from the corner of my eye into his pillow. Dammit. I didn't want this psychopath to see me cry.

"Now, I'm going to tie your legs to the chair in case you get any ideas about surprising me again, but I'll leave your hands free so you can have your drink and feel comfortable." The futon squealed as he stood.

I thought about punching him in the groin, but I wasn't sure it was worth getting raped. He still had hold of my hair, and I couldn't count on him to let go when I punched him.

He pulled me up, set the chair upright, and pushed me down into it. "We're just going to talk?" I asked. "You promise that if I don't scream, you won't hurt me?"

"Rape you," he corrected, his voice sounding so businesslike that I shivered. He kicked a bin out from under his bed, dragging it over with his foot while he kept a tight hold on the hair at the base of my neck. "Now, lift your feet back here so I can tie them to the back legs of the chair. That way, your feet won't touch the ground, in case you get any ideas about running. This will be your first test. How scared are you to get a little wang in your poontang?"

Every instinct in my body told me to run like a scared little bunny, but I knew he was too strong and too fast. Even if I made it through the door, I hadn't seen anyone on the tiny street for the entire two blocks we'd walked from the library. I didn't know if anyone lived in the other apartments in the long, low building. And if they did, I didn't know if they were home, or if they'd help me.

Clenching my teeth with rage, I forced my legs to go limp as Joaquin pulled them back and tied them to the chair with some rope he'd pulled from the bin. As he was tying the second one, my phone rang again. I dove for it, my hands shaking so hard I didn't know if I could get it out of the side pocket of my backpack.

I grabbed it out, relief flooding through me when I saw the name on my screen. *Zeke.*

As I tapped my thumb on the screen to accept the call, Joaquin's hand shot out and smacked the bottom of mine. The phone flew into the air, and a cry ripped from my throat, my hands shooting out to catch it.

I didn't catch it, though. Joaquin did.

His eyes locked on mine, full of malicious fury. "Dude, what's the emergency?" he said into the phone in his obnoxious surfer-dude voice. "How am I supposed to impart my smarts to your sister when her phone's ringing right and left?"

He paused, holding a finger to his lips.

I could scream. Zeke was just down the street at the school. He'd be here in five minutes.

But by then, the damage would be done.

Still, at least I'd live…

Maybe.

"Of course she's fine," Joaquin said. "She's just too nice to tell you to leave her alone. Here, talk to her."

He reached into his pocket, pulled his hand out, and a six inch blade slicked out of a knife. He held out the phone, stepping behind me and grabbing a fistful of my hair. With one hand, he pulled my head back against his chest, holding the blade against my throat with the other. When I swallowed, I could feel the cold steel pressing into my skin.

"Gwen? You cool?" Zeke asked.

"I'm cool," I said, wincing at how uncool those words sounded coming from my mouth. "Just…studying."

"Sweet," Zeke said "I…I don't know why I called. Just making sure you made it okay."

Joaquin's fingers tightened in my hair. "Tell him you have to go."

"I should go," I said as Joaquin bent lower,

angling the tip of the blade under my chin.

"Joaquin's not doing anything too...*Joaquin?*"

Like holding a knife to my throat? Nope. Not at all.

"Just studying," I said again.

"Get off the phone," Joaquin said through clenched teeth, the knife point pricking my skin.

"I'll let you go then," Zeke said. "I just had this weird feeling, I don't know, I guess it was stupid."

"It's not stupid," I said. Would that be enough? It would have been enough for Eliot.

But Zeke was not Eliot.

I closed my eyes, praying harder than I'd ever prayed before that the first call had come from Eliot, not Zeke. That Eliot had wondered why I didn't pick up. He'd said he was the anxious type, and we'd shared a connection before. He'd sensed when I was in trouble at school, and that was just a couple mean girls. This was a psycho with a knife.

Joaquin yanked the phone away from me and hung up, dropping it into his pocket. "Now, where were we?" he said, his eyes bright with fury. "Oh, yes, you were learning to be a good guest. A good guest doesn't answer her phone in the middle of a conversation. Now, what shall your punishment be? My choice or yours. We'll take turns choosing."

"I'm bleeding," I pointed out, feeling a warm trickle down my neck from where he'd poked the knife into me.

"My turn," he said, his eyes lighting on the spot. He stepped between my knees, grabbing the hair at the crown of my head and yanking my head back. In one movement, he bent and ran his long tongue from my collarbone up to the nick he'd made in my skin.

Releasing me, he stepped back, shaking a clump of hair from his fingers. There was more on the floor and the bed from where he'd dragged me across the room. The sight of the clumps of hair made my stomach turn more than the fact that he'd just licked blood off my neck.

"What are you?" I whispered.

"Didn't your mommy tell you?" he said, his long tongue flicking against the tip of his switchblade. "I'm your worst nightmare."

"A demon."

He grinned. "I guess Mommy did tell you. But I ask the questions here, not you."

I tried to remember things she'd told me, but most of what I knew about demons was to run away from them. I probably knew as much about demons as human boys, so it really didn't give me an advantage one way or another, but just having some knowledge of what I was up against gave me courage.

"Fine," I said. "I thought we were having a conversation. Usually, those go both ways, but if we're going to drop the pretense and call this an interrogation, that's cool, too."

"Shut up and take your drink." Shoving the

cup into my hand, he sat on the edge of the bed and watched me take a sip. His whole face changed, relaxing and rearranging into the casual, dopey face of the surf rat I'd met on my first day. "So, Gwen," he said, leaning forward like we were sharing a secret. "Where you from?"

"Around," I said warily.

He flipped his switchblade closed, then open again, wiggling his eyebrows at me. "Ready for more?"

"I was homeless," I said quickly, fighting a shudder at the thought of his tongue on my skin again. "We traveled around the country. I was born at Mass General."

"Ah," he said, nodding. "Same as me. Interesting. What about your brothers?"

"I don't know."

"Hmmm." He ran the tip of his tongue along the sharp edge of his blade. "I don't think I like that answer."

"Wait," I said, holding up a hand when he stood. "I think they were. Yes, I remember now. Neil did mention that."

"Did he now?" Joaquin said, stalking around me. "What else did he tell you? Did he tell you you're special? That you're a god?"

"What? No."

"But you are, aren't you?" He lifted a lock of my hair and buried his nose in it. "I can smell it on you. Which one are you? Baldur? No, he's dead. Freya the Slut?"

"I'm not a god," I said. "I'm nothing."

"That's what your brother said on the street back there," he said. "Oh, yes. I heard you. I have excellent hearing, Gwen. It's part of being a good listener."

"Then you know it's true."

"False," he yelled, lunging towards me.

I jerked back in my seat, and Joaquin laughed maniacally.

"What do you mean?" I whispered.

"I heard you both admit you were pieces of the gods. Now I just need to know which one. You're not one of the good ones," he mused. "Not part of me."

"Wait—you said you're a demon. You're a god, too?"

"Who said I was a demon?" he asked with a smirk. "Maybe I'm a demon, maybe I'm not. I could be Loki. He likes to cut hair. Maybe I'll give you a buzz cut. See if your brother wants to fuck you then."

"What?" I asked, pulling back.

"Are you stupid? I told you, I saw your little lover's quarrel with the prodigal son."

"Xander hates me."

"Xander hates everyone," he said, circling me. "Didn't they tell you?"

"Tell me what?"

"Why he's such a vile human waste."

I opened my mouth to defend him, then

stopped. The damn Keens with their damn secrets. I'd followed this nutcase home to get answers to questions they could have told me themselves. If I could keep Joaquin talking, though, maybe I could buy enough time...

"No," I said slowly. "Xander doesn't tell me anything."

"That's too bad," Joaquin said, turning to look over his shoulder at me, then spinning on his toes to face me. "Tell you what. We'll gossip after you tell me what I want to know."

"What do you want to know? I really think you have the wrong person. I don't know anything."

"How many of you are there?"

"Five," I said automatically. Then I remembered that I hadn't counted myself, but I didn't correct my statement. I didn't know why he wanted to know, but it couldn't be for anything good. I was going to feed him as many half-truths as I could get away with.

"So it's just you and all those Keens," he said. "Neil's been collecting them for ages. I've tried to get to them, but this is the first time I've had a real opportunity like this. Let's make it count, shall we? Now, spill your guts, or I will." He wiggled his eyebrows and flicked his pointy tongue out to touch the tip of his switchblade again.

What good was it to be part of a god if I couldn't do anything with it? What good was it if it didn't work unless we were all together? I closed my eyes and screamed inside my head, as loud as I could into the emptiness of our connection.

"What are you doing?" Joaquin demanded.

Because I didn't know what else to do, and he wasn't wasting time talking, I talked. I told him about being on the run my whole life, about Mom's mental state, about things I'd never told anyone. I could have made up something, but it was sort of a relief to get it out, to tell someone and not care if he thought I was a freak. He was probably going to kill me, and if he didn't, I seriously didn't think he cared that I'd been a homeless, socially-stunted, uneducated weirdo whose best friend was a fictional Civil War widow.

I couldn't tell my new family those things. I wanted them to like me, to think I was worthy of being part of the Keen family. I didn't care what Joaquin thought. Let him think it. As long as I kept talking, he'd keep his knife put away.

Finally, I ran out of things to say.

"And what happened when you got here?" Joaquin asked. "Anything strange?"

"Nothing," I said.

"Wrong answer," he said, circling behind me. He grabbed my hands and yanked them behind my back. The Grape Drink tumbled out of my lap, splattering across the matted, stained carpet. Joaquin bound my hands tightly, then stepped back. "Now you lost privileges. So what happened?"

"Nothing," I said again.

"Nothing?" he asked, stalking around me, his

eyes narrowed. "No blown out windows at home? I guess that just happened at school, huh?"

Shit. How had I forgotten that the whole school had witnessed that?

"Just at school," I said quickly, not sure where he was going with this. I had no plan but to stay alive as long as I could and hope the others would find me.

Heimdall, help me, you nine-mothered bastard!

"Now it's your turn," Joaquin said. "I bound your hands. What punishment would you like?"

"Nothing," I said. "I'm telling the truth."

"Bullshit." He strode forward and grabbed my hair at the crown of my head again. "I always did like blondes," he said. "How about a kiss? You never had a boyfriend when you were homeless, right? Think of all you've missed out on."

"No," I said, trying to twist my head away.

Joaquin grinned maniacally, yanking my head straight, leering as his face approached mine. I sucked in my lips and bit down on them as his mouth smashed against mine, his tongue wiggling along the seam of my lips, trying to get inside. At the corner of my mouth, the tip of his pointed tongue wormed its way inside, slithering along my teeth before retreating.

At least my first kiss was memorable.

Joaquin sat back and licked his lips. "Want some more?"

"There was nothing except the one day at school," I burst out.

Joaquin paced the tiny apartment, flicking his

knife open and closed and muttering to himself. "There should be more of you. One piece is the key. The others form the lock around the key. Who else could be part of it?"

I shook my head, confused and wary at once. What was he talking about? Heimdall had mentioned an essence, but he hadn't explained it. Was that the key? The key to what? And if I was the key, and Joaquin killed me, did that mean he'd be killing the god itself? What would happen to the other pieces if Heimdall died?

"It must be someone at school then, if it only happened there," he said, stopping in front of me. "Someone you met before your brothers. Maybe on your way into town."

I shook my head again. "I don't know."

"Last chance, Gwennie. Who's enamored with you besides your brothers?"

Enamored with me? What was he talking about? Sure, I had a spark with my step-brothers, but I couldn't be sure it was more than the god bond. And it was hardly strong enough to call it enamored.

"No one," I said.

A malicious grin twisted his mouth. "Then it's my turn."

"No," I said quickly. I wracked my brain, trying to think of a single person I knew at school besides my siblings. "Um...you?"

He snorted, but he didn't move to touch me.

"It's you," I said quickly, relief rushing

through me. Why hadn't I said it earlier? If he was part of me, surely he wouldn't kill me.

Joaquin snorted with laughter.

"You're the only person at school who talks to me besides them," I insisted. "And we did meet. Maybe. At the hospital, when we were born. Does that count?"

"It can't be me," he said, pacing the room again. "I'm supposed to kill you. Who else wants to get in Gwennie's tight little pants?" He smacked the blade of his knife into his hand as he paced back and forth again. Outside, I heard a motor. Should I scream now? If it was a neighbor getting home, would they come to investigate?

"Your sister," Joaquin yelled, rounding on me. "Your sister is a dyke."

He slid onto my lap, his thighs straddling mine. "You sneaky little liar," he said, drawing my chin up with the blade of his knife. "Now I get to pick your punishment. I like blood. All that red. It's my favorite color. What's your favorite color, Gwennie-Gwen?"

My heart slammed in my chest so hard I thought I might black out. "White," I whispered.

"Oh, that's good. The walls are already white. I think it's time for a change, don't you? Let's paint the walls *my* favorite color." The knife pierced through the skin under my chin.

I flinched, muffling a cry of pain in my throat.

"That makes me so hungry," Joaquin said,

making a slit in my skin.

Clenching my teeth, I squeezed my eyes shut, willing myself not to scream. "It's you," I rambled, my voice shaking. "You're part of us. Part of me. We need you."

"A man's got to eat before he goes to work," Joaquin said, grabbing my hair again and yanking my head back. "I'll eat now, paint later."

His mouth descended on the cut he'd made, pulling at it until it felt like my skin was turning inside out. My mouth opened, a ragged sob of pain leaking out.

"Remember, if you scream, my knife won't be the only thing inside you tonight."

I clenched my teeth, choking back sobs as he slid his knife through my skin. "Don't kill me," I begged when the knife reached my jugular.

Joaquin licked the tip of the knife, splitting open the tip of his pointy tongue. "Sorry, baby, I can only handle so many at once. Your brothers will be here in thirty minutes, so that's all the time we got. I can't risk them all showing up at once. When you're all together, you're a freaking god. I can't compete with that."

"You don't have to," I whispered.

He shoved my chin up and started eating my blood.

I screamed. I screamed so loud that every car alarm in Wellfleet went off at once, along with a lonesome foghorn.

The lights overhead blinked out. Joaquin's hand clamped over my mouth, and the door exploded inwards. My chair shot backwards, crashing to the floor. The knife skittered under the bed. Joaquin's weight crushed down on me.

Zeke dragged Joaquin off my lap and threw him on the floor. Xander leapt onto him, pounding Joaquin in the face with his fists. Peyton ran to me, peeling off her hoodie and holding it against my bleeding throat. Finn stood frozen in the doorway, his mouth hanging open, his eyes wide with shock while Eliot tipped my chair upright.

Eliot yelled at Finn to help untie me, and they both knelt behind me.

As soon as I was free, I leapt onto Xander's back. "Don't kill him," I said, wrestling with Xander's arms. "He might be the missing piece of us."

Xander stood up, stumbling backwards and ripping himself from my grasp. His eyes were glazed, like he was only halfway here.

"He's being controlled by the fire giant," I said. "It's not really him."

"Don't tell me what he deserves," Xander growled, flexing his fingers.

"We all deserve forgiveness," I said. "No matter what we've done."

"Not all of us," he said, and he turned and walked out.

CHAPTER THIRTY-FOUR

Gwen

Eliot called Neil from Joaquin's place while Peyton and Zeke hovered, asking if I was sure I was okay. I didn't want anyone to touch me, and I couldn't stand another minute inside that death trap apartment, so I fled. Apparently, we'd caused a blackout through the whole town. I stood in the dark on the empty pavement outside the apartment, breathing in the fresh, cold air and relishing the sting of salt on the breeze.

Xander had gone, but Finn stepped out of the apartment after me and stood a few feet away, not speaking. We were still standing in silence when Neil's Mercedes SUV pulled up. Before it even rolled to a full stop, Mom tumbled out the door, sprinting for me.

"Gwen," she wailed, throwing her arms around me and keening like a wild animal. "The fire giant found you, I should have seen, I should have known…"

I stood there with my arms hanging at my sides.

"The giant, is he still here?" she asked. "Has he been driven from the host? Did you see a raven today, Gwen? Have you seen them on the Cape?"

"No, Mom," I said, my voice robotic. "I didn't see a raven today."

For maybe the first time in my life, I wasn't freaked out about her freaking out. I was too tired, too drained, to even feel anything about Joaquin and what had happened. I wanted to pass out, not deal with my shrieking mother. For once, I just wanted to get away from her. I didn't want to be the strong one, to reassure her and talk her down.

"You kids should get home," Neil said firmly. He'd climbed from the car, along with Rosa. "We've got a generator, so you'll have power at the house. Gwen, do you need to go to the hospital?"

I touched my neck, but my fingers came away with only a smudge of blood. The wound itself had disappeared. Apparently there were a few perks to being a god. I shook my head, weariness settling into my bones like stone. "I'll get Mom calmed down," I said. "Once she wears herself out, she'll zone out for a while."

"Don't worry about Olivia," Neil said, resting a hand on my shoulder. His face was kind, and I was too tired to read anything into it. After the day I'd had, I should have been questioning my judgment of people and their motives, but I was tired of my own paranoia. And the truth was, it was a relief to let him take over.

She was still wailing, holding onto Neil, when Peyton touched my elbow. "Let's go," she said softly, sympathy replacing her usual exuberance.

Without another word, we piled into Zeke's car and rolled through the silent, dark streets of Wellfleet and towards home. I turned my face to the window, watching the dark shapes of trees blur by. Xander was out there somewhere on his bike, alone and angry. I wished for once he'd stayed, that he would stop pushing us all away.

My thoughts looped back to Joaquin's, where I'd left Mom with Neil. I'd abandoned her in the middle of a fit. No matter how angry I was, how frustrated, I'd never done that before. Though I thought Neil could handle it, guilt still gnawed at me. Guilt for tonight, but also for the last ten years. I should have been able to help her. She was my mother.

But I couldn't deny the truth. The stark reality was, Neil was better with her than I was. Admitting that, even to myself, crushed me. I should have known what to say, what to do, to get her help sooner. I'd never even tried—not really. I'd been afraid to contradict her, afraid I'd make it worse. And to me, that was just who she was. I hadn't spent much time trying to change her or even help her. I'd accepted her as she was and built my life around surviving her strange madness.

Now, suddenly, she had help, and she didn't need me. There was a terrible loneliness in that, in knowing that it wasn't the two of us against the world anymore. I'd lost my partner in crime. It was just me now, finding my way in this normal world that made less sense to me than my mother. And even though I was surrounded by my new family, even though we were literally pieces of the same whole, I still felt the emptiness of the space beside me where Mom had always been.

*

When we got home, Xander was sitting in the hot tub, his head laid back on the rim and his eyes closed.

"Let's get in," Zeke said. "Gwen, we need you to tell us exactly what happened before we got there."

When we'd all changed and climbed into the hot tub, I filled them in on my evening with Joaquin.

"I knew something was wrong when you didn't answer your phone," Eliot said. "I should have listened to my anxiety."

"You came when you could," I said.

"When we heard you calling," Eliot said quietly. "Not soon enough."

"Do you think he's one of the pieces of Heimdall?" I asked. "He was born at that hospital, and he told me he was a piece of something, too."

"Or maybe he's just a psycho," Peyton said.

"You're his friend," Eliot said, turning to Finn. "What do you think?"

"So I should have seen this coming?" Finn asked, sounding less than chill for the first time since I'd met him. "I didn't know he was possessed by a demon."

"No one said that," Zeke said. "It's cool, bro. Nobody blames you for what happened to Gwen."

When we'd climbed in the hot tub, Zeke had put his arm around me, and I finally let myself relax. I felt safe next to him, like nothing could hurt me again.

"What I was going to say," Eliot said slowly, watching his brother with a frown. "Is that maybe you were drawn to him because he is a piece of us. And I was going to ask if you thought that. Not tell you this is your fault."

"You think I didn't want to help Gwen," Finn said quietly.

"Bro," Zeke said. "No one thinks that."

"Because I was just standing there," Finn said, ignoring Zeke and staring at Eliot. "That's why you yelled at me to help."

"It's not your fault," I said, slipping away from Zeke and sliding over next to Finn. I took his hand under the water and laced my fingers through his. "Sometimes, you just freeze up when you're surprised," I said. "I know you'd do anything for me."

"I would," he said softly, his eyes grateful. He

stroked my hair behind my ear, his fingers lingering for a second too long as sparkles raced through the water around us. Slowly, he leaned in, his eyes on mine. No one breathed as he drew even closer, then turned slightly, letting his lips brush across my cheekbone.

My whole body seemed to melt, and blue sparks raced like bubbles around our bodies, illuminating them under the water.

"Thank you," he whispered against my ear.

My attention was pulled away by the water pouring off Xander, who had stood. He stepped out of the tub and abruptly left the deck. He hadn't said a word the whole time I spoke, hadn't asked questions or even insulted me.

I sighed. "Should I go talk to him?"

"Let him be," Zeke said quietly.

"It's not you," Peyton said, giving me a sympathetic smile. "He's got issues."

Just then, lights illuminated the driveway out front. "Speaking of," I said. "I should probably go make sure Mom's okay."

"You don't have to take care of her anymore," Eliot said. "That's Dad's job now."

I shrugged, not wanting them to think I was immature for needing to be near my mother so much. "It's always my job."

I grabbed a robe and headed in. Mom was sitting on the couch, as glassy-eyed as Xander had been when I'd pulled him off Joaquin.

"She doesn't seem to want to talk," Neil said from the across the huge room. For the first time since I'd met him, he looked uncertain, with worry lines creasing his brow. He might be good with her, but I'd known her longer. I knew that blank stare.

"She'll be okay," I said, crossing the living room and curling my body against hers, pulling her arm over me. "She's always like this after an episode."

At last, I felt like I was on the same team as Neil, not like he was trying to get between me and my mom, or take her away from me. I cuddled against her familiar body as I had so many times before. Until I'd come here, these moments were my only physical contact with another human being. No wonder I was starved to touch all my stepsiblings. It wasn't just that our pieces felt better together. I needed to make up for lost time.

Slowly, Neil approached and sat on the edge of the loveseat. "Is she having one of her visions?"

"No," I said. "Probably not. Those are loud with lots of ranting."

Neil nodded thoughtfully. "Back at Joaquin's, then."

"Or on the way there."

"I wish she hadn't been quite so good at hiding," he said. "I'm afraid what she's seen and experienced has taken a toll on her ability to differentiate between what's real and what's part of the visions."

"I always knew she was mentally ill. I can deal.

At least now I know why. I know that there's truth to it, even if it's made her like this."

Neil nodded. "You're right."

"What about Joaquin?" I asked. "Is he going to be okay?"

"I can't answer that," Neil said. "Rosa is keeping watch on him now. She's casting a rune-spell to keep him subdued for now."

"A what?" I asked. After seeing Heimdall, I didn't think anything could really surprise me, though.

"There are other entrances into the nine worlds," Neil said. "Rosa came through one of them."

"Wait, so she's hosting a god, too?"

"Not quite," Neil said. "She came through whole, as she is. Rosa's a dwarf. She casts spells with runestones."

"Of course she does," I said. "You couldn't have anyone normal living here."

"Just me," he said with a rueful smile.

"So you collect creatures from other worlds," I said. "That must be what Xander meant when he called me your new toy."

Neil grimaced. "I'm sorry about that. I wish I could say he doesn't mean anything by it, but I'm afraid he doesn't think very highly of me."

"Yeah, what's that about?" I asked.

"I think you should let Xander tell you that."

"Like he'd tell me anything," I muttered.

Neil sighed and ran a hand through his hair,

looking tired and haggard. "I hope you'll learn to get along," he said. "He could use a friend like you."

"What, an easy target?"

"One who's not going to get him into any more trouble."

I didn't know what to say to that. If Xander got in trouble, it was probably his own doing. But maybe parents were oblivious to that kind of thing. I looked at my mother's blank face. I was used to watching her and worrying, waiting. I was used to taking care of her, not running off with my new friends. Tonight, I'd chosen them over her. I still wasn't sure if that felt good or horrible.

The concern in all their eyes when I'd told them about Joaquin had scared me a little. To be fair, Mom had always worried about me, too. But suddenly, five other people were worried for my safety. I wasn't in this alone anymore. Along with the relief, though, came a terrifying amount of responsibility. Five other people were counting on me to be okay. For the first time in my life, I was part of something that didn't involve my mother. I wasn't sure I knew who I was without her as my other half. But I was willing to find out.

"I'm going upstairs," I said, lifting Mom's arm and sitting up. "Call me if she needs anything."

"I'll take care of her."

I pulled the damp robe around me and headed for the stairs. I paused at the foot of the winding staircase and turned back, though. "Does that mean we're out of danger?" I asked. "Since we've got Joaquin?"

"For now, we're all safe," Mom said dreamily.

"Do you think he's a part of what we are?" I asked.

"That, I don't know," Neil said. "You can probably answer that question better than I can."

As I climbed the stairs, I wondered how we could find out. Maybe summoning Heimdall again would give us the answer. For tonight, I needed to sleep and forget about the psycho with a knife and the fact that our powers seemed to be getting stronger. We'd knocked out the electricity of a whole town. So far, no one had been seriously injured by our power surges, but I worried what would happen if they continued.

On the third floor, I headed for my room. When I got to the door, I hesitated. Music reverberated through the upstairs, the vibration enough to tremble my blood. That couldn't be healthy.

Against my better judgement, I found myself standing outside Xander's door. I tapped three times and waited, but of course he couldn't hear me. He probably didn't even have eardrums left. Twisting the knob, I eased the door open and peered into Xander's room.

Or music studio. He had enough equipment to produce records in there, along with mixing them, and playing a one-man band. Twisting around, he caught sight of me and slammed his hand down on the strings of the electric guitar he had looped over his shoulder. Ignoring the feedback whine from his amp, he tore his headphones off and glared at me.

"What do you want?"

"I didn't know you played music."

"Because it's none of your damn business."

"You kind of make it everyone's business when you play so loud the house shakes."

He pulled the headphones from around his neck and dropped them on a desk with a thousand buttons and lights all over it. "Fine. I'll stop playing. Happy now?"

"That's not what I meant."

He sighed and shut off the amp. "So fill me in. What do you want? You must have come up here for something. Otherwise, you'd still be getting cozy in the hot tub with people you actually like."

"I might like you, too, if you didn't go out of your way to be a complete asshole at all times."

He studied me, his fingers playing across the strings of the guitar. Dammit, why did he of all people have to play guitar on top of everything? He already looked like a freaking god.

The thought made me smile, and he plucked the cord from the end of the guitar and started winding it around his arm. "So that's it? You came up here to tell me you'd like me if I wasn't me? Okay, awesome. Got it. I could have saved you a trip because I'm pretty sure even a guy who had to repeat senior year could figure that out."

"I didn't come up here because I want anything from you," I said. "As shocking as this must be for you, not everyone is out to get you, Xander. Not everyone wants your money, or whatever else you think I'm after. I just came up to see if you were okay. So what's your problem?"

"Nothing," he said, his voice wilting. He sat down on the edge of the bed and dropped his head into his hands. "I don't have a problem. You didn't have to come up here. I'm fine."

I stood there a minute, not sure what to do with myself. "Is it because of what I said earlier? Because I'm sorry."

"Me, too," he said without lifting his head.

"Okay," I said, backing towards the door. "Cool."

"Wait." His hands fisted his hair. "Don't run away."

"I'm not running."

He lifted his face. "You're always running away."

"Yeah, well, you're always giving me a reason to."

For a moment, we sized each other up. It didn't take him long. There wasn't much of me to go around.

"Fuck," he said, raking his hand through his hair before slapping his palm down on his knee. He looked up at me, and I had to take another step back from the anguish on his face. "When I opened that door and saw your hair all over the bed, and your hands tied up behind that chair…"

"I'm fine," I said.

"I would have killed that guy."

"But you didn't."

"I wanted to."

"You hate me."

"Jesus Christ," he said, jumping up from the bed and prowling around the room. He stopped in front of me, his hands resting on my shoulders. "You really think that?"

I shrugged, staring straight ahead at his chest instead of looking up at him. "Do I think you hate me? Well, yeah. Kind of. Do I think it's my fault? No."

"I don't hate you," he said, his forehead dropping down to rest against mine. He closed his eyes, his voice a whisper of defeat. "You scare the hell out of me, Gwen."

My name was a trapped bird inside his mouth, beating against the bars of a cage, dying more each second of its captivity. I almost cried out in despair at the sound of it. I wanted to save that bird, but I didn't know if it was him or me.

"I thought you didn't know my name," I whispered, barely able to speak.

"I know your name, Gwenevere Penelope Keen," he said, pronouncing each word slowly. "I probably know more about you than you know about yourself."

"So tell me." My heart was beating so hard I couldn't breathe, my head swimming with dizziness at being so close to him. It felt so right, after so long, to finally touch him like this, without fighting my inescapable attraction. It was as if we were two magnets, and all this time, we'd been trying to force the repellent ends together. At last, we'd been turned around, and his magnetism was irresistible. I reached up to wrap my hands around his forearms, anchoring myself.

He straightened a bit, pressing his nose into my hair and dragging in a deep breath. "I know your smell. I know how your laughter builds like a scream inside you until you can't hold back any longer. I know how your whole face lights up when we go fast on my bike." His hand circled my waist, flattening against the small of my back, drawing me against him. "I know how it feels to hurt you, and have to see it all over your face."

"Then stop hurting me," I whispered, my fingers skimming up his arms, over his strong shoulders.

He drew in a ragged breath. "I can't."

"And I can't stop showing it when you do," I said. "I'm not going to hide myself for you, Xander."

"You shouldn't," he said. "I deserve that."

"You deserve worse than that."

"I shouldn't have left you with him," he said, his hands raking up my back suddenly. He lifted his head, his tormented eyes finding mine. "I'll make it up to you. I can make it all go away. I can erase where he's been, make it like it never happened."

Wordlessly, I slid my hands further around him, flattening them on his shoulder blades as I pulled him closer. My body responded, every part of me finding the place it fit against every part of him. Heart pounding, I held his gaze. My throat tightened, closing off my breath. I could only nod.

His strong hands slid over my shoulders and up my neck, lifting my chin. Cradling my face in his hands, he pulled me up, bending to claim my mouth with his own.

CHAPTER THIRTY-FIVE

Gwen

A minute later, Xander turned our bodies and walked me to the bed, his mouth never leaving mine. We fell onto the bed, our limbs tangling, his lips showing mine the way. Instinct took over, and I let my hands roam over his shoulders, his throat, his lush hair. I couldn't stop if I wanted to. My hands were starved for more of him, as if all those years of not touching anyone had left me dry as a desert that only he could quench.

I tugged at the bottom of his T-shirt, wanting more of his skin. My fingers skimmed the top edge of his jeans, and I sucked in a breath. He grabbed my hand, his grip crushing, and his mouth jerked back from mine. "Don't," he said, his eyes blurry with hunger.

"What's wrong?" I whispered, shame twisting in my gut. My throat constricted, and tears threatened behind my eyes.

"I don't hook up," Xander said, sitting up and turning his back, dropping his head into his hands again.

"Don't do that," I said, sitting up beside him and resting a hand on his back. I couldn't let go of that glimpse I'd seen of the real Xander, the one behind the stiff shoulders and hardened voice. "Please don't go back to hating me. I didn't mean anything. I wasn't trying to…I mean, I don't hook up, either."

"Obviously," he said, lifting his head and scowling at me.

"Tell me what's wrong," I said. "Don't do this again."

He sighed and shook his head. "Nothing's wrong."

"Then why are you like this?"

He snorted. "I can't tell you that. You're the only person who doesn't know. I'd like to keep it that way a little longer."

"Well, I'm tired of being the person who doesn't understand anything. I want to understand you, Xander. I…I really like you." The words sounded so lame, so insufficient.

"Exactly why I can't tell you," he said, shrugging my hand off his shoulder.

"I want to know," I said, coaxing his chin around so he was looking at me. "Help me understand. I want to know everything about you.

Even the ugly parts. You saw mine."

The corner of his mouth twitched. "Your scars?"

"Let me see yours."

He dropped back on the bed, crossing his hands behind his head and squeezing his elbows together over his face. "Why don't you ask one of the others?"

"Because I don't want them to tell me. I want you to." I lay beside him, nestling my head against the side of his chest.

He was quiet a long moment. "Fine," he said, scooting his arm under my head. "It's probably better if you don't get any ideas about me being a decent guy."

I slid my arm over his chest and my leg across his, marveling at the way our bodies fit together like they were made for this. "Too late," I whispered.

"This shit is all ancient history," he said. "It was years ago, when Mom was really bad. Instead of being by her side, I was in a courtroom with some girl I didn't even know."

I swallowed, dreading what he was going to say next. The instinct to run washed over me, and I tensed, my body telling me to do what I always did. To run away, to tell him I'd changed my mind and I didn't want to hear this after all. But I knew if I did that, I'd be closing this door forever.

"What happened?" I whispered.

"It was at this stupid party," he said. "I was

trying to forget about Mom, and I got fucked up and ended up in bed with some chick I didn't even know. I don't remember any of it. Just waking up the next morning with her."

His voice was flat, completely devoid of emotion, his eyes fixed on the ceiling as he spoke. "She said I got her drunk."

I swallowed the sour taste in the back of my throat. "She said you raped her?"

"No," he said. "Worse. She said I got her pregnant."

I bit back the words that I knew not to say, to ask if he did.

"Who was she?"

"It doesn't matter," he said. "You don't know her. She doesn't go to school anymore. But she did then. We had to tell my parents, and her parents. Mom was...not doing well. Dad didn't need to deal with this shit on top of it. But he did. We had to."

"What did you do?"

"Dad wanted me to get rid of it," he said, his voice harsh.

My stomach was shaking, but I couldn't hold back the question this time. "Did you?"

"No," he said. "She wanted to keep it. Chelsea dumped me, but the girl... She had a boyfriend, and they stayed together. They were going to raise the baby. They just wanted me to pay for everything."

Xander tried to take his arm from around me,

but I held on, clinging to him. "I'm not going anywhere."

He sighed. "I didn't blame Chelsea for ditching me. She wasn't going to walk around school every day seeing some chick her boyfriend had knocked up. We're cool now. We're friends."

"I know."

We were quiet for a minute. "The girl's boyfriend hated me at first," he said. "Got me kicked off the football team. Not that I wanted to play, anyway. I just did it because it was something to do. He made a big deal about how I'd slept with his girlfriend when she was drunk, said she could press charges, and did the coach really want a player like that on his team. But she never said that. She said we were both drunk. She wasn't a bitch about it. They just didn't have any money."

"And you do."

"Yeah. I didn't mind. I got used to the idea. I was only sixteen, but it was kinda cool, thinking about being a dad, seeing it grow in there. Her boyfriend stopped being a dick when I stuck around, paid for everything, went to all the doctor appointments and shit. Everyone at school thought we were crazy, but the three of us were friends. We shared this cool thing that no one else shared. We were all in it together. It could have worked out."

I swallowed, gripping a handful of his T-shirt to anchor myself. "Why didn't it?"

"Dad was pissed. He told me not to pay for

anything until the baby came and we knew for sure. But I wanted to. We fought all the time. It was hard on Mom. My brothers and Peyton didn't know what to say to me. I didn't like being home. I spent all my time with the girl and her boyfriend. Planning this whole life. Even Dad finally agreed I could use my trust fund to get them this nice little place not far from here, so I could see the kid. I guess I was kind of excited about it by the time it came. I was there when she had it. I was trying to do the right thing."

"They took off with your money?" I asked.

"No," he said, scowling. "Dad made them get a DNA test. The kid wasn't even mine. Turned out, they had planned the whole thing. She was already pregnant the night of the party. I don't even know if we really hooked up. They just wanted someone to pay for shit, and look, there's a rich guy who looks dumb enough to do it."

A tear slipped down my cheek and dripped onto his T-shirt, and I pressed a kiss against it, against him. "But you're not stupid."

"It doesn't matter," he said. "Life goes on. I was free."

"That's a good thing, though."

"That's what everybody said. But nine months is a long fucking time. Everything had changed. I'd changed. I'd let that idea of the future consume me. I'd dropped everything else for an entire school year. I'd believed the whole lie, not just the baby. All of it. I saw this life ahead, and then it was gone. I couldn't just go back to the way things were."

"Why not? It wasn't your fault. It wasn't your responsibility."

"I wanted that life," Xander said quietly, his fingers tangling in my wet hair. "I didn't want to sue them and get the money back. I wanted what they'd said to be true. But that wasn't an option."

"And being this way is better?"

Xander let out a low, bitter laugh. "Dad made me go to court, and I had to sit there and see them. My friends. My only friends, by that point. They wouldn't even look at me. Dad got the house back, just kicked them to the curb. I would have gone with them, but they didn't want anything to do with me if I wasn't going to pay for shit."

"What happened them?"

"I don't know. I don't care. Dad sent me away to a boarding school because he didn't want to see my face. When I came back the next year, they were gone. Those assholes didn't deserve anything more than what they already got from us."

We were quiet for a moment, Xander's hand absently tugging at a knot in my hair. Tingles traveled from my scalp all the way down my body from his touch. Finally, I pushed myself up on one elbow and looked down at him. "I just have one question," I said.

Xander swallowed, his dark eyes guarded. "Yeah?"

"Why would any of that make me think less

of you?"

He frowned, opened his mouth, and then closed it. I searched his grey eyes, darkened now with brooding. "I don't know," he said at last. "Everyone at school knows what happened. I'm the sucker who got taken in by those people. I actually believed we were friends. I'm the joke."

"But you didn't do anything wrong. They did."

"I ditched that kid."

"It wasn't your kid."

We stared at each other a long moment. "We aren't like them," I said. "We didn't come here looking for money. We didn't even know you had it until we got here."

"I know."

I brushed my fingers over his forehead, smoothing the creases of his frown. "I'm not going anywhere without you," I whispered. "You're part of something real this time, Xander. We all are. It's not a lie."

He caught my hand and pressed it to his chest, closing his eyes and taking a deep breath. "How do I know that?"

"Because I'm not running."

I slid my body onto his, pressing my cheek against his strong chest, listening to the reassuring, steady thrum of his heartbeat. His legs intertwined with mine, his arms wrapping around my body, his hips fitting mine with unbearable perfection. My belly moved in rhythm with his as we breathed, like two parts of the same being, two broken pieces that had finally found their way back to the place where they belonged.

FROM THE AUTHOR

Resources

Mental health

There are millions of people all over the globe who suffer from various mental illnesses. In America, it is one of the most commonly dismissed diseases, so people too often suffer in silence. Those suffering may be afraid to speak out as there is still enormous stigma surrounding these illnesses. If you or a loved one needs help with your mental health, please do not hesitate to reach out and seek the care that you deserve!

If you're in crisis or feel suicidal, go to your nearest emergency room or call this toll-free number, open 24 hours a day. **1-800-273-TALK (8255) or text MHA to 741741.**

For non-emergencies, you may want to start here: http://www.mentalhealthamerica.net/finding-help

Homelessness

It's not the sexiest topic on the news, so homelessness doesn't get a lot of media attention, but there it is estimated that over half a million people in the United States alone suffer homelessness. Of those, about a quarter are children. If you or a loved one is experiencing homelessness, here are two organizations to get you started. Most libraries allow people to sign into their computers with a guest log-in that does not require a permanent address.

www.nationalsafeplace.org/homeless-youth

https://youth.gov/youth-topics/runaway-and-homeless-youth